ROBERTA L. SMITH

SIMONE'S ghosts

For Kylie

Enjoy !

Roberta Smith

ISBN-10: 1534763988
ISBN-13: 978-1534763982

www.bertabooks.com
www.nevermoreenterprises.com

Nevermore Enterprises

For the misunderstood, and those trying to do better.

It is wonderful that five thousand years have now elapsed since the creation of the world, and still it is undecided whether or not there has ever been an instance of the spirit of any person appearing after death. All argument is against it; but all belief is for it.

SAMUEL JOHNSON, *The Life of Samuel Johnson*

Bullying is a national epidemic.

MACKLEMORE

Also by Roberta L. Smith

The Secret of Lucianne Dove

Chapel Playhouse

The Accordo

The Dreamer of Downing Street

Bouquet of Lies

A Year in the Life of a Civil War Soldier: the 1864 Diary of Frank Steinbaugh

Distorted: Five Imaginative Tales on the Dark Side

Visit www.bertabooks.com

SIMONE'S ghosts

CHAPTER 1

ANOTHER NEW SCHOOL and I won't know a soul.

Simone hurried along the sidewalk that ran parallel to the boulevard busy with rush-hour commuters. A gray SUV whizzed past a little too close to the curb and kicked up a breeze that stirred her long dark hair. The sun had just risen, and even though it was September in Southern California, she felt a slight nip in the air. It would be gone by midmorning.

The convenience store was a quarter mile from the apartment where Simone lived with her mother, Anna. Simone had noticed they were out of coffee, and if there was one thing Anna needed before work, it was coffee. Simone had just enough time to buy some, hurry back, and get ready for school.

She frowned, thinking of the day that lay ahead.

So what if I don't know anybody? It isn't as if any of the souls at my last school were peeps I wanted to waste a thought on.

She jogged the last few feet, threw open one of the glass double doors, and rushed into Mr. H's Mini Kwiki. A little tune alerted a middle-aged Asian man behind the counter that a customer had entered. He glanced in her direction for the briefest of moments, then returned his attention to the woman buying lottery tickets, a can of Diet Coke, and a donut.

Simone knew exactly where the coffee was shelved, but found none. They'd rearranged the store. *Great,* she thought unhappily, and she began searching up and down the aisles.

The little tune went off again, over and over. People were stopping for goodies on their way to work, or paying for gas inside the store because the outside credit card reader wasn't working.

"Get that thing fixed, dude," one young man complained.

"We working on it," came the reply.

Ah. Coffee!

Simone grabbed a can and hurried to the counter to pay. There was a line now and only the one clerk in the store. Her mother could have bought Starbucks on the way to work or even had the bar's yucky stuff—her mother's words, not Simone's—once she made it to the Rip Rap Room where Anna did everything from bartending to waiting tables. But Simone was trying to make up for butting heads with her yesterday. Anna never made it home from work until after three in the morning and needed to sleep in. So it would be nice to have coffee in the apartment when she got up.

It would also be nice if she woke up early this morning at least, Simone thought. As babyish as it sounded, Simone would like to see her mom before heading off to her latest academic stomping ground.

The line moved at a snail's pace.

"Sorry," she heard the clerk say. "Larry call in sick."

So that was the hang-up.

Simone hugged the can of coffee to her chest and tapped her anxious foot. She sighed and stared at the floor. This would be her third high school and she was only starting her sophomore year.

Life had been stable when she was younger. Then at the

age of eleven, everything changed. Her stepfather died suddenly, money became a problem, and she and her mother moved a lot. For a while they lived with a girlfriend of Anna's who only wanted money for utilities and food. Anna saved for a decent apartment, but then she met a guy and they moved in with him. That didn't work out so well and they rented a room in a house, which seemed like a sweet deal until the landlord wouldn't stop making passes at Anna even after she told him she wasn't interested.

Finally, her mother found a job that paid well, and they moved into the apartment where they lived now.

The line edged forward. A couple of customers just wanted gas. But then one guy came back for a receipt and took cuts.

So Woodruff Senior High makes three. Yep. Three high schools. Count 'em.

This time the new school was her fault. She'd gotten suspended for throwing the first punch in one kick-ass brawl. Except it didn't exactly happen the way everybody said, and she'd warned the girl to shut her mouth. It wasn't Simone's fault the girl kept egging her on and calling her names. She'd even yanked Simone to the ground by her backpack. In the end, both of them were suspended for what the school called "mutual combat." The threat of expulsion was made, and to avoid that, Anna had taken steps to enroll her at Woodruff Senior High.

"Just try to fit in," her mother begged when they had their latest blow up.

What happened to "be who you are," huh, Mom?

And what if being who you are didn't allow you to fit in? Then are you supposed to hide who you are?

Finally, it was her turn to pay. As luck would have it, no

one was behind her; she was the last in line. If they hadn't moved the coffee she'd be long gone by now.

"Why you do that to your hair?" the clerk asked.

Simone put the coffee on the counter and said, "What?"

"The color. It dark. Week ago it blond. You a pretty girl. Why you color it like that?"

She had dyed her hair dark brown just yesterday, and if he didn't like her hair then he definitely wouldn't like what she planned to wear to school. Black boots. Dark purple leggings. Black skirt. Black sweater trimmed with red. Ivory-white makeup, black shadow and deep-purple lipstick. The finishing touch would be a black choker with silver studs—nothing spiked, so it wouldn't clash with the dress code. It would be a new look for her. Dressing to fit in hadn't helped her find friends. This would keep people away on her own terms, she hoped.

The clerk continued to stare at her hair, and Simone felt the need to snap him out of it.

"Your hair's black," she commented. "Maybe I wanted to be more like you."

He narrowed his eyes and then decided she was being funny. He laughed and rang up the coffee. "Eight dollar . . . "

Two teenage boys entered the store amid a tumult of noise from their horsing around. They accidentally rammed a display of gum and candy, which made a box of Sugar Babies smack the floor.

The clerk pointed at the candy in the aisle. "You. You boys. Pick up what you mess up."

But the teens just laughed and continued farther inside the store to get whatever it was they were after.

The annoyed clerk looked at Simone. "Eight dollar and eight-seven cent." She handed him a ten and accepted her change. By then another customer was ready to make a purchase, keeping the clerk busy.

Simone walked to the glass doors. After glancing around to be certain no one was watching, she stared at the candy on the floor. With deep concentration, she stared hard. The box of Sugar Babies rose in the air and landed back where it belonged.

§   §   §

Simone took the back-row desk nearest the classroom door, dropped her backpack in the basket at the rear of the chair, and slouched in the seat. Trying not to be too obvious, she watched as students filtered in and found where they wanted to spend the next hour of their lives: eager beavers near the front, loners near the back or to the side, people happy to be in class together next to each other.

The teacher, Mr. Erickson, stood along a wall that was full of windows. He was tall and wiry, like her stepfather had been, and was around her mother's age, Simone thought. He had an engrossed look on his clean-shaven face, and was obviously sizing up the kids he would be dealing with for the next semester. A couple of guys started clowning with each other. First a punch in the arm and then a friendly insult: "Sit over there so I don't have to smell you, Rodriguez."

Mr. Erickson sprang into action. "Hey, knuckleheads. Close your mouths so I don't have to hear you."

Both guys snickered, but they sat. "Yes, sir," one said before he shut up.

Erickson nodded slightly. *Well, that worked. For now.*

Oh, great, thought Simone. *The teacher has one of those brains that can infiltrate mine.* She waited to see if any more of his thoughts seeped in. They didn't. *Good.* That sort of thing didn't happen often, but it happened enough to be annoying.

The bell signaled it was time to begin, and before Erickson took roll call he warned the class about cell phones. They would not be tolerated. Period. If he heard one ring, if he saw one being used, if he smelled one outside the student's backpack, it was his until the end of the week. If he spent too much time having to monitor them, then he'd take everyone's cell phones and return them at the end of the week. Capeesh?

With the nodding of heads, he started handing out papers. "This is a survey designed to tell me about you. I want silence in this room as you answer the questions and as I read them over. Then I'll let you in on what happens next."

"Psst."

Simone looked to her left. A curly-haired guy wearing a red plaid shirt whom she hadn't noticed before was leaning back in his seat, staring at her. The students in between didn't pay him any mind.

"Hey, you like English Lit?" he semi-whispered to her.

She glanced at the teacher to see if he'd heard. Evidently not, because she saw no reaction. She returned her attention to the kid, but he was no longer there.

Simone closed her eyes and suppressed a long sigh. She'd heard the school was haunted. Apparently the rumor was true. Now she had *that* to deal with, too.

CHAPTER 2

BACKPACK OVER HER shoulder, Simone traipsed toward the quad, hugging a book to her chest as if it were a shield. Kids seemed to rush every which way to catch up with their besties for lunch. Simone glanced up at the clear September sky. Despite the strangeness of the teacher, she decided that English Lit was going to be her favorite class. She liked reading. She thought it cool that Erickson cared enough to match literature to the need of the student by putting together a survey. Well, the need as he saw it, which might be all wrong. But still, it took extra effort and that was worth a few points in Simone's book.

She found a bench where no one else sat, relieved her shoulder of the backpack, and took out the lunch she'd made the night before. Cafeteria food made her gag. It was better to bring something she liked. Peanut butter and grape jelly wrapped up in a tortilla. Quick and tasty. She took a bite and looked around at the clusters of kids. There were a few loners like Simone. Well, not like her. Those dressed like her were in their own tight-knit group of five, with one guy occasionally glancing her way.

"Why don't you go over and introduce yourself, gorgeous?"

Moving her eyes and not her head, she spied the plaid-shirt

ghost next to her. Keeping her voice low and trying not to move her lips too much, she answered him. "Why don't you go wherever it is you're supposed to go?"

"You mean into the light?" He laughed. "I didn't see any light. You know what that means."

"Not really."

"Wha? You don't follow such things? A girl like you?"

"Nope. And why do you keep bothering me?"

"Because you can see me, gorgeous. Why d'ya think?"

"I think you should go away." Her tone had risen more than intended.

"I just got here." That wasn't the voice of the ghost. Simone looked up to see a boy from her English class standing in front of her. Immediately she remembered the teacher had called him Dalton. He was cute. He was beyond cute, and he was looking at her with deep blue eyes, thinking she'd just told him to get lost.

"Uh, sorry. I, um. Sometimes I have this bad habit of talking to myself," Simone said.

"You told yourself to go away?" He looked amused.

"No." Simone felt her heart pound. Why was she so nervous? Was it just that she wasn't used to other kids being nice to her? Or could it be that she sort of liked him? Oh, that wasn't good. "Never mind. I was just thinking about something."

He nodded and sat beside her where the ghost had been. She felt her pulse rise. "Hey, I noticed that Erickson assigned us the same five books to read."

"He did?" Now why did she say it like it was a question? She'd noticed as well. Other kids might have gotten one or two of the same, but not all five. She quickly amended her tone. "He did. Yeah. Yeah. I saw that, too."

"You did. Well, I was thinking we might collaborate. Like, read the same book at the same time and talk about it before we have to discuss it in class or write a paper."

Simone's breath caught in her chest, and she hoped he wasn't noticing that her eyes had grown big, because she could feel that they had. This was stupid. Why was she acting this way? She let the air out of her lungs, diverted her eyes, and pulled on the edge of one of her boots. She shrugged. "Collaborate? I guess. I'm not really good at working with others, though. I . . . I should warn you."

Dalton chuckled. She looked at him. Was he laughing at her? No, his face was friendly. There was no derision in his expression.

"Okay. Well, I'm glad you told me. Wouldn't want to be caught off guard. But I have a feeling we'll get along fine." He stood and smiled at her. "I'll see you later."

Simone didn't say anything. She watched him walk away. Suddenly her appetite vanished. She tossed the uneaten tortilla wrap in her lunch sack and was about to throw it away when out of the corner of her eye she spotted two girls standing only a few feet away.

She looked at them, knowing their conversation was meant for her ears.

"It's cute how Dalton is nice to everybody."

"I know. Even the weirdos."

Simone had heard enough. She wasn't going to engage. They didn't like Dalton talking to her? Tough. It was a free country. She stood and started walking away, but the two girls followed. She could hear them behind her.

"Oh look, she's running away."

The two girls laughed. Simone quickly put on the brakes and spun to face them. The two pretty girls stopped as well.

They wore trendy, short-short dresses. Their makeup looked perfect. Any blemishes on their skin were hardly noticeable. The one with long blond hair crossed her arms. The one with long dark hair did the talking.

"Dalton doesn't like you. He's just been taught good manners."

"Unlike the two of you," Simone shot back.

"Don't talk to us that way," the blonde chimed in.

"I'll talk to you however I like. And if he doesn't like me—"

"He's going with Jenna."

"Well, tell *him* that." Oh, geez. Why was she doing this?

"He knows," the blonde said.

They're just taking a little break from each other.

The thought had come from the brunette. One of those times when Simone's brain connected with someone else's. Okay, here was her chance to just walk away. But the feisty side of Simone wouldn't let go.

"Well, he asked me out for Saturday night. So . . . " She paused and looked at the brunette. "*If they're just taking a little break from each othe*r, then our date should be harmless."

The brunette's brow furrowed. She'd caught what Simone was putting down, word for word.

Why had Simone taken the bait? She was just making things worse. And what would happen when one of them asked Dalton about it? Her stomach started to churn.

"We don't believe you," the blonde said.

Yeah, I don't believe me either. Mom should have named me Trouble.

Simone walked away and the brunette's thoughts came with her. *She couldn't have heard me, the freak.*

"Come on," Simone heard the blonde say. "Let's tell Jenna

what she said."

§ § §

Finally, it came. Simone's last class of the day, World History. A quick stop at the girl's restroom meant Simone was thankful she could still nab a desk in the back, even though she arrived later than most.

She spied Dalton near the front, chatting with another student, a jock named Gary. By now Simone knew who some of the kids were; at least she knew their names. This and English Lit were the only classes she shared with Dalton. He didn't notice her. She wondered if he'd acknowledge her if he did happen to turn around. She wondered if he already knew about the story she'd made up.

And then it happened—in walked Jenna, long hair flowing, platform sandals clacking. She made a beeline for Dalton.

"You're in my seat," Jenna told a heavy-set girl sitting to Dalton's right.

"Um, what?" The girl looked at Jenna. For a second her face turned stony and she looked like she might stand her ground, but then it softened and all she said was "Sorry." She began gathering her things.

"You don't have to move, Hannah," Dalton said.

"Yes, she does," Jenna responded, her gaze stuck on the displaced girl.

Hannah found a desk three rows back, and Jenna slid in beside Dalton. Feigning a grateful heart and sounding very artificial, she called out, "Thank you, Hannah," and mouthed a kiss.

The girl in front of Simone turned around. "I wouldn't

have moved. Would you?"

Simone felt herself straighten up. "Uh. Don't think so."

"Why do you dress like that?" the girl asked, a genuinely puzzled look on her face.

"Why do you dress like *that*?" Simone snapped right back.

The girl smiled. "Touché." She turned back around.

Simone really did wonder why. The girl's dress was sleeveless and shapeless, the fabric bright with busy horizontal stripes. Her gold-blond hair was short, just to her neck, but ratted high upon her head. It certainly wasn't becoming. She was pretty, anyone could see that, but the clothes and hair were distracting. It was different when you tried to not look attractive on purpose. But this girl didn't give that impression . . . *I wonder what her name is*, Simone thought.

As if on cue, the girl turned around. "I'm Kim." She smiled again and returned to face the front.

Okay, that was strange, Simone thought. *Or maybe not. Probably a coincidence.*

I thought you didn't believe in coincidences, came a voice in her head that wasn't her own.

Simone froze and listened, but no more thoughts came. She decided it was best to forget it and turned her attention to Jenna, who was chatting at Dalton. "At" seemed the appropriate word, because while Dalton nodded at things Jenna said, he didn't return the chatter. Simone wondered if Jenna's friends had told her about the "date" yet. Probably. Enough time had passed. Simone sighed quietly. Why had she opened her big mouth? Making up things like that only led to headaches. And Jenna would think she was after Dalton when she wasn't. *He'd* talked to *her*.

Well, she couldn't worry about it. Wouldn't worry about it. What doesn't kill you makes you stronger; that was

Simone's motto and had been for a while. Not that she liked the process of being made stronger. In fact, she was rather sick of it.

The bell rang and the teacher, Mrs. Kent, stepped from around her desk and started to talk with a voice so squeaky it made fingernails on chalkboard a preferable sound. A couple of snickers and a few soft groans reached Simone's ears. Perhaps Mrs. Kent realized her voice was a problem, because she didn't talk long. Instead, after handing out the syllabus informing the class what they'd be learning during the semester, she pulled down a screen and asked Simone to turn off the lights.

Great, Simone thought. If Dalton and Jenna didn't realize she was in their class, they knew now.

She stood and did as she'd been asked. She retook her seat without looking at the two people she had never meant to antagonize.

"Let your fingers do the walking, let movies do the talking . . . ," Kim sang very softly, then giggled.

Simone wondered what in the world Kim was singing about.

Mrs. Kent started a DVD that would delineate the root causes of World War I. It began with a scratchy recording of "Pack up your troubles in your old kit bag, and smile, smile, smile."

With the lights dim, Simone worked up the courage to look at Jenna and Dalton. He had his eyes on the film. Jenna's were pointedly aimed at Simone.

Simone thought, *The root cause of any war simplified: Nations are made up of people and there is always someone who likes to start trouble. Now smile, smile, smile.*

She smiled at Jenna.

CHAPTER 3

SIMONE MADE THE bus trip across town and strolled home. She picked up the mail from the mailbox and trudged up the steps to the apartment. Inside she dropped the mail on the coffee table, her backpack on the couch, pulled off her boots and opened the blinds and windows to let in some fresh air.

Anna wasn't home. Wednesday was her day off and she'd left a note to say she'd gone shopping with a friend and was going out to dinner. Simone wasn't fooled. She knew her mother had a boyfriend she hadn't met yet. Anna was probably making sure this relationship was going to work out before bringing him around her daughter.

Really, Mom? Isn't it better to be up front with me than to lie?

Dropping the note on the dining table where she'd found it, she decided that technically her mother hadn't lied. She *had* gone out with a friend.

Simone grabbed a Coke from the fridge, her backpack from the couch and went into her room—her sanctuary. She threw herself on the bed and for a couple of minutes and rested face down with arms splayed.

The first day at her new school and she'd already made enemies. What was it about her that made that happen? She could probably make things right with Dalton. Tell him she'd lost her cool and he would understand. In her limited experience it seemed that guys found things like what happened with Jenna's friends more humorous than serious.

Girls, on the other hand, were such drama queens.

Simone pushed off the bed and immediately came face-to-face with the plaid-shirt ghost.

"What are you doing here?" Simone demanded. "You can't follow me home."

The ghost shrugged and lifted his eyebrows. "Well, technically I can. I mean, I'm here." He began to roam the room, examining things, even picking them up.

"Don't touch my stuff. I want you to get out!" She took a stuffed bear away from him and tossed it on the bed.

"Is that any way to treat a friend? I came to help. You seemed so sad at school."

"I'm not sad. I'm mad. Go away. Now!"

"Simone. Let's start over. We haven't been properly introduced. I'm Jimmy. Some people called me Jimbo. But I like Jimmy."

He was as solid as any person. Simone had encountered ghosts before, but mostly they were invisible or shadowy and they communicated with thoughts. She'd only met one other ghost that appeared as solidly as Jimmy did and that had been when she was four. Her stepfather had caught her talking to what appeared to be thin air. When he asked her who she was talking to and Simone told him it was a little girl named Lizzy, that she was her friend, he'd nodded and said, "Uh-huh." And then he'd suddenly yelled: "Go away, Lizzy! In our house, we only want people we can see." Lizzy vanished and never came back. A part of Simone never forgave her stepfather for that, although she liked him. She thought he was a good guy.

"Jimmy. Jimbo. I don't like either," Simone said. "This is my room! I don't want you here."

"Okay. Okay." Jimmy put his hands together and moved them reverently, bowing his head. "How about this? I'll give you time to get used to me and then I'll come back."

"No. I don't want you to come back. And don't come back invisible either. I'll know."

"What? You think I'm a perv? No way." Jimmy grinned. "Just remember, I'm here to help." With that, he vanished.

Simone calmed herself with a couple of deep breaths. *Help with what?* she thought. Did he know something she didn't? It was possible. She had no idea what "the other side" was like, what they knew and didn't know. She couldn't believe he'd followed her home; it was a total invasion of privacy.

She sat on the bed and pulled her backpack closer. Doing homework would take her mind off things. She dumped the books and folders full of assignments on the bed. She'd read. She and Dalton hadn't decided on which book they'd start with . . .

She stopped and rolled her eyes. He probably wasn't going to want to study with her now. What was she thinking? She picked up the book that interested her most, *Cyrano de Bergerac*, and began. A couple of hours later she decided she was hungry and used the microwave to cook one of those small cheese pizzas her mother kept on hand.

Around six-thirty she removed her makeup and changed into more comfortable clothes: soft, stretchy shorts and a tank top. She did her algebra homework, then got on the Internet. She didn't have a Facebook page. She'd taken it down after kids at her last school started leaving creepy messages. She didn't have friends anyway, so what did she need a page for? She did have an Instagram account where she could post photos she'd taken that she particularly liked.

She opened it. There was an old one, of Anna with Simone's stepfather, Terry, that Simone loved to look at. But almost all of her pictures were of sunsets or sunrises and shadowy streets devoid of people. She also liked to look at the public photos people posted of abandoned buildings, places and things. The objects in these pictures always seemed angst-ridden even though that couldn't be, since they were made of brick, mortar, wood, or manmade materials. Buildings that had been beautiful when they were in use were now beautiful in a different way. Without maintenance, Mother Nature cloaked floors in fallen debris, peeled paint from ceilings, felled plaster, and destroyed woodwork.

If this is what happened to manmade things, Simone always thought when she stared at such images, *what happened to the human heart when it was no longer cared for?*

CHAPTER 4

SIMONE STARED AT her cell phone and felt pathetic as she rode the bus across town. Some teenager she made, she thought sarcastically. She didn't have anyone to call or text, so all she really did with it was play games and take pictures. She snapped one of the interior of the bus. Since she sat in the rear, all faces were turned away from the shot.

Simone's mother wanted her to have a phone for safety reasons, and so Anna could call her. It made sense. But she didn't love her phone. Not like normal teenagers who were always texting and chatting . . . *and playing games.* The last thought made her smile.

Simone started a session of *Angry Birds.*

Suddenly her phone played *Phantom of the Opera.* Someone was calling her and the caller ID did not say "Mom."

"Hello?"

"Hey, Simone. How's it going?"

"Who is this?"

"Dalton. Who else?" He chuckled.

Simone felt her heart pound. "Oh, hi." The surprise caller made her lose her tongue for a moment, but she quickly recovered. "How'd you get my number?"

"Oh, no. If I tell you, I'd have to . . . old joke. Sorry. I kind of have a way with the ladies in the school office. Dee gave me your home phone number, swearing me to secrecy. I called your house and your mother was more than happy to give me your cell number. Cool mom, by the way."

Simone nodded. Oh, yes. Her mother would have done that in an instant. She wanted her daughter to be more social. And a boy calling, that would be icing on the cake to her.

"I think I woke her up. Tell her I'm sorry," Dalton said.

"She works nights," Simone explained. Well, last night the late night had been a date. She didn't explain that. "It's okay, though."

"So I wanted to talk to you before class."

"Why?" Oh, that didn't sound right. It sounded defensive, a bad habit she was trying to break.

"Why?" he repeated back.

"Sorry. I didn't mean it the way it sounded." She closed her eyes for a second. "Wha . . . what is it you wanted, um . . . " She paused. She'd fumbled the sentence and felt stupid again.

Just don't care. It doesn't matter. It doesn't matter.

She could feel that Dalton was smiling on the other end of the line and that helped her relax. He wasn't laughing at her. He was just trying to connect.

"I picked a book last night and started reading. I thought it made for a cool experiment in case you started reading, too."

Simone smiled. "Yeah, I did start a book."

"*Cyrano?*"

"Yes!" Simone almost laughed. How funny was that?

"Okay, we *are* on the same page. Pun intended. Mr. Erickson must have a sixth sense or something."

"Well, we did take a survey," Simone said.

"The other thing was, I thought we should figure out where to go Saturday night."

Simone swallowed. So he did know about that. She lost her tongue again.

"Hello?" Dalton said.

She took a deep breath.

"Simone? Are you there?"

"Yes. Look, I don't know why I said that. I—"

"Come early to first period and—and we'll talk."

He hung up. She stared at the phone and listened to her pounding heart.

§ § §

As Simone walked down the corridor toward her English Lit classroom, she spotted Dalton with Jenna's two friends just outside the door. Her first thought was this was some kind of setup. Her second thought was, duck into the restroom.

She did . . . almost. But she decided it was better to not show fear. Be fearless. *Semper fi!* her stepfather would sometimes shout. He'd tried to teach her courage and to have pride in herself. Too bad he'd died before he could finish the job.

She lifted her chin and was about to approach the dreaded threesome when Jenna's friends walked away, leaving only Dalton. She continued to watch. Just because he was alone didn't mean she was out of the woods. Maybe they were trying to teach her a lesson and he was part of it. She might believe that, except he didn't seem like that kind of person. And why would he ask her to come early only to see him with Lynette and Shelly and then see them walk away? That didn't make sense.

Well, she thought. She could analyze this to death, or she could start using some of the special abilities she had shoved away as being unethical. If there was one quality Simone knew she had, it was that she was a fair person. It was also true that she could read minds. Not everyone's mind. And not all the time, but then again, she'd tried to kill off that ability. Sometimes thoughts slipped through, like Mr. Erickson's and Shelly's, but never because she asked. Now she was going to ask. She was going to dust off the old I-can-read-your-mind skills, starting with Dalton, if only for a little while. If only to save herself embarrassment.

"Hi," she said as she approached, not waiting for Dalton to speak first.

He smiled broadly and she thought he might have the brightest, cutest smile she ever saw. There went her heart again, beating too fast. She really didn't have any defenses against this guy if he was going to be nice to her, and apparently she couldn't read his mind either. She'd opened herself up fully and nothing was coming through.

"Hey, there you are." He took a step toward her. "How's it going?"

"I just talked to you." There she went again, saying the wrong thing. "Everything is just . . . whatever," she corrected, perhaps with a bit of sarcasm that she hoped only she detected. It was best to take the bull by the horns—another saying her stepfather had favored—and just say what was on her mind. "You know I only said that thing about, you know, you asking me out because they were being nasty to me and I wanted to bug the bejesus out of them."

"Bejesus?" he laughed.

"Bejesus. You never heard of it?"

"Of course, but . . . it doesn't matter. You're cute."

"Well, a lot of times people use the words they heard growing up even if they're not hip or dope or whatever the cool words are now. All I'm trying to say is, I was sorry the minute I lied to them."

"Don't worry. I figured it was something like that. They were so anxious to make sure I knew." He kind of laughed and shook his head. "Girls. So, where should I take you Saturday night?"

"Didn't you hear me? You're off the hook."

"I don't want off the hook. I like you. I want to get to know you. Dinner and a movie is pretty standard, but you can't talk in a movie. You can do other things . . . " He smiled and his expression looked a little different this time. He started talking again.

Simone suddenly couldn't hear what he was saying. Her ears, her brain, everything had spaced out. She liked him. For sure, she liked him, but she didn't want him finding out what a weird person she was. They could talk books, that appealed to her. But a real date? She'd never even been on a date. And he was joking about what you could do at the movies. She'd never been kissed either. Did she want him to know that? No.

"I don't think my mom will let me go on a date." The words popped out of her mouth without her having thought of them.

"Simone. I don't bite. And your mom gave me your address. You worry too much." He stepped closer to her and his eyes moved over her face. "Another thing I know about you. This makeup and these clothes are not you. Otherwise you'd be hanging out with the other kids who like this dark stuff." He took a lock of her hair and rubbed it between his thumb and index finger. "Not that if this *was* the real you, I wouldn't like you." He smiled and let go. "I'll figure Saturday out. We'll have a good time. Does six sound good?"

Before she could answer he turned and walked inside the

classroom.

§ § §

Plaid-shirt ghost said, "So you have a date, gorgeous."

It was lunch time and Simone had found a tree to park herself under, by herself, of course.

"I told you not to come around."

"Uh, correction. You said don't come to your house."

"That was *at* my house. At lunch yesterday, I told you to leave me alone."

Jimmy scrunched his face in complex contemplation and tapped a finger to his chin. "No. I really don't remember it that way."

"I don't care how you remember it. I'm not every ghost's best friend."

"Well, I should hope not. I just want you to be *my* friend. And I think we should talk about this Dalton guy. I don't trust him."

Jimmy didn't trust Dalton? Simone considered that for about one second. She took a deep breath and let it out. "Why?"

"He's a guy."

Simone couldn't help it. She laughed out loud and then caught herself. She was alone and if anyone saw her doing that they'd think she was crazy, unless she was reading a book . . .

Good idea.

She pulled *Cyrano* from her backpack and glanced around. Yep. There they were: Lynette, Shelly and Jenna. It was the first time she'd seen them together. They huddled at a table, just the three of them, once in a while glancing in Simone's direction. And they would laugh, naturally.

She turned away. Jimmy was gone. For a moment she wondered about him. The school was supposed to be haunted and Jimmy was proof that it was. She didn't know the story behind it. She could ask him the next time he popped up, because no matter how many times she told him to go away it was clear he was going to come back, but she didn't want to encourage him. He'd think she wanted to be friends.

She looked at her book, but the sun glared on the pages. Maybe she'd hang out in the library for the rest of lunch time. She looked at Jenna and her entourage. They were still laughing at her. Yep. The library sounded good. She hadn't actually been there yet and needed to get her bearings. She looked across the quad toward the buildings and for a second experienced what could only be described as double vision. She rubbed her eyes and took a deep breath. Her sight returned to normal; at least she thought so. The buildings were in focus and they looked the same, but different. The color was off. Maybe she'd been in the sun too long, but it wasn't all that hot.

About to toss her backpack over her shoulder, she spotted Kim walking along a hallway with two girls who dressed in the same style as Kim: knee-length dresses, ratted hair, strappy flat shoes—and no backpacks. Instead, the girls held their books crooked in their arms against their torsos. They looked out of place and yet they walked along with confidence.

Simone stared until she heard the giggling voices of her newly sworn enemies. She'd waited too long to make her getaway. They were on their way. But then as they approached, she saw Kim walking toward her, too—minus her friends. And the buildings in the background were back to their normal color.

Kim was closer than Jenna and her pals, which for some reason made Jenna, Lynette and Shelly stop walking. Maybe they'd had a run-in with Kim and Kim had bested them. They seemed kind of afraid of her.

"Hi," Kim said. "I thought I saw you."

Simone responded softly. "You saw me. It's me."

Kim smiled. "It's a nice day to eat outside."

"Yeah, I'd say so." Simone's eyes flitted to Jenna. She and her friends were staring in what could only be construed as awe.

"What class do you have next?" Kim asked.

"Algebra."

"You know what? I always liked algebra. That surprises people for some reason." Her smile widened. "I have psychology. But honestly, the stuff that teacher talked about yesterday went straight over my head. I thought we'd study practical stuff about people, you know?"

Simone didn't know what to say. "I guess."

"Okay, well, I just wanted to say hi. I'll see you in World History." She turned and headed back, but not exactly in the direction she came. She veered toward the three gaping teens who moved out of the way.

Now that's weird, thought Simone. *Really weird.*

She took the opportunity to escape to the library, all the while thinking she really needed to come up with her own name for Jenna and her crew.

CHAPTER 5

EXCEPT FOR A few arm bumps in the hallways between classes, thanks to the ever-must-I harass-you efforts of Jenna et al, Friday passed without incident.

JEA. That's it, thought Simone. *Jenna et al—Jenna and friends—would be JEA. The Jeapests.* It would be her own private word for Jenna, Lynette and Shelly.

She lay on her stomach on her bed, legs kicking as she listened to music from *Wicked* through her cell phone. Her mother was at work and she was alone on a Friday night. Tomorrow was the big date. She'd already finished reading *Cyrano.* Dalton said he had, too. At least she knew they had that to talk about. Still, she was nervous. What if they ran out of things to say?

And what was she supposed to wear? He'd already let her know he didn't think much of what she wore to school. She rolled off the bed and opened her closet doors. She had a lot of clothes. Regular clothes. Maybe she'd just wear jeans and a cute tee shirt with an overshirt. And she wouldn't hide behind a lot of makeup. She removed a soft blue top from a hanger just as her cell ringtone announced that she had a call. It wasn't her mother and there was no caller ID. She didn't recognize the number. Curious, she tossed the blouse aside and picked up the phone. Suddenly Jimmy was there, his head next to Simone's, listening in.

"Hi girlfriend . . . not," Jenna's voice came through.

Simone held her breath. She didn't know what to say. She turned from Jimmy, but he came around and stuck his head to the phone again.

"I'm just calling to let you know I'm having a party tomorrow night. No, I'm not putting you on the guest list. But Dalton will be there. I guess you could crash it, but I doubt that would be any fun for *you*. So sorry to mess things up for that little study-group-of-two date you had organized, if it could have even been called a date. But, you know, these things happen. Oh, and Dalton asked me to break it to you. Ciao."

Jenna hung up.

"How'd she get your number? Huh? Huh? Huh?" Jimmy looked pretty pleased with himself. "I know you told me not to come here," he continued, then sang in a melody Simone had never heard, something about dropping in to see what condition she was in.

"What does that mean?"

"Hey! We've made progress. You asked me a question. You didn't tell me to get out."

"Get out." Simone turned her back to him.

"I'm just saying. Who gave her your number? The only person who has it. Dalton."

Simone stood still, pressing her lips together and thinking. She tossed the phone on the bed. Yeah. How would she have her number unless Dalton gave it to her?

"What are you going to do?" Jimmy asked.

"Nothing," Simone said. "It's no big deal. I never asked for a date in the first place."

"Yeah, but, she shouldn't get away with treating you like that."

Simone shook her head in tight little movements. "I can handle it." She felt her eyes grow hot, and tears began to form. "Would you go away now? Please."

"I'll go. But I think—"

"Just leave me alone." Simone wiped her eyes. When she looked again, Jimmy was gone.

"Well," she said. "Guess I don't have to worry about what to wear."

She lay back on the bed and began listening to music again. She wished her mom would come home. She wished her stepfather hadn't died.

§ § §

Simone slid out of bed early on Saturday. She hadn't slept well and was glad to see the sun shining through the window. She remained in her stretchy shorts and tank top, her favorite sleeping attire, and made her way to the kitchen. After pouring herself a bowl of Frosted Flakes, she turned the television on low to watch cartoons on Netflix. Watching cartoons was a habit she'd never outgrown. Cartoons made her laugh.

Anna stepped out of her bedroom at ten, tying a soft, white robe tightly around her small waist. She yawned and drew her fingers through her shoulder-length ash-blond hair. "Good morning, Sunshine," she said.

"Coffee's made," Simone told Anna from her seat on the living room floor.

"Oh, I keep forgetting." Anna disappeared into her room and re-emerged with four plastic shopping bags from Marshalls and Target. She rained them down into Simone's lap, gave her daughter a kiss on the top of her head, then went into the kitchen and poured a cup of black Folgers.

"What's this?" Simone asked, stealing a look into one of the bags. She saw clothes. Black clothes. She pulled out one of the items. A dress. It was gorgeous. Her mother did have great taste. Clothes were what they'd fought about, the day before school started. Anna didn't want her daughter crossing to the dark side; she wanted her to "fit in."

Anna walked in bare feet from the kitchen into the living room and sat on the couch. She was thirty-four, petite and very pretty. Sometimes people thought she was Simone's sister, which Anna loved. Simone, not so much.

"I owed you school clothes."

"You already bought me school clothes."

"None you're willing to wear."

I'll wear them. Eventually. Maybe. "I know," Simone said.

"Well, I remember how hard it was being fifteen. I'm sorry we had to fight about it."

"Me, too."

Simone had babysat a lot over the summer and bought the goth stuff with her own money. She'd gone to thrift stores and done the best she could. But she really didn't have her mother's flair.

"I just thought if you're going to wear bland black all the time, at least it could be stylish. You may not have noticed, but I took back most of the nice things I bought you. Most. Not all."

Simone felt guilty. Her mother tried to understand her, but how could she when Simone hardly understood herself? And she wasn't anything like her mother. Her mother was great with people. Personable. Friendly.

"So my little girl has a date tonight," Anna said between sips.

Simone stopped breathing for a second, but kept her eyes

on the TV screen. She knew her mother would bring that up and as silly as it sounded, she didn't want to disappoint her with the bad news that Dalton was taken.

"You aren't nervous are you? He sounded like a very nice guy."

"I guess," Simone said.

"Where are you going?"

"It's more of a study date. We have English Lit together." Simone closed her eyes. Now she was lying. "I don't really want to talk about it."

"Why not?" Anna leaned back to finish her coffee. "What are you going to wear?"

"I don't know yet."

"Want me to help you pick something out?"

Simone took a deep breath. "You know, it may not even happen."

"What do you mean?"

"He has a girlfriend and he may go to this party she's having instead."

"Well, that isn't very nice. He asked you out, right?"

"Mom, can we just not talk about it?" She hardly knew Dalton, but if feelings were a gauge of attachment, she was attached.

Simone felt her mother come up behind her and stroke her hair. "Well, he doesn't know what he's missing." She kissed Simone on the top of her head again. "I'm going to take a shower. And then we can paint each other's nails."

"Sure, Mom." They always painted each other's nails and most of the time Simone liked it. But today she'd do it just because.

Anna left for work at one. On Saturdays she worked a double shift. She made good money on Saturdays.

Simone turned the store bags upside down and allowed her mother's purchases to fall onto the bed. She found black leggings edged at the ankle with black lace, a high low skirt, a black lace top, a lacey corset top with a zipper that ran completely up the front, a gossamer lacy dress, black jeans, a deep-burgundy shrug-collar top . . . Some of this might have come from Marshalls or Target, but not all. She searched for the receipts and couldn't find a single one. Either her mom was making really great tips or her new boyfriend chipped in some cash. For her mom to take the money meant he must be a keeper.

Simone tried everything on and looked in the mirrors that made up the sliding closet doors. Everything fit perfectly. "Thank you, Mom," she whispered.

There was homework to do, but she'd leave it until Sunday. The sun was bright and inviting. It was a perfect day to laze around the apartment pool. She looked out the living room window to see how many little kids were playing and didn't see a single soul.

She changed into her bathing suit, grabbed what she needed, and hurried down the stairs in cheap flip flops. She placed a beach towel on one of the lounge chairs and a can of Coke on the concrete, and sat and rubbed sunscreen on her skin. Then she lay back, closed her eyes and relaxed.

Catching some rays? came a female voice in her head. It sounded a lot like Kim. She opened her eyes. No one was around except a couple of older women, and by older she was thinking in their thirties, who were setting up on the other side of the pool.

Kim? Simone thought.

Natch.

Apparently there was something different about Kim

besides how she dressed.

You're talking to me with your mind. Simone's thought was a statement, not a question.

I say, if you've got it, flaunt it. Don't you think it's kinda groovy?

Groovy?

Yes, groovy. We're talking with our thoughts, Simone.

Where are you?

What difference does it make? You shouldn't stay out here more than an hour.

I won't burn. I put on sunscreen.

In my day, we used baby oil.

Simone sat up. *In your day?*

There was no response.

Kim?

She was gone. Simone rubbed her forehead. Was she hallucinating? Was she crazy? Or had what she thought just happened actually happened?

It happened, Simone decided. But was Kim another spirit? She could just be someone with abilities like Simone had, except for the "in my day" remark. Two ghosts. Really? Jimmy acted like a ghost, while Kim hung around like she belonged, albeit in her own unique way. And had the Jeapests seen her? They must have, to have acted the way they had.

Simone couldn't relax. She didn't want to be a magnet for ghosts. She'd never liked ghosts. Well, except for Lizzie when she was little and that hadn't lasted very long. She started to gather her things to go back in the apartment, but realized that she didn't want to be alone in a closed space. The outdoors was preferable.

She lay back down, and when a group of four children accompanied by an older teen showed up at the pool, Simone was happy for the noise that followed. She didn't want to think about anything.

Throughout the afternoon, more and more people came to enjoy the pool. Simone moved into the shade after a while and people-watched. Finally she grew bored, and since nothing more happened to disturb her peace of mind, she took her towel and lotion and went back to the apartment. She took a shower to get rid of the sunscreen and the chlorine, since she had braved the water for a little while.

Finished with the shower, she combed her hair and didn't blow-dry it. She changed into her favorite home clothes even though it was only five o'clock and lay on the bed. She pulled a second book from her backpack—*A Tree Grows in Brooklyn*. She would read.

At six o'clock there was a knock on the door. Cautiously Simone put the book down. She looked out the peephole and her heart leapt. It was Dalton.

CHAPTER 6

SIMONE THOUGHT ABOUT not answering, but only for a second. Sheepishly, she opened the door and poked her head out. "What are you doing here?"

He stared at her and shook his head. "I know you didn't forget."

"No, but . . . um." Simone took a deep breath. "I thought you were going to a party instead."

"Yeah," he said softly and not very happily. He put his hands in his back pockets. "I tried to call you all afternoon. I left messages."

"Oh. I was down at the pool and I didn't take my cell phone. So you showed up because you couldn't reach me? I mean, Jenna called and told me—"

"Jenna doesn't speak for me. Please remember that for future reference."

Future reference?

"Come on, get ready. We have places to go and a book to talk about and I hope you're hungry because I sure am."

Simone let him in and he sat on the couch while she went into the bedroom and closed the door. What was she supposed to wear? She could hardly control the giddiness that riddled her body.

Don't think about it, just grab something, she told herself.

Jeans. Jeans. Where were her favorite jeans? *In the drawer, dummy.* Okay, she was being crazy. She grabbed them and pulled them on. Then she took a soft pink sweater top, one of those items her mother had bought and hadn't returned, and yanked that over her head. She hurried into the bathroom to do something with her hair and to apply some makeup. She pulled her hair into a ponytail because she hadn't blow-dried it and that's about all she could do in a hurry. Makeup was applied quickly as well. Mascara, blush, lip gloss. She looked nothing like she did at school.

She sighed deeply because she was actually tired from rushing.

After walking into the living room, she stood there for a moment expecting him to say something about how she looked. Instead he got off the couch and said, "Let's go."

She was glad he'd turned his back because she was certain she'd turned five shades of red. She'd stood there like a prom date expecting him to comment on the fact that she'd dressed "normal" and he hadn't even noticed. Or he didn't care. Had she dressed this non-goth way just for him but kidded herself it was because she needed to hurry?

Idiot, she thought.

He opened the door and waited for her to go first.

She felt awkward as they walked silently down the steps. He was in some sort of mood, she could feel it, but even though she once again tried to open herself up to his thoughts, she couldn't read them.

"Where are we going?" she finally asked. "And how are we getting there?"

"I'm seventeen," Dalton said. "I've had my license a year. I'm legal to drive you in my car without supervision."

Simone frowned. "Wait. You're seventeen?"

That got a chuckle out of Dalton. "Before you get the idea I flunked, I was sort of a hyperactive kid. My mother waited to enroll me in kindergarten."

"Oh," Simone said.

"I like that sweater you're wearing, by the way."

Simone smiled. He'd noticed.

Dalton's car was a sleek 1969 Camaro, chrome and deep-purple paint shimmering under a nearby street lamp.

"Wow," Simone said softly.

"You like?"

"It's groovy," Simone commented, thinking of the comment Kim had made, using the term as a kind of inside joke.

"Groovy? Try awesome!"

"Yeah, that's what I meant," Simone said.

Dalton opened the passenger door for her and hurried around to the other side. They both buckled up. He reached to turn the ignition key and paused. "I feel like I need to clear the air. I was in a bad mood when I got to your apartment. I'm sorry. I don't like to be manipulated."

A surge of guilt passed through Simone. "You think I manipulated you? I really don't cling to my phone like most kids do. And I didn't expect you to call."

He looked at her and shook his head. "Not you. I don't get a manipulation vibe from you at all."

Oh, Simone thought, feeling foolish.

"Jenna. She can be a nice person when she wants, but she's insecure."

"Jenna? Insecure? Are you sure about that?" Simone heard an edge in her voice.

"Very. She surrounds herself with people who idolize her because she needs that to feel good about herself. Appearances are everything. And I know that's normal for fifteen." He paused. "I sound kind of full of myself, don't I?"

Did he? Simone thought. *Maybe a little.*

He nodded, answering his own question. "I just thought I should explain since she's been trying to control you, too. We hung out over the summer. Nothing serious. But as school neared she told me she wanted to break up. I didn't even realize we were a couple. I wasn't dating anyone else, but I thought we were just hanging out. Most of the time her friends were with us. Honestly, I drive, and I think that was the appeal."

A number of questions flew through Simone's mind, but she didn't ask them. He might tell her they were none of her business.

"So then, the day before the first day of school she calls to say she'd changed her mind. I told her I hadn't. Summer was fun, but blah blah blah. You know?"

No, I don't know, Simone thought. She wished he'd tell her, but he didn't.

"Anyway, she cooked up this party and told me I was expected, which was a load of you-know-what. She'd grabbed my phone, kidding around, on Friday and I just knew she'd found your number and called you, because she can be like that. So that's it. That's why I was annoyed when I got to your apartment, and I'm sorry about that."

"It's okay," Simone mumbled. "It's not your fault."

He started the car and didn't say anything else for a while. Simone watched him drive. He didn't speed or show off, but he didn't drive like an old lady either. The radio was on, but turned low to KIIS FM. The music came through speakers in the back. She liked that Dalton had his license and that because of his age, he acted more mature than most of the guys at school. At least, it seemed so to her.

"What do you do when you're not at school?" she asked. "Like what do you usually do on a Friday night?"

Dalton shrugged. "I don't have a usual Friday night. Sometimes I hang out with friends. Sometimes I do, you know, whatever. What about you?"

"Oh, me? I really do read a lot. During the summer I babysat." She felt so boring. She didn't feel like telling him she watched a lot of videos on YouTube or that she liked cartoons and old musicals like *Wicked* and *The Phantom of the Opera.*

"I have a job, too," Dalton offered when Simone didn't say more. "Sundays at Napa's. I work on my car a lot. Not because it breaks down. I like to tinker with things and keep it super clean."

She could see that. The interior was completely dust-free and paper-free. There were no stray items of any kind. Anna's car was always littered with a few things.

"I read . . . " Dalton gave her a quick look with a smile. ". . . of course. And I'm on the swim team. JV."

Simone had been on a swim team when she was younger, but she didn't tell him that. She preferred he just talk about himself.

"I'll never be a Michael Phelps or anything." He shrugged. "But I swim second in the four hundred free relay, which means I'm the weakest of the four, but it also means I swim faster than most of the team."

"Oh," was all Simone managed to say. They drove in silence for a little while with neither speaking until Simone felt too uncomfortable. "I really do like your car," she said.

He glanced at her. "You're into cars?"

"I don't know anything about cars. But this one is super

nice."

"As opposed to groovy?" He smiled.

She smiled back.

"Actually," he said, "there are those that would argue 'groovy' is the greatest slang term ever. Although there are those who think it's uncool. I prefer 'awesome' myself."

"As in 'your car is awesome.' Which it is."

"Yes, it is."

"Groovy." Simone laughed.

Okay, they seemed to be breaking the ice. At least they were laughing.

"I was going to take you to this one place for dinner," Dalton explained. "But I changed my mind. We wouldn't really be able to talk there. Do you like the beach?"

"I was raised in southern California. What do you think?"

"Okay, then." They were at the 605 freeway and Dalton took the onramp to drive south. "Do you like seafood?"

"I like fish tacos."

"Awesome."

"Groovy."

They both laughed, even though the joke had gotten a little stale, and then there was silence again. Dalton seemed to be into his own thoughts. This was one of those times when it would have been good to keep up her mind-reading eavesdropping skills.

"What are you thinking about?"

He flashed a smile. "Okay, you caught me. I was wondering about you."

"Wondering why you asked me out? This isn't exactly going so well, is it? We don't seem to have anything in common."

"Au contraire. We have books! And the night is young."

Simone giggled. "Okay. If you say so." She was quiet for a second. "What were you wondering? You can ask me anything. Doesn't mean I'll answer if I don't like the question."

He glanced her way again.

"All right. That's fair." He paused a moment. "You know, most people heard about you. That you were kicked out of your last school." He paused again. "I thought you'd be a bully, but that's not what I see. What was the fight about that got you suspended?"

CHAPTER 7

OH, BOY. SHE didn't see that coming. A full confession would involve admitting to some of the strange things she could do. *Well, you see, I can move objects without using my hands. I can see ghosts. I can read people's minds, sometimes. And if anybody gets wind of it, or just hears a rumor about it, I get called a liar. Which I can handle until it goes too far. And this last time it went too far. This girl kept saying, "Prove it, you liar." And she knocked me to the ground. I beaned her. I broke her nose . . . with my mind. I didn't mean to. If I'm calm I can direct my kinetic abilities. But if I'm too far gone, as in extremely upset, angry, mad, or scared, the feelings get so strong they're like a laser I can't control. And even though no one could have seen me "throw the first punch" because I didn't, that's what everyone said I did.*

Simone sighed. How much could she say? He'd never believe the truth. She could just make up a story, but why should she?

"Maybe we should stick to books," Simone said. "How about that Cyrano? Did he hate himself or what?"

She laughed, but Dalton didn't. *He seriously wants to know,* she thought.

"If I told you what happened, you wouldn't believe me," Simone said.

"How do you know? I'm fairly open-minded."

"You have to be *completely* open-minded. And nobody is that. Not that I think they should be. Then you're just an airhead."

She saw him nod with a thoughtful expression on his face.

"What?" she asked.

"Nothing. I'm trying to figure out what could be such a big secret. Were you going to say it wasn't your fault? I'd actually believe that."

It wasn't a good idea to confess to him, Simone was certain of that. He'd either run like she had the pestilence, tell other people she was nuts, or, who knew? She stared at him. She really did like him and she'd be risking losing him as a friend, but then again, if knowing her secret made him reject her, then it was better to get that over with now before she got any more attached.

"Okay," she said. "Allow me to demonstrate. When I say 'go,' take your hands off the wheel."

"Uh?"

"You have to trust me."

His brow furrowed and his eyes slid in her direction.

"You can always grab it if you get scared."

"Scared? Me?"

She giggled. "Yes, you."

"I don't scare easy." He started to remove his hands.

"Not yet!"

He grabbed hold.

"I have to be ready." She stared at the steering wheel. After a couple of seconds she said, "Now."

Dalton let go and Simone looked out the windshield, gauging traffic. She glanced out the back window and then the side window beyond Dalton. A Honda Civic passed before it was clear.

"We're going to change lanes. Don't grab the wheel," Simone ordered.

The wheel turned enough to guide the Camaro left into the next lane.

"You can take control again," Simone said.

Dalton took the wheel. "How'd you do that?"

"My little secret."

She waited for what would come next. But apparently Dalton was at a loss for words.

§ § §

They cruised west on Main Street, a street alive with people enjoying their Saturday evening, looking in the windows of boutique stores, gift shops, and galleries, or patronizing the bars and restaurants, or just walking straight ahead for the Seal Beach pier. It was nearing seven, and the sun was low in the sky, creating a vista of gold, orange, purple and pink.

Dalton spotted someone pulling out of one of the parking places that angled to the curb. "Good timing," he said as he swung the Camaro into the spot. They were close to the ocean and Simone could hear the crashing of the waves and smell the salt air. It was refreshing and a little chilly. As soon as she stepped out of the car Dalton was right there, taking her hand, shooting her heartbeat into overdrive. He was touching her. Her skin warmed immediately.

"The restaurant is across the street," Dalton said. They had to wait for three cars to pass and then they made a dash for it.

He didn't cancel the rest of the evening. He didn't run away. And he's holding my hand. Simone's heart continued to race.

Dalton opened the restaurant door and guided her inside. It was a little noisy because it was packed and they had to wait ten minutes for a table, but that wasn't bad. Once they were settled in, they looked over the menus.

"Order anything you like," Dalton said with a grin. "I'm a working lad and my parents pay the rent."

Simone smiled. She had actually lost her appetite, but she knew guys hated it when girls didn't eat. She tried to read the many options on the menu, but couldn't concentrate. "How about I have what you have?" She closed the menu.

"Fish tacos?" he asked rather timidly.

"No, order what . . . " She took a deep breath. "I really only like the fish tacos from Del Taco." She slammed her palms over her face, hiding. "I know. I'm such a kid. I only like Kraft macaroni and cheese, chicken nuggets from Wendy's, and pizza? Only with cheese."

She lowered her hands. Dalton was laughing quietly, his eyes squarely on her. "So at a nice restaurant like this, a hamburger would be a safe bet."

"With fries," she said meekly, feeling stupid. In case she didn't like the hamburger, she could always nibble on fries.

"Hamburgers it is."

He put his menu down. "Now, about that little trick you pulled. Stunning. I know magicians never reveal their secrets, but, um, what was that? And how did that get you kicked out of school?"

"You think it was a trick."

"A good one. Since you put our lives in danger, I think I deserve to know."

"Our lives were never in danger."

"You didn't somehow hypnotize me when I wasn't looking and I was really steering the car with my knee but didn't realize it?"

"You can think that if you want. But *that* would be a real talent."

"You aren't going to tell me."

The waiter arrived. "Good evening. How are you? I'm Charlie and I'll be your server tonight. Can I get you anything to drink? Any appetizers to start with?"

"Cokes?" Dalton stared at Simone and she nodded.

He placed their order without appetizers.

"Maybe I should ask *you* a few questions," Simone said.

"Ask away."

His eyes were all the more vividly blue because of the overhead lights that made them sparkle. And she loved the way his mouth curled up when he smiled, revealing dimples so sweet she had to hold herself back from poking a finger into his cheek. Her mind went blank. She had a million questions and they'd vanished in the flash of an attentive stare.

"I can't think of any at the moment, but when I do, you'll be the first to know."

"Want to discuss books, then?" he offered, and she agreed.

They talked about *Cyrano*, a book that every tenth grader had to read, the reason obvious to any thinking student. Cyrano, embarrassed by the size of his nose, could not see past it to truly understand his self-worth.

"What would you pick as the thing you'd most want to change about yourself?" Dalton asked.

The thought came fast, although it remained unspoken. She'd get rid of her "special" abilities. They made her weird, and not in a good way. "I suppose I'd want smaller feet," she said, which was true, too. "What about you?"

"I'd like to be the fastest swimmer on the team."

"Why is that?"

"I'm no different than anyone else. I like to be on top."

"Ever notice, though, that when you're the best, some people are so jealous they hate you?"

Dalton shrugged. "That's their problem. Anyway, it was only a for instance. I'm actually pretty happy with who I am."

Simone nodded. She could see that.

When they finished their dinner, Dalton suggested a walk on the beach. They stopped at the Camaro to grab two jackets that he'd brought along, and as they walked toward the pier, and then made their way to the sand, they left *Cyrano* behind and discussed what they'd read next.

"Well," Simone said, "I kinda already started *A Tree Grows in Brooklyn*."

Dalton groaned. "That was the one book I didn't get Erickson passing off on me. It's such . . . it seems like girls should read it."

"You might have something there. It's my favorite book of all time and I'm a girl."

"I thought you said you just started it."

"I did. Again. I read it over the summer. You might like it if you give it a chance."

"I might like limburger cheese if that's all there was to eat."

"Okay. But you have to read it, so you might as well get it over with."

She heard another groan, softer this time and suddenly his arm went around her shoulder and he pulled her into him as they continued to walk. It was nippy and the breeze was growing bolder. Maybe he was just cold. She looked up at his face and saw that his eyes were not on her, but directed toward the rolling sea. He'd put his arm around her so comfortably, as if they'd been friends for years, with his thoughts elsewhere.

She liked it and didn't pull away.

"Let's read something else first since you've already read *Tree*. What do you say?" He looked down at her.

She shrugged. "Okay."

"Hey. I thought you said you were tough to work with."

Must be your smile or your eyes. It must be you, Simone thought. She shrugged again. Now that he was this close to her she detected the scent of a light cologne. She didn't know anything about men's colognes and couldn't say what it was, but she liked it. And mixed with the scent of the sea, it was something she'd always remember.

He looked as if he suddenly realized he had an arm around her, but happily, he didn't look shocked either. And he didn't remove it. She hadn't given him reason to; she hadn't protested. But then he said, "I think it's time we head back. You must be cold and I have to work tomorrow."

Did he really think she was cold, wrapped in his jacket and his one-arm embrace? She wasn't. She was warm and tingly all over.

§ § §

Dalton walked Simone up the stairs to her apartment. She continued to wear his jacket, and even though she wasn't the tiniest of girls, it still drowned her. At the door she reached in her purse for her key. "I'll start reading *The Outsiders*."

"Okay," Dalton said. "And we can talk at school."

"I'm kind of a fast reader."

"I'm sure I can keep up," Dalton responded with a smile.

She looked down. "I didn't mean it that way."

"I know." He grinned.

"What?" she asked.

He shook his head, reached out and gave her hair a gentle tug. "Good night, Spooky."

"Don't call me that." Her voice was terser than she intended.

"Okay . . . Sorry. You don't like nicknames?"

"Not that one. It's what kids at the last school called me."

He nodded as though he understood. "All right. I'll call you Simone. Good night." He turned away.

"Good night. I had fun," she called.

He paused and looked at her. "Me, too."

CHAPTER 8

SIMONE CLOSED THE door and leaned against it.

"Well, that was a disaster," a male voice said. She looked up to see Jimmy grinning at her.

"What do you mean?" Simone said defensively. "I had a good time."

"You hardly ate a thing, you were so nervous."

"You were there? Get out. Get out now!"

"You might have sensed I was around if you hadn't been so nervous. You said you'd know, remember? You didn't, and that worries me. You need to sharpen your instincts."

"If you don't leave right now—"

"Who you gonna call? Ghostbusters?" He laughed.

"No. I'll light sage. I'll bring in a priest, five mediums, ten mediums!"

"Whoa. Whoa! Slow down, gorgeous. I told you I'm here to help."

"Help me with what?"

"You never know. You've got enemies now. You need to be prepared."

He vanished before her eyes.

§ § §

Waking up on Sunday morning was a joy. Despite Jimmy showing up when she'd come home, Simone felt good about last night. She hadn't said too many stupid things that she recalled. She'd shown Dalton one of her abilities and he had swept it away with rationalization. But that was fine by her. She didn't want anyone to know what she could do. Calling her "Spooky" had freaked her out a little. She sort of wondered if he'd heard about the nickname from someone. But that was just her being paranoid. At least she hoped so.

As the day wore on, she felt less and less positive about the evening. She wanted the phone to ring with Dalton on the line telling her he'd had a good time, or let's do that again.

Stupid, she told herself. He never said he'd call her. And it wasn't a *date* date.

She finished her homework and read half of *The Outsiders* before it was evening and time to go to bed.

If Sunday turned into a "self-stress" day, as she called them when nothing was wrong but she stressed anyway, Monday was more so.

What was she going to wear? Something "normal" that Dalton would like? Or should she continue with the dark stuff that wasn't really her? Compromise?

No. She wasn't going to compromise. And Dalton wasn't her boyfriend.

She went into the bathroom and took the time to color a streak of purple into her hair. Then she grabbed the front-zippered black corset blouse from a hanger. This was her. At least for now. When it came time to apply her makeup, she painted her eyes and lips extra dark.

Dalton snickered when he saw her walk into class, and even shook his head. The snicker bothered her a little, but when she'd dressed she'd also put on an emotional shield and was determined to be strong.

Be who you are and this is who you are right now, she told herself.

A loner with a chip on your shoulder. How attractive is that? Kim responded. She wasn't manifested, but she was there.

Are you reading my mind? Simone thought back.

Natch.

Well, stop it.

I know. It isn't polite. But you and I seem to be connected. I can't remember anyone I've been connected to like this. I'll see you later.

I can't wait, Simone thought, her anger at Dalton spilling over to others.

Dalton never talked to her, not before the bell rang and not after. She walked slowly out the door and took her time heading for second period. But, except for the snicker, Dalton ignored her. What had she done wrong? Kept his jacket? That really was an accident.

When it was lunchtime, Simone found Kim, a full-blown apparition, walking beside her toward the quad.

"As long as I'm with you, those girls won't bother you," Kim explained.

"You mean people can see you? They know you're a . . . "

"Ghost." Kim laughed. "You can say it, I don't mind. And you can see me. That's for sure. But others? When I'm like this, most people only see a dark mist or something like that. Or they feel me. It's kind of fun to watch them scurry away. Like, notice no one sat in that chair in front of you in history? They might start to, but they always change their mind. Not because they see me."

"Because they feel you. And I thought they didn't want to

sit near me."

"Nope. It takes a lot of energy to stay in this form. I've worked at it forever—well, since I died. I've managed to maintain for as much as an hour, that's pretty much my Guinness Book of World Records. What I was hoping to do, once I realized our connection, was hang with you enough so that you thought I was alive and then spring it on you."

"Well, you sprang it on me."

"Did I?" She sighed. "Not exactly how I wanted to, but I've learned. You can't have everything."

"My stepdad used to say, 'Simone. You have to learn to live with disappointment. But that doesn't mean you don't keep trying to kick butt.'"

Kim laughed.

Simone stared at her ghostly friend. Now that she really studied Kim, she could see that her apparition had some haze around the edges. "You're so young," Simone said softly. "How did you die?"

Kim's image flickered like a satellite dish on the blink. "Um. Well." Kim disappeared and reappeared. "Oh. I . . . I'm not . . . "

She didn't look as opaque as she had. Simone watched and after a second, Kim was gone. Simone half expected Jimmy to make an appearance, but he didn't. And, for some reason, she wanted him to. He was starting to grow on her.

Also, she felt lonely.

She paused in the corridor. Kids were everywhere, but hardly any were by themselves like she was. If they were, they were soon joined by someone, and always seemed relieved when that happened.

Nope. Wouldn't want to be a geek-head, untouchable loner like me.

The goth kids didn't mind being friendless, though. Some of them sat alone, smileless. Always smileless. Like if they did smile, it might fissure their skin.

She'd watched one of those YouTube channels about how to fit in on your first day of school. Do this, say that. Try it, someone will like you. She'd tried it at her last school and been shut down pretty quickly. If there was such a thing as having "it," was there such a thing as having the opposite?

Well, she wasn't really it-less. She had made a couple of friends. Ghosts as they might be, they still seemed to be friends.

And then there was Dalton. But was he a friend? What was that snicker about? Were they still going to meet to discuss books?

She started walking, head down, all books in her backpack, none shielding her chest. "Probably not," she said aloud at just the moment she practically bumped into Jenna, Shelly and Lynette.

"Talking to yourself?" Jenna mocked.

"Why not? She doesn't have anyone else to talk to," Shelly said.

"How was your *date*?" Lynette asked with a fake innocent expression.

"But before you make up some other lame lie," Shelly said. "We already know."

"Know how we know?" Lynette asked, her smile growing wider.

"He told us," Shelly said.

"He came to my party," Jenna explained. "After he left you."

Simone's heart grew suddenly heavy and sank. He'd said he wanted to end their "date" because he had to work the next day. He'd lied to her.

It doesn't matter. It doesn't matter . . . Simone repeated to herself before the thought hit her that this would be an excellent time to read minds. She shifted her gaze from Jenna to Shelly. Shelly was the one whose thoughts had slipped through the first time they'd met. She was her best bet to read what was truly going on in a Jeapest's head.

"He said he was bored out of his skull, and that he shouldn't have wasted his time." The glee in Jenna's voice hit its mark. Simone felt a stab to her insides. But she remained determined to read Shelly's mind and stared at her.

"He stayed until two in the morning. I had to practically push him out the door," Jenna said.

Shelly giggled. *Good one,* she thought, glancing at Jenna before looking at Simone.

"What are you staring at?" Lynette asked.

Shelly frowned. *This girl is a freak*, she thought. *Why are we even bothering with her?*

Simone smiled slightly. She liked that Shelly felt uncomfortable and that her thoughts had come through.

"Three against one. It hardly seems fair," Jimmy said.

Simone broke contact with Shelly and looked to her side. There he was, in living plaid. Simone looked at the Jeapests. They didn't act nervous as they had when Kim walked toward them. They couldn't sense Jimmy, she decided. She wondered if Jimmy could read her mind like Kim.

They can sense Kim, but not you, she thought.

"Kim is advanced in some ways and not so much in others," Jimmy said.

Then you know each other.

"Yes."

And you can read my thoughts like she can.

"Yes. But it's much easier for me when you just talk normal."

Simone felt a push that almost caused her to hit the concrete.

"Pay attention, dork," Lynette said.

Simone found her balance. "Don't put your hands on me."

"No?" Jenna said, her brows raised, a challenge in her tone. "What's with the sexy top?"

Simone's heart jumped. She hadn't been going for sexy, but maybe her mother had. She'd grabbed the corset blouse as a quick thing to wear and thrown a black lightweight sweater over it. "I don't know what you're talking about."

"You thought Dalton would like it, you big freak?"

"No. I wasn't thinking about Dalton."

"Yes, you were," Jimmy said.

"Shut up," Simone demanded of Jimmy, speaking aloud without thinking.

"You shut up," Lynette said.

"If you think it's so sexy, maybe everyone should see." Jenna reached out and pulled the zipper of the corset blouse completely down.

Simone heard laughter rise around her. Any kids who were nearby, and there must have been at least twenty who'd ventured close enough to watch the Jeapests dish out their brand of fun, watched in complete amusement.

Simone didn't rush to zip up her blouse. She'd put a camisole on that morning and so the most embarrassing part of the whole encounter was that someone was messing with her, trying to hurt her. Simone slowly and purposefully zipped the zipper. "Are you done?" she asked, maintaining her cool. She didn't need another episode like last year that had gotten her kicked out of school. If her temper flared, who knew what bone she might break this time. Maybe Jenna's neck. The Jeapests had had their moment. Maybe now they'd leave her alone.

"Sure, Spooky," Jenna said. "We have better things to do."

"Spooookeeeee," Shelly and Lynette mocked.

The word plunged like a sword into Simone's midsection. How could Dalton have told them? That hurt more than anything these girls had done. He'd pretended to be a friend when he was anything but.

The Jeapests walked past Simone, bumping her in the process. Simone whirled around, eyes on their backsides as they walked away. Their clingy blouses and tight-tight pants were a blur. Simone eyes were wet as an onslaught of emotions filled her chest and made it hard to breathe. She felt betrayed and humiliated. She was angry, too. As her feelings grew stronger she knew she needed to suppress them quickly or something she didn't want to happen would—

Rrrriiippp.

"That's one," Jimmy said.

Oh, no, thought Simone.

Rrrriiippp.

"That's two."

Rrrriiippp.

"And that's three."

Simone heard the bellow of laughter around her, only this time it was at the expense of Jenna, Shelly and Lynette. Thanks to long splits at the seams of their tight pants, all three had exposed panties. Jenna wore a pink thong. Lynette's panties had a leopard print. Shelly's had Snoopy. They whirled around and faced Simone. At least she hadn't broken anyone's nose and she was yards away from them. Still, the rumor mill would begin. Simone just knew she'd be blamed.

Jimmy roared with laughter. "Man, that was great. I couldn't have done better myself."

Simone wiped her eyes.

"You!" shouted Jenna, pointing a finger reminiscent of Charles Dicken's Ghost of Christmas Yet to Come. "You did this!"

Shelly and Lynette put their hands behind them, covering the exposure as they inched backward toward a girls' restroom.

"Maybe you should lose some weight," a voice in the crowd shouted.

"Or buy bigger clothes," another voice said.

"I'm too sexy for my pants," a boy changed the words to the popular song as he came forward with gyrating dance moves. The kids whistled and hooted.

Jenna lifted her chin, put her hands on her hips and looked at everyone with defiance.

The dean of girls, Mrs. Nagel, arrived to put an end to the disturbance and also to find out who had started what. She eyed the crowd, zeroing in on who was present and who she should talk to.

Jenna pointed once again at Simone. "It was her. She started it, Mrs. Nagel. She split our pants." Jenna whipped around and strutted away, disappearing into the girls' restroom just behind Shelly and Lynette.

CHAPTER 9

SIMONE SAT ON a bench outside Mrs. Nagel's office. Fifth period had nearly ended before she'd been called in to talk to the dean and told to wait in the hall—a familiar tactic. Make 'em sweat before you bring 'em in for an interrogation. The Jeapests deserved what they got, but that didn't make Simone feel better. She had a reputation because of what happened at her last school, and most likely things wouldn't go well.

Mrs. Nagel's door swung open and two boys exited. They both glanced at Simone, saying nothing. "Simone. Will you come in, please?" Mrs. Nagel said.

Simone slid off the bench and stepped inside, her stomach tied in an enormous knot. For a second she thought she might even throw up.

"Take a seat." Mrs. Nagel patted a vinyl armless chair, orange in color, that had been arranged in front of her massive, dark-wood desk. Its twin sat next to a credenza along the north wall. Mrs. Nagel settled into her black, high-back leather chair and, rather than look at Simone, studied some notes neatly written on one of those yellow legal pads.

Simone wished the tightness in her chest would ease up. She took a deep breath and eyed the decor. The overhead lights were off and blinds on the windows were closed. Slivers of light through the slats and a lamp on a side table gave the room a murky glow. Above the table were framed certificates of merit and Mrs. Nagel's college diploma from many decades ago. On the table sat a leafy potted plant beside a framed photo of a teenage girl. *A niece*, Simone thought. Although she didn't really know.

The dean's desk, highly polished and neatly organized, supported a phone, an in/out tray, a stack of folders and a square glass vase that held a number of pencils. Simone had cooled her heels in a few vice principals' offices and by comparison, this room felt sterile and ominous, as if the room were more important than anyone who might enter. The only bright color came from the orange chairs, putting anyone who sat in those chairs under an interrogation spotlight.

Mrs. Nagel continued to review her notes, and Simone got the feeling that part of her punishment was waiting to see what her punishment would be. The dean had been at this game a long time and no doubt knew how to twist the knife in passive-aggressive ways when she wanted. Woodruff Senior High School had been the place of her employment for forty-something years. Simone didn't know how many years Mrs. Nagel had walked the planet, but she guessed that the dean had to be in her mid-sixties, old enough to retire if she wanted. *Thin, attractive, probably beautiful when she was young,* Simone decided. She wore her dull-blondish hair in an old-fashioned French roll and dressed in a classic eggplant-colored pantsuit. Her skin was taut, but there were many lines in her face, especially around the red-lipsticked mouth that she held in a scowl.

Just when Simone thought she might have to sit there for the rest of her life, Mrs. Nagel lifted her head. "Simone, you've been exonerated."

"Huh?"

"I heard the girls' side of the story, and two of their friends corroborated what they had to say." She paused. "That you grabbed Jenna and Lynette by their clothing, causing it to tear. And when Shelly tried to stop you, you laid into her as well."

Simone sucked on the inside of her cheek waiting for more.

Mrs. Nagel tented her fingers and leaned back. "But when I called in six unbiased witnesses, a few at a time, I think I got an accurate account of what happened. Their pants were just too tight and inappropriate for school. I don't appreciate bullying and have no tolerance for it, just as your last school had none."

The look Mrs. Nagel gave Simone put the fear of God into her. She had, after all, by all inaccurate accounts, broken a girl's nose at her last school.

"I will have a serious talk with Jenna, Shelly and Lynette as well as the students who lied for them. I'm glad to learn that what happened today was not your fault. It would be a shame to have to expel you. Keep your nose clean, Simone."

Simone nodded, and the tightness that had made a home in her chest eased up a bit. Jenna might be queen bee, but not everyone was willing to curtsy. Some kids had told the truth. At the same time, Simone couldn't help but wonder how much good a talk with the Jeapests would do. It wasn't "no tolerance," but at least it was something.

"If they pull any more of these stunts, I want you to tell me," the dean instructed.

Great. I'll be labeled a snitch. "Sure," she said.

§ § §

Simone left the administration building and traipsed down the corridor toward sixth period. It would be half over and she didn't feel like being around anyone, not even Kim. But what else could she do?

The corridor stretched before her, empty except for one of the goth loners crouched against the side of a classroom, directly in Simone's path. He had tats and a ring in his nose. His black hair hung long and looked greasy. He wore black eyeliner and smoked a cigarette. When he saw Simone he stood up.

What now? thought Simone.

He nodded at her as she came near. "You're in the clear," he said, not remotely expecting a response. He dropped the cigarette, crushed it with his boot and headed somewhere, presumably class. Simone stood completely still, not knowing what to make of the boy.

When she entered World History, she found the room had been darkened once again for a film. She didn't see Kim or Jenna. Dalton sat in his assigned seat, the one he'd had since the first day of class, because that's how Mrs. Kent liked it. Several kids looked at Simone, stared at her in fact. Dalton gave her a quick, small smile and a nod. That was all.

Simone took her chair.

The video narration droned on with a British accent and a photo of a muddy battlefield with a water-filled trench and filthy soldiers standing nearby.

" . . . Then we marched back again. But we were still fairly well behind the line. There the sergeant, whom we hated because he snarled every time he spoke, was unlucky, for a flying piece of iron caught him in the liver. Somehow we found we were sorry when he died, because when he had gone we discovered there were a lot of things he had done for his platoon that weren't done for anyone else . . . "

A caption appeared on the screen: From the diary of Alfred Willcox, a private in the Royal Sussex Regiment.

Nobody knows anybody, Simone thought. *Certainly no one knows me, yet people hate me. I can honestly say I don't* **hate** *the Jeapests. I don't like them. I don't understand them. I don't want to be their friend. But I don't hate them.*

Simone thought of Mrs. Peterson, a teacher at her last school whom everyone hated, including Simone, because "mean" seemed to be her middle name. She often embarrassed her students. Simone thought she had no business being a teacher and that, as an adult, she should have a better handle on her behavior. This one girl in class had a mother who told her to try and find something good about Mrs. Peterson. The girl said she honestly couldn't do it. There was nothing—absolutely nothing—good about this teacher.

Then, four months into the school year, Mrs. Peterson wasn't there anymore. Everyone cheered. But then the students learned that her thirty-year-old son had attacked his mother and put her in intensive care. He wanted money for drugs and when she said no, he beat her to a bloody pulp.

Most of the kids felt sorry then, but they still didn't like Mrs. Peterson. Some of them continued to hate.

When the bell rang, Simone rushed out. She reached the bus stop in record time and tried to chill as she waited. She took out her phone and turned it on, thinking music might help her mood. She'd had a bad run-in with Jenna and pals, and even though it had turned out in her favor, Simone still worried about what tomorrow might bring. Jenna could find someone else to do her dirty work if she couldn't do it herself.

The phone came to life with an alert she had a call. Dalton's name appeared in the window. A sick combination of excitement and fear pricked her skin. What did he want? To feed her more lies? She wanted to trust him, and that was a problem. If he did feed her more lies, she might swallow them hook, line and sinker, as her stepfather used to say.

She decided not to answer.

Let him leave a message.

The bus arrived and she rode the lumbering mode of public transportation across town. It took twenty-five minutes to reach her destination, although the time had passed in what seemed like an instant, her mind so full of competing questions.

Had Dalton corroborated Jenna's story? Would Jenna leave her alone now? Why had Dalton told Jenna about her nickname? Who had backed her up with Mrs. Nagel? Why was everything such a mess?

About ten yards from her apartment she spotted Dalton's purple Camaro parked in front of the building. She stopped walking when she saw him hop out of the car, forcing him to come to her.

"I tried to call and tell you I'd give you a ride home. We need to talk about things."

"No, we don't." She sounded hostile because that's how she felt. She saw no need to hide it.

"Okay, I knew you were mad about something the minute I saw you in English Lit."

"No, you didn't."

He chuckled. "In some ways you're like an open book. In others, not so much. The piled-on makeup after we had a good time on Saturday night. A big clue."

Had his smirk been about that? "I heard you were bored out of your skull," she said.

"What?"

"Jenna said you came to her party after you left me and

told her that you'd been bored out of your skull."

"And you believed her?"

"I did."

Dalton put his hands on his hips and looked at the ground with a big groan. "I did go to the party. That's true." He looked at Simone. "But I stayed less than five minutes. Long enough to tell Jenna . . . okay, I'm not trying to be a knight in shining armor or something like that. I just know that Jenna's harassing you because of me and I thought if I told her to lay off—you and I were just friends—she'd calm down. But she tried to make me drink the Kool-Aid, her special punch for drunks, and I wouldn't. Then . . . never mind that. I think I pissed her off even more, if that little stunt she pulled at school is any indication. I told Mrs. Nagel what I saw happen, by the way. A lot of kids did. I don't know why you think everybody hates you."

"I don't think that."

"You act like it. But, maybe hate is too strong a word. People do like you, as much as they like anyone else. And they don't like you as much as they don't like anyone else. You need to start liking yourself."

"Don't lecture me. And who says I don't like myself?"

He sighed this time. "You're right. Who am I to give you a sermon? But, I blew off swim team to come talk to you. I should be there right now. Coach won't let you be late. If you're late, you don't even show. And if you aren't sick, you swim thirty-two laps before you even get to work out the next day. So I'm screwed right now. You got any cookies and milk?"

Simone suppressed a smile. She wanted to believe him. In fact, she did believe him. He'd broken through her shield. It wouldn't hurt to have him come in for milk and . . . "No to the cookies. Yes to the milk. We have cereal."

"Unless you want to go to Wendy's for chicken nuggets."

Simone almost said yes and then she remembered her makeup. "You sure?" She pointed at her face.

"I can handle it. Come on."

He led the way to the Camaro and opened the door for her. The closest Wendy's was ten minutes away.

Dalton drove for a couple of minutes before he spoke. "Jenna's right about one thing. That blouse you're wearing is sexy." He shook his head and kept his eyes on the road.

The comment surprised her and she felt her face grow hot. It wasn't that she didn't like what he said, exactly. But it made her self-conscious.

"Sorry," he added. "Was that a weird thing to say?"

She gave a little shrug. "I don't know what's weird and what isn't anymore."

Dalton glanced at her and smiled.

Silence filled the car. Simone stared at him. This would be a good time to bring it up, she decided. "Why'd you tell Jenna about 'Spooky'?"

"What are you talking about? I didn't."

"She knew it."

"Maybe she called you that by accident, like I did."

"Nope. They all said it, and in a way . . . someone told them."

"Well, it wasn't me. I promise."

She sighed quietly and hoped he was telling the truth.

Dalton pulled into the Wendy's parking lot. "Drive-through or walk-in?"

"If you wanna drive through because of how I look, that's fine." She'd used that chip-on-her-shoulder voice. *Stop it,* she told herself.

Dalton parked the car. "Walk-in, it is." He turned off the engine and hopped out. Simone stepped out as well before he could run around and open her door. "You know, I have two sisters," he said. "The older one says it's nice when a guy opens the door for her. The younger one, well, she's twelve and I call her 'snippy.' She says it's stupid. I guess you're in agreement with the twelve-year-old."

Simone shrugged. "I never thought about it. I'm capable of opening the door."

"Got it," he said.

They went inside and he ordered chicken nuggets for the two of them. As they ate, Simone decided she wanted to know more about him. "How old is your other sister?"

"Marceline?"

"I don't know her name. You said one was twelve. The other?"

He laughed. "Marceline. She's twenty-three. My parents spread us out. Can't tell you why."

"Are you close to them?"

"Mmm. I used to be very close to the younger one. Cindi. She looked up to me for the longest time. And then she turned twelve and something changed. Now she acts like I'm the enemy half the time."

"And Marceline?"

"We're pretty close." He grabbed another chicken nugget. "You? Any siblings?"

"It's just Mom and me."

"And you're close."

Simone shrugged. "Sometimes she feels like a big sister. She tries."

"I kind of got that when I talked to her. I don't think my mother would give out Cindi's cell and address to a boy she'd never met, even if Cindi was older. And my dad? Forget it. He'd want to know everything about the guy, including his blood type and social security number, before he would let Cindi skateboard in front of the house with the kid."

Simone pressed her lips tightly together. Her mother—not the overprotective type, that was for sure. She felt her defenses go up. What could she say? Anna was Anna. She did things her way.

"I've been thinking about that trick you pulled in the car Saturday night," Dalton said.

Simone braced for what might come next and stared at the chicken nuggets on her tray.

"It wasn't a trick, was it?"

She met his eyes. "Of course it was a trick. What else could it be?" Simone popped a nugget into her mouth and looked over at some people at another table.

"Telekinesis."

Simone looked back at Dalton. "Do you believe in that sort of thing?"

"I don't think it matters if I believe. I saw you do it."

She pressed her lips together again. Should she say more?

"You trusted me enough to show me. Maybe you should trust me enough to admit what you did."

Her guard began to melt. She had shown him, so why not admit it?

"It's no big deal. I can do certain things. Like turn a steering wheel. Shut off a light. I can bend a spoon despite what some people say about that. Things are made up of energy and for some reason if I picture something in my mind in just the right way, I can make it happen. I was born that way. My mom said she almost changed my name to Tabitha. You know, the baby on *Bewitched*. That old show."

"So your mom knows you can do this?"

"Sort of. I guess as a baby I could make the blanket cover me if I was cold. Or I'd make a toy float in the air and come to me. When I was five or six, I figured out people didn't understand, and I pretended I couldn't do things like that. My mom quit asking me about it somewhere along the line, and we don't talk about it. I don't talk about it."

"Can you do bigger things?"

"Like break a girl's nose? Or split the seam in some very tight pants? What do you think?"

"I think you can."

Simone answered slowly and quietly. "I didn't mean to break that girl's nose. And I didn't split those pants on purpose."

"I wouldn't blame you if you had. Well, I don't know about the nose thing."

Simone studied him. "But I didn't do either on purpose. I really didn't."

"Then you didn't. Hey, did you start *The Outsiders*?"

He'd changed the subject because her discomfort must show. *Nice*, she thought. But she needed reassurance. "Don't tell anyone, okay?"

He gave her an understanding smile but no words.

"What I just told you," Simone said. "Don't share it. People think it's weird."

"Hey, don't worry. It's our secret, okay?"

She bit her lip. Would he really keep it a secret?

Dalton leaned across the table and tugged her hair. "Don't worry. I won't tell anyone."

She nodded, finally believing him.

"Guess what book I started?" he asked.

She shook her head.

"*A Tree Grows in Brooklyn.*"

"Why?"

He smiled and shrugged. "Because you really wanted me to. But, I must confess. I've only read five pages."

Simone laughed.

Dalton drove Simone back to her apartment and left the car running while she snatched her backpack from the car floor and reached for the door handle. "Thanks for the chicken nuggets." She pulled the lever.

"You're welcome. You know, I was thinking. I can't drive you home from school because of swim team, but I could give you a ride to school. It would save you one bus trip a day, anyway."

What had he said? Ride to school? Every day? A thick sense of fear overwhelmed her and she suddenly felt sick to her stomach. If she did that, she'd start trusting him even more than she already did. She liked him. She liked him a lot. Probably in a way he didn't like her. What if he turned out to be like Chris Hecker, that jerk from her last school? She'd thought he was a friend. Not a boyfriend, just a friend. But she'd trusted him.

Her fear turned to irrational anger. "No. I don't think so. It's a bad idea. I'm fine with the bus."

Simone hopped out of the car, slammed the door and hurried into the courtyard of the apartment building. She ran up the stairs as if something were chasing her, and fumbled with the key to unlock the door, even dropping it once. She liked Dalton way too much. Riding with him every day to school? She'd get attached, and she'd probably talk about herself too much. And what about the Jeapests? They'd really go crazy.

Rushing through the door, she thought about what had

happened with Chris—the class clown at her last school. A real cut-up who made people laugh. He also got in trouble a lot, always wound up in detention. But he'd talked to her like a friend. He'd turned on the charm and hung around her at lunchtime and break.

She never saw it coming. When Chris said, "Let's tell each other our deepest, darkest secret," she told him about her childhood friend Lizzy, the ghost. He frowned and said, "Come on. Kids always make up friends when they're little. Tell me about something going on more recent."

After a short debate with herself, she confessed she could move things with her mind.

"Oh, yeah? Show me," he said with a big smile on his face. "That's cool."

Simone didn't like to demonstrate. It made her uncomfortable. But they'd been hanging out at lunch for over two weeks and he'd shared all the "bad" things he'd done that got him in trouble. Simone didn't see the harm. She thought they were friends.

She spotted a Coke can someone had left on a table and pointed. "I'll make it jump into the trash," she said.

She stared and after a couple of seconds the can rose in the air and flew into the receptacle. She smiled and looked at her friend. She expected him to laugh, do a high-five, and say something clever like he always did. But not this time. He frowned and looked around, which made Simone look around. There were kids everywhere, watching.

"Thanks a lot, Spooky. You just cost me twenty bucks," Chris snarled.

"What are you talking about?"

"Jay saw a folder jump into your hands. I told him he was nuts. We made a bet."

Chris stood up and left her sitting there by herself. It was the first time she ever heard somebody call her Spooky.

CHAPTER 10

FOR THE NEXT three days, Simone caught a break. The Jeapests acted like she didn't exist. There was no "accidental" arm bumping or anything like that in the hall. Mrs. Nagel's talk with the girls must have done the job, but Simone knew she still had to wait and see.

Dalton made it a point *not* to sit beside Jenna in World History. He must have asked Miss Kent for permission to move.

He politely smiled at Simone in and out of class. They even met at lunch once to discuss *Cyrano*. Erickson had given the class their assignment for that book and had told everyone to partner up. Dalton had still only read five pages of *A Tree Grows in Brooklyn*. He didn't flirt. He didn't tug her hair. He didn't bring up dates or driving her to school. He wasn't cold, exactly, but he clearly wanted to give her lots of space. She didn't like it, especially after Jimmy paid her a visit at home and told her he'd changed his mind about Dalton. "He's an okay dude."

"You could have told me that at school," Simone said sourly, pouring herself a bowl of cereal, her favorite after-school snack.

"You should be glad I'm willing to travel all the way to your place."

"All the way?" Simone said. "You take a bus or something?"

"It's a joke, gorgeous. Where I reside, there is no time, there is no space." He made cheesy spooky sounds, wiggling his fingers at her.

"Shut up," Simone said with a smile in her voice. She sat at the dinette table. "I haven't seen Kim lately. Why's that?"

Jimmy scrunched his face in an expression that said *huh*. "Why are you asking me?"

"Well, isn't it obvious? You're both, uh, how to say this politely?" She jiggled her spoon and looked toward the ceiling. "Both in the same non-physical condition." She smiled at Jimmy.

"Since when are you polite?" He took the chair across from her.

"Ha, ha."

"Kim does her thing and I do mine."

"What's her thing then? I know yours is hanging around to annoy me."

"I do not annoy. I help. I'm the James Bond of the spirit world. Without the guns and girls and shaken-not-stirred."

"Why don't you want to tell me? What's the big secret?"

"I refuse to speak ill of the dead." He laughed.

"You aren't going to tell me about her."

"She needs to tell you about her. I wasn't even born when she died."

"Hmm. Then tell me about you. Start with your full name and what happened to you." She took a spoonful of Frosted Flakes.

Jimmy sighed, as if explaining himself amounted to some sort of torture. He put his hand over his heart. "My name is James Thomas Poole. Which is ironic, you see, because I drowned in the school swimming pool."

"When?"

"What? No sympathy?"

"Of course I'm sorry. But it's ancient history now, right?"

"Not to my parents."

"Are they still alive?"

"No. But if they were, they'd still be grieving."

"I'm sure you're right."

"Okay, then. Let's have some empathy for the dearly departed."

"All right, dearly departed. When did you die? I've been trying to figure it out."

"Oh, you've been thinking about me."

"Not often."

"Well, what did you come up with?"

"It's tough. You sang that one song: *I Just Dropped In (To See What Condition My Condition Was In)*. I Googled it. Nineteen sixty-seven. You're old, Jimmy."

"My mother liked that song."

"Oh."

"I died in nineteen eighty-eight. Look it up if you want to know more. In fact, you should. It might assist you in knowing why I hang around trying to help kids like you."

"Like me? You mean because I see ghosts."

"No. I've helped kids who don't even know I'm there. Here's the deal. I can't see everything that's going on all the time. But I've noticed that you have unique skills which you've mostly buried. *We* are going to develop them *together* starting this weekend."

"No we're not," she sing-sang.

"Yes we are," he sang right back.

"No way."

"Yes, way. If I have to scare you into it, I will."

Simone laughed. "Scare me? Ghosts don't scare me."

"That's not how I meant it."

"Besides. I have a lot of homework and—"

"Just count this as one of your assignments." He started to fade away instead of merely vanishing in one fell swoop like he usually did. "Oh, and I'm buried in Rose Hills, if you want to pay your respects."

He was gone.

"Pay my respects?" Simone mumbled. "Help me? Help me what?"

She finished her cereal, rinsed the bowl and spoon, and put them in the dishwasher. She eyed her laptop. Time to figure out Jimmy, and apparently that started with his death. She opened the computer and Googled yearbooks for her high school. She discovered that she didn't have to purchase a membership, but if she registered with Classmates.com, she'd have access to them.

Jimmy had died in 1988, so it was a safe bet he'd be in the 1987 book. She pulled it up, paged through and found him in the junior class. She went to the 1988 yearbook and clicked until she came across a memorial page for him that included his senior picture.

Jimmy Poole smiled for the camera, looking rather handsome in a suit and tie with his dark curly hair carefully combed. In print above his picture were the words: "We love you, Jimmy! You'll be missed." Below his picture were the years he'd lived: August 3, 1970–March 17, 1988.

Because the yearbook was a used copy and for sale on the site, there were also handwritten messages on the page. Many were what you'd expect: *Gone, but not forgotten - TH;*

I'll miss those hijinks - JJ.

Someone had drawn a flower with a frowny face and a tear.

Two messages struck Simone as more meaningful: *Hey Jokester, guess the last laugh's on you - Killa. ♡Babycakes♡ you'll always be mine XX Kaci*

Simone moved to the senior section to look for who Kaci might be. Only one girl claimed that name: Kaci Black.

Nothing in the yearbook said how Jimmy died. He'd have to tell her the details, or . . . an idea popped into Simone's head. She went to findagrave.com and typed in Jimmy's name and date of death. She found him immediately. The page included a picture of his grave and of him. And someone had added a bio:

> Jokester Jimmy. In the early morning hours of March 17, 1988, James Poole, a senior attending Woodruff Senior High School, went to the school's swimming pool with a bucket and several ounces of green pool dye. Known for his pranks, he was going to dye the water for St. Paddy's day. Come daylight, a maintenance worker found him in the pool, floating face down. He had a knot on his head and water in his lungs. It was ruled an accidental drowning, although some disagree.

How is this information supposed to help me? I can swim

and I don't pull pranks. Jimmy, aka Babycakes, had more explaining to do.

She laughed. "Babycakes," she said aloud.

§ § §

On Friday, Simone's worst nightmare came true. She knew how Jenna had found out about her nickname Spooky: Chris Hecker.

During the twelve-minute snack break students were allotted after second period, Simone hurried to the girls' locker room where she'd forgotten her choker necklace after gym class. As she approached the door to enter, she heard giggling. Not the kind that indicated someone was laughing at her; the more intimate kind, like cooing birds showing their approval of each other. Simone looked in the direction of a building catty-corner to the gym, around thirty feet away. Jenna's back pressed against the building with her arms resting on Chris's shoulders, hands clasped behind his neck. He leaned toward her, his hands flat against the building on either side of her head. They smiled into one another's eyes, talking low. When they kissed, Simone ducked inside the gym.

Wow. Wow! was all she could think. Had Chris been at this school since day one? Almost four thousand students attended Woodruff Senior High, so it wasn't a stretch that she hadn't spotted him before. What she couldn't understand was, if Jenna liked Chris, why had she made a big deal out of Dalton talking to her? It was petty and stupid and made no sense. But that was Jenna.

And Chris is no prize.

Terry, Simone's stepdad, had said it best: "Birds of a feather flock together."

Simone made her way to the locker she'd used during gym class, opened it and found the choker near the back. She grabbed it and fastened it around her neck. She'd have to leave the way she came. Hopefully, she could time it so neither Jenna nor Chris would see her.

She sat on a bench between two rows of lockers as another question swirled in her head. Did others know Jenna and Chris were hooking up? Maybe not, since they appeared to be hiding. Of course, they could have just wanted privacy.

Nah. It seemed like kids sought the spotlight in all things. They wanted to show others they had a life.

The more she thought about Jenna with Chris, the more her heart raced. She felt scared. *Okay, good*, she thought, suddenly glad Jimmy wanted to help her this weekend. She needed to stay one step ahead of Jenna. She took a deep breath and blew it out. "Babycakes," she whispered, smiling at the pet name she'd read in the yearbook. "You were right."

"Who's Babycakes?"

Simone looked around. Kim's perfume scented the air, but Kim wasn't visible.

"Jimmy Poole. You two know each other, don't you?"

"Oh, him."

"Don't you like him?"

"He's sort of a know-it-all. He says I'm confused."

"Are you?"

"I don't think so. Well, maybe sometimes."

Kim started to appear, but only partially. Simone could see her head and face and part of her torso in that striped dress she always wore. She was hazy.

"What are you confused about?" Simone asked. "You know you've passed. You know you're a ghost."

Kim stared at her. "I know." She looked away. This was

not the cheerful Kim that Simone had come to expect. "It's just that sometimes I'm back at school the way it was, with the people I knew. With lockers and lots of rules about clothes and behavior. And it seems so real I have to remind myself it's not real. I guess that means I'm not confused." She suddenly smiled. "Right?"

"Sounds right to me. Kim, I don't mean to be blunt, but when did you go to school here? When did you die?"

"I was Homecoming Queen. Did you know that?"

"No," Simone said. "I don't know anything about you."

"Well, I was. And Scotty Ohanian was king. He was a doll, I can't even tell you, and all the girls were bummed when we started dating. His ex was majorly ticked off. She tried to start rumors that I was a druggie. And she turned into a big rat fink, too."

"Rat fink?"

"Yeah. Scotty had shared some stuff about himself and she told. Tried to get him in trouble. She was a real scuzz."

"What year was this?"

"Nineteen sixty-eight. You know, the last thing I remember is talking to her. I went to this party and Leslie was there."

"That's Scotty's ex?"

"Uh-huh. She cornered me and said she wanted to talk. She said she wanted to apologize. I didn't really believe her, even though I wanted to. I wanted to think she'd changed. Especially since the friends I had at the party had already left and I didn't know if I could take her, you know, saying rotten stuff to me. So I tried to be cool and I remember I said, 'That's nice.'"

"What did she say?"

"She smiled and said, 'No, really. I'm very, very sorry.'"

"Was she?"

"I don't know. I don't remember anything after that."

The warning bell rang and Simone knew she had all of two minutes to get to class. But learning about Kim seemed more important. As long as Kim wanted to stick around, Simone would, too.

Kim remained quiet for a while. Her eyes had a faraway look. "Sometimes everything seems like a dream, though. I'll be at school back in nineteen sixty-eight where I belong and I'll think, 'Good. I woke up.' I'll be walking with friends, going to class. Sometimes I'm with Scotty and we talk about going to that party. But he wouldn't go. And then suddenly I'm at school and it isn't my time anymore. The kids are all different and they dress strange and I think '*This* is a dream.' But I know it isn't. It happened so often that I started trying to be visible so I could mingle with the kids. It was a relief to discover you could see me, Simone. As I am. No mist. No shadowy energy. You saw me."

Kim smiled.

Simone was two minutes late for third period and the teacher wasn't cool. She got a detention slip, to be served next Monday after school.

CHAPTER 11

DALTON STORMED INTO the house, slammed the door, and raced toward his room. His energy was so pervasive, Cindi poked her head into the hall from her bedroom and yelled, "Keep it down, snot nose!"

Dalton spun around, causing alarm to materialize in his baby sister's eyes. "What did you call me?"

"Nothing. I was kidding." She shut the door.

"That's what I thought."

Normally, Dalton let anything and everything Cindi said run off his back. She was a preteen and going through whatever preteen girls went through. But right now he was pissed.

He entered his bedroom, tossed his gym bag into a corner and threw himself onto the bed. He jumped off the mattress and grabbed a basketball from the closet. He lay back down and began tossing the ball into the air, catching it over and over. His mind spun in circles. "Yeah, yeah, yeah," he said to himself. "Yeah."

He threw the ball so hard it hit the ceiling and shot back at him.

"A couple bad swims. One missed practice. One time!"

He threw the ball at the open closet. It knocked into clothing, boxes, and shoes, setting up a racket before it was caged. "Coach should have given me a second chance." He sat up, swung his feet to the floor and put elbows on knees. He rested his head on two fists. "I'll show him he made a mistake."

"Who made a mistake?"

Dalton looked over at the door. Cindi leaned against the casing, her mouth biliously fixed.

"Coach," he answered.

Cindi took the response as permission to enter. "Wha'd he do?"

"He kicked me off the four hundred free relay. Put Egan in. I always beat Egan's time. Except this week." He shook his head in disbelief.

"Well. You can get back in. Right? Just do better next week."

"There's a meet tomorrow. And . . . never mind. I was being dumb."

"What?"

He eyed his little sister. For a second he considered confiding in her, then thought better of it. "You're right. I'll do better." He looked away. "Egan buckled down this week, but usually he's a screw-off."

"That's not what you were going to say."

"Sure it was."

"Nuh-uh." She stared at him.

He sure did want to get things off his chest. He could talk to his friends but they'd make fun and the way he was feeling was anything but fun. He didn't need their ribbing.

"Is it girl trouble?" Cindi asked.

Dalton's jaw went slack. "What made you ask that?"

"Well. My friend saw you at Wendy's the other day with one of those goth geeks. And you're acting weird."

"Two and two makes five, huh?"

"Four. Because I'm right."

"She's not a geek. I don't even think she's goth, if you want to know the truth."

"Of course I want to know the truth."

Dalton didn't know what else to say. How could talking to a twelve-year-old help? Being kicked off the relay team bothered him, but Simone bothered him more. He'd been thinking about her so much he'd skipped one day of practice, and couldn't focus on swimming when he *was* in the pool.

"Dalton?"

"It's nothing."

"Why are you so woeful?"

"Woeful?" He laughed. "What have you been reading?"

"Poetry. We have to write poetry with words our teacher chooses." She stepped farther into the room, then sat cross-legged on the floor and looked up at him, her long brown mop of hair making her look a little like a grown-up Cabbage Patch doll. "Don't think of me as your little sister. Think of me as your therapist. I help all my friends." Her face was somber, almost deadpan.

"Who helps *you*?"

"I'm serious. Tell me all about it."

Dalton cracked a wide smile. It was wacky to hear his sister talk this way, and even wackier that he was thinking about telling her what he had on his mind.

"Okay, I have a question for you. Why would a girl who has to take the city bus to school, turn down my offer to drive her? And. And!" He held up a finger. "Be mad about it?"

"I don't know. If it's that goth geek—" She stopped herself and held up both hands. "*Girl.* Maybe she's just weird."

Dalton shook his head. "No. Something was bothering her. It was like I scared her or something."

"Hmmm." Cindi appeared to think very hard. "I got nothin'. But . . . You could just ask her. Ever think of that?"

"Of course," he said.

He'd thought of it and decided against it. As comfortable as he was with most girls, he had felt shut down by Simone, and he didn't like the feeling. It was foreign to him.

"What did she say?" Cindi wanted to know.

"I said I thought of it. I didn't say I asked."

She shook her head. "You must really, really like her." The doorbell rang and Cindi jumped to her feet. "That's Jill. We're going to make videos. Update at nine?"

Dalton contorted his face. "No. There's nothing to update."

Cindi looked at him with an expression that said she knew better. She flew out the door.

Dalton remained confused, but surprisingly he felt better. He slipped his cell phone from his pocket. Why not just ask Simone why she'd reacted like she did? What was he afraid of?

Nothing. Grow a backbone, he told himself.

But it took two tries before he actually punched in her number.

§ § §

Simone sat at her desk looking for Kim on findagrave.com. She'd learned her last name during their talk in the gym and hoped that lightning would strike twice. She'd been able to discover the facts surrounding Jimmy's death using the site; maybe she'd get lucky with Kim Blue.

Except Kim wasn't listed, and Simone was forced to give up. She typed in the URL for YouTube and began watching music videos. That's when she heard her cell play *Phantom*. She grabbed it and saw Dalton on the ID. Her heart began to pound.

"Hello?" she said, bracing herself against her feelings. She couldn't imagine why he was calling. They'd talked about *Cyrano* on Thursday because Mr. Erickson had given the class that assignment and afterwards said they'd talk the next week. And Dalton had casually said, "See you Monday," when they'd left their last class of the day. Maybe he'd remembered something he forgot to say. She hoped that wasn't it. She wanted him to talk to her like he used to. But she'd put a stop to that when she'd turned down his offer of a ride to school. She'd been stupid. She should have said yes. But she didn't know how to take back her instant reaction.

"Uh, hi." He had to clear his throat. "Hi. It's me. Dalton."

"I know. Hi."

He paused. "I was, um, thinking." He paused again. There was a long silence on the phone and Simone's hand began to tremble. She was picking up the sense of an injured animal. He still didn't talk and she realized now how much her reaction had wounded him. At the time all she'd been focused on was her own feelings. It never occurred to her when she'd slammed the car door that it would have a hurtful effect on him. She needed to apologize and she owed him an explanation.

"Um, Dalton?"

"Yeah."

"I need to say something."

"Okay."

"The other day. When I slammed your car door, um. I was being stupid." It was her turn to pause.

"You were?"

"If I tried to explain what made me do that, I'd sound even stupider. So can I just apologize and let's forget it?"

Her hand quit trembling. She took a deep breath and released it.

"Okay. It's forgotten."

Another pause.

"Why'd you call?" She squeezed her eyes closed. "Did you think of something for *Cyrano*?"

"No. I'd sort of forgotten about that. Did you think of something?"

Simone laughed. "You called me."

Dalton laughed, too. "Right. Well, I have a swim meet tomorrow. Do you want to come watch?"

"Watch? Um, yeah. I guess so. What time?"

"I'll pick you up at seven. As in seven a.m." There was excitement in his voice.

She felt the same.

§ § §

Simone's emotional shield was up again and she'd dressed in black with heavy makeup. There was no point in making him think he was changing her. Dalton didn't seem to mind how she dressed. He made one light-hearted joke about it—*oh, my goth!*—and acted like his old self. Simone felt happy about that, although she did her best not to show it, and that was making the drive to Lakewood where the meet took place a little like their first-date-that-was-officially-not-a-date. Dalton did the talking, explaining which events he'd swim in and when they would occur.

Simone wasn't allowed to sit with the team on the deck of

the indoor pool, so she sat in the bleachers, high in a corner where she could be by herself. The other onlookers appeared to be mostly parents and younger siblings of the swimmers. Five schools were competing, but the stands weren't crowded. Dalton had explained on the drive over that this was a practice meet. It didn't count toward anything official. Swim season geared up in October. But you had to practice in September if you wanted Coach to take you seriously.

She watched the swimmers warm up in the pool. A part of her envied their camaraderie when they sat on towels together, talking, stretching and doing their best to quell the butterflies that ravaged their stomachs. She knew about those butterflies from swimming on that city team until the age of eleven when her stepdad had died. He came to all her meets and practices and said that butterflies meant your adrenaline was pumping and proved that you wanted to do your best. It was good to have butterflies. After he was gone, she'd lost interest in swimming and dropped out. Her mom couldn't afford the dues anymore anyway.

She caught Dalton's eye a couple of times. Once he waved at her. She wiggled fingers back.

"Hey, gorgeous. Aren't you supposed to be at home awaiting my arrival?"

She turned to see Jimmy sitting next to her. "I don't think so. I had something to do."

"It would appear so. Well, it doesn't matter where you practice. You can do it here."

"Here? Like what? Drain the pool while they're swimming?"

She noticed a woman three bench seats down twist and look at her. She stared back until the woman returned her gaze to the swimmers.

I forget I can talk to you with my thoughts, Simone told him.

"People are a little too close," Jimmy said. "You can talk. I actually like it better when you talk. Just keep your voice down."

I have a better idea, she thought. *Don't come around when I'm in public.*

"I need to talk to you when I need to talk to you. I'll get rid of some of these people."

Simone watched Jimmy scramble down the benches to the woman who'd turned to look at her. He lifted the woman's hair and blew in her ear. Simone had to stifle a laugh as the woman shot glances all around, grabbed the little girl next to her and scurried away.

Jimmy moved to a man who was nearly as close as the woman had been. He pointed with an outstretched knuckle, looked at Simone, and then dug into the man's lower back, moving up the spine. After screaming like a child, the man also changed seats.

Five more ghostly assaults later, Simone had a wide berth around her.

"Now where were we?" Jimmy sat beside Simone again. "Oh, yes, draining the pool. That would be a good trick but I don't think you're that advanced."

"I was joking." Simone kept her voice low.

"You're actually pretty good at moving stuff, except when you're excited. Ripping those pants was golden, but you weren't really in control, now were you?"

"Jimmy, Babycakes, I have a simple solution." She glanced around to make sure she was talking softly enough. "Why don't you just tell me when you think something's going to happen so I can avoid it?"

"Simone, gorgeous, I can't see the future. I observe what's happening and get a pretty good idea what might come next."

"Might?"

"I don't know when. I don't know where. But you've gotta be prepared. Look what happened to me. And don't call me Babycakes. That was her name for me."

"Kaci?" Simone saw the lady with the little girl glance at her again. She'd spoken too loudly.

"Ah. I see you did your homework."

Do you visit her? Simone decided talking to Jimmy with her mind was the safest bet.

"No."

Why not?

"She's married. She's happy. She has a life."

Jimmy looked like he had tears in his eyes. Simone was surprised.

Can ghosts cry?

"I emulate it without trying. I'm not sure it's crying. Although I have seen Kim cry."

I had a long chat with her yesterday. She says you think she's confused.

"She is confused."

But she knows she's dead.

"There's more than one way to be confused."

Like?

"Can we just focus on you . . . Uh-oh."

Jimmy suddenly disappeared. It was as if he had only so much juice and it ran out.

Simone had come to like their little talks, and this one had been enlightening. He thought something bad was going to happen, but didn't know what. He couldn't see the future any more than she could. There was Casper the Friendly Ghost.

Maybe he was Jimmy the Suspicious Ghost.

She shifted her attention to Dalton. She was at his swim meet after all, and she'd come to watch him. Thus far, she'd hardly paid attention.

But he was paying attention to her. He waved again and she wondered if he'd seen her talking to Jimmy. She hoped not. How would she explain talking to herself?

A voice came over the loudspeaker. "We begin with the men's two hundred medley relay . . . " Five teams of four swimmers approached the starting blocks and the voice announced the name of the school for each lane.

Dalton had told her his best chance for a win was in the 200 freestyle which would happen right after the medley relay. He'd need to be among the top three in his heat and then swim it again later with others who'd won their heats.

Simone was happy when Dalton made it to the final in every one of his swims. But he came in second in the final race of the 200 free and didn't medal in the 100 free or the 100 butterfly. His frown, as he climbed out of the pool after each loss, said it all.

"My times in the one hundred free and butterfly were a disaster," Dalton said as he drove onto the freeway to take Simone home after the meet.

It was easy for her to see he was depressed. She hoped she could cheer him up. "But you came in second in the two hundred free. That's good."

"I *did* better my time there."

"Hey, that's great," she said. "You should be proud."

He flashed a lukewarm smile. "I wanted to do better." He hesitated. "I wanted to impress you."

"You did impress me."

"No. I wanted to impress you with a win because . . . "

Simone kept still, her eyes on his face. She watched him take a deep breath and let it out.

"What?" she said.

"Well, if you haven't figured it out by now, I guess I'll have to confess. I really like you."

Simone's mind went blank after she heard Dalton's declaration. She knew immediately how she felt about it, however. She liked him, too. But she didn't say it. The words stuck in her throat as if they were just too big to emerge. She felt panic, at the same time. It was that trust issue she had. It insulated her from others.

"Well?" he said. "What do you think about that?"

Simone found her voice, although it was pretty soft. "I'm glad. I like you, too."

Dalton pulled to the curb in front of the apartment building and shut off the motor. He turned and looked her in the eye. "Want to go to the movies tonight?"

"Movies? Uh, sure."

He smiled. "Good. You pick the movie and text the time, okay? I'd choose something too sci-fi or shoot 'em up, and I know that's not you."

"How do you know?"

He gave her an are-you-kidding look. "Give me a little credit."

"All right," she said, reaching for the door handle.

"Wait." He took out his phone. "I think it's time." He pulled her close to him, stretched his arm and took a selfie of the two of them. He checked it. "We look good. I'll send it to you."

She nodded and he gave her hair a tug.

"See you tonight," he said.

She climbed out of the car.

§ § §

Dalton thought about Simone the entire drive home—with a smile. He parked the Camaro in the driveway, jogged into the house and headed straight for his room where he immediately slowed to a stop.

Jenna sat on his bed, fooling with her phone.

Dalton tossed his athletic bag aside roughly which made her look up and smile broadly.

"I was in the neighborhood," Jenna said. "Baby sis let me in."

"Of course you're in the neighborhood, you live three blocks away. What's up?" He stayed in the center of the room, hands on hips.

Jenna dressed seductively—a constant theme with her. She looked good in short-shorts. There was no doubt about that. But her thinking was shallow and one-tracked. If the topic wasn't Jenna, then she changed the subject so that it was.

Dalton had driven Jenna and her friends to the beach a lot over the summer, and it was fun. He'd even made out with her a couple of times. The night of the big bonfire with over forty kids partying had been memorable. Jenna had gotten drunk—drunker than he'd ever seen anybody get—and she'd flirted with everybody.

Then, as the night wore on, she clung to him. They'd settled into the sand, Jenna seated in his lap, both facing the fire. At some point she tilted her chin skyward, the top of her head pressed against his chest. He looked down into her eyes, swimming with moonlight and booze. "I know you lahhv me," she said sloppily, the alcohol she'd consumed in full effect. "Let's . . . get . . . married." She twisted around so that she faced him on hands and knees and leaned in for a kiss. The taste of vodka was not appealing. He knew her proposal was pure game-playing and he decided then and there that she needed to play games with someone else.

"I'll call the preacher tomorrow," he'd responded and she quickly demonstrated that she didn't like his sarcastic tone.

"You think I was serious?" she said, all flirtation gone. "I was kidding!" She hiccupped. "You know what? I was gonna break up with you tonight. What do you think of that?"

The announcement surprised him. He knew for a fact she'd gone out with other guys over the summer and had never thought they were exclusive. He supposed that in the condition she was in, it was better to humor her.

"If that's what you want," he responded. "I want you to be happy."

"It makes me very happy." She managed to get to wobbly feet, kicking up sand as she staggered off. It wasn't long after that he spotted her kissing Brian.

Jenna stood up from the bed and sashayed toward Dalton. "Don't you think it's time we buried the hatchet? I know you're mad at me for breaking up with you. And I don't blame you."

"Jenna, I'm not mad. In fact, I couldn't care less."

Her face hardened.

"I would have thought you'd moved on," Dalton added.

Her eyes narrowed to slits, but then she smiled coyly. "I have. I was just worried about you. That I'd really hurt you. I mean, that *thing* you've befriended." Jenna shook her body as if Simone creeped her out. "Something strange is going on there."

Thing? Jenna needed a dose of the truth, but Dalton knew it would make things worse. He merely said, "Duly noted. Look, I just got back from a meet and I need to eat—"

"I'm hungry. Where should we go?" Jenna blinked at him innocently.

"I'm grabbing a sandwich here. You need to leave. I'm kind of busy."

She stared at him for a second before she nodded and gave him a crooked smile. "Okay. I have things to do myself." She strolled forward, kissed two fingers and touched them to his cheek. "We can talk later." She sauntered out, and he heard the front door close when she left the house.

Dalton took out his phone and looked at the selfie he'd taken with Simone. He so looked forward to tonight.

§ § §

Simone heard her cell phone chirp. She had a text from Dalton. He'd sent her the selfie with a message to check Facebook. She pulled up his page. He'd posted the selfie online. It made her grin. They were truly friends, maybe more. *Wow. Wow!*

She stared at the picture. They did look good together, like he'd said. But maybe she'd tone down the makeup, if only a little. For their date, at least.

Simone went to work at figuring out the perfect movie, one they'd both enjoy, hopefully. She liked action films as long as the story made sense and there was comedy. She picked one that started at seven-twenty and sent a text to Dalton. Then she stared at the clothes in her closet and tried on almost everything. By the time she'd decided, the floor and the bed looked like a whirling dervish had hit the room.

Dalton arrived a little early, but Simone was ready. In fact, she was eager, although she still felt a knot in her stomach.

"You look great," Dalton said.

She was dressed in mostly black and goth, but it was

stylish, thanks to Anna.

Dalton opened the car door for her and closed it after she was seated. He walked around, stepped in from the driver's side, and buckled up.

"Feeling better?" Simone asked when Dalton didn't talk first.

"Better?"

"About the meet."

"Oh." He started the engine and pulled out. "Yeah." He shrugged. "It would just be nice to finish first for a change."

"You've never finished first?"

"Oh, sure. With the relay. We finish first a lot. And sometimes I win when I'm not up against the high-power swimmers. I'd just like to swim with the best of them and finish first instead of second or third or fourth."

Simone nodded. Everyone wanted to be the best at something.

"You ever watch old movies?" he asked.

Simone shook her head. "Not really. Well, sometimes my mom likes me to watch Fred Astaire and Ginger Rogers movies with her. *Top Hat*'s her fave."

He smiled. "Well, there's one I saw. It's called *Amadeus*."

"I never heard of it."

"It's pretty good. I hate to admit I've seen it more than once. This one character calls himself "the champion of all mediocrities." When I heard him say it, I laughed because I feel like that sometimes."

Simone felt surprised. "You aren't mediocre. You're anything but."

He glanced her way and smiled.

The line outside the movie theatre was long. Most, if not all, of the moviegoers were teens on their cell phones—

texting, taking selfies, checking the Internet. Simone recognized lots of kids from school. A few stared at her and Dalton as if they couldn't believe what they were seeing. She supposed it would be all over school that Dalton had taken her to the movies. That would be a new kind of rumor for her; something she liked.

Dalton took her hand, and Simone's breath caught in her chest. This was the second time they'd held hands, and it felt just as amazing as the first time . . . until she heard Jenna's laugh, and a chill ran down her spine. She closed her eyes. She couldn't believe it. Jenna was there. Why did Jenna have to be there? *Why?*

With any luck, she and Dalton wouldn't be spotted, but that seemed highly unlikely.

"Hey, you guys." Jenna had found them.

"Hey." There was Lynette.

"Hey." And there was Shelly.

Simone turned to face them. She didn't like to play games and said nothing.

"Ladies," Dalton said with no expression.

"You." Jenna looked into Dalton's eyes and tapped his chest. In response he pulled Simone against his side and put his arm around her waist. Jenna's smile faltered a fraction of a second. "Did you get everything done you needed to this afternoon, sweetie?"

"What are you talking about, Jenna?" he asked.

She turned her eyes on Simone. "I was over at his house today. We were going to have lunch, but I had to go. He really didn't want me to. He looked like such a sad, sorry puppy dog. But then he relented and said it was okay; he had things to do, too."

I wonder how much of that is true? Simone thought,

clutching Dalton's arm. And then she couldn't help herself from asking, "Where's Chris?"

Jenna looked faintly surprised. "Chris Hecker? I'll see him later." Her eyes flitted to Dalton, who remained impassive.

The line started to move. Jenna, Lynette and Shelly didn't ask but stayed with them, effectively taking cuts. "Hey. We should all sit together," Jenna said.

Simone heard a loud whistle. "Hey! Worthy. Up here." It was Andy Egan with Jay Browning and Angel Fragoso—Dalton's swim-mates—closer to the front of line. "What are you doing here? Shouldn't you be practicing? I keep beating your sorry ass."

"That'll change. You just wait." Dalton called back.

"I'll wait. And wait. And wait." He laughed, but Simone could tell it was friendly.

"Hi, Andy," Shelly called out with a coy smile.

"Hey, Shelly," he called back. "What ya doin'?"

She shrugged and he smiled before turning away.

Jenna rolled her eyes. "He's a bozo. Stop giving him the time of day."

Simone wondered what Andy had done to deserve Jenna's disapproval. Maybe nothing. Maybe she was just keeping Shelly in line.

Once inside the theatre, Dalton led Simone to the crowded snack bar. "You *do* eat popcorn?"

Simone laughed. "Yes."

"What a gentleman," Jenna said, standing behind them in line along with her BFFs. "Would the gentleman buy popcorn for all the ladies?"

"Only brought enough cash to be a gentleman for one, Jenna."

Jenna's comments continued, but Simone tuned them out.

Dalton appeared to do the same since he didn't respond to any more of her remarks. She resorted to talking to Lynette and Shelly.

Dalton bought the largest tub of popcorn and two Cokes, and he and Simone took the opportunity to find seats without room for the Jeapests to join them. Simone caught sight of them farther down front just before the lights dimmed and the endless previews began.

The movie kept them in stitches for two hours and she felt proud of herself for choosing it. They left just after the credits began. Without saying a word, both of them seemed to have the same idea: *time to go, in case Jenna tries to catch up with us.*

"I haven't seen anything that funny in a long time," Dalton said as they walked toward the Camaro holding hands.

"You know what I'd like to see?" Simone said.

He looked at her.

"*Amadeus.*"

"Really? I'm sure it's on Netflix."

"We have Netflix," Simone said. "And cheese pizzas in the freezer."

"Sounds good." Dalton opened the car door for her.

§ § §

Dalton cooked an individual-sized cheese pizza in the toaster oven. "We'll have to do them one at a time, but it's still faster than waiting for the regular oven to heat up."

Simone called back from the living room where she searched for *Amadeus* on the TV. "I just nuke them."

"Then they taste like cheese on cardboard." He'd offered to buy a pizza from her favorite pizza place on the way to her apartment, but Simone had declined.

"I guess I'm used to it," she said. "Ah ha!" she added when she found *Amadeus*. "Success!"

She walked into the kitchen just as the oven dinged. She handed Dalton a plate and a pair of tongs. He pulled the pizza onto the plate and cut it into four pieces. Then he popped a second pizza into the oven. "We can work on this one while the second one cooks."

Simone nodded and grabbed a couple of paper towels to use as napkins. They walked into the living room where Simone had pushed the coffee table away so they could sit on the floor with their backs against the couch. The floor was her favorite seat in the house. She reached for the remote but stopped when her phone chirped.

"Go ahead," Dalton told her.

She reached for her purse on the couch and fished out the phone. The text was from Jenna. Simone's chest tightened. *Jenna, again? What was her problem?* She glanced at Dalton.

"What?" he asked.

"Jenna," she said.

Dalton shook his head.

Simone read, *SRY :) about b4. LJBF :-)*

"Let's just be friends?" Simone repeated, showing Dalton the phone. She immediately thought of Leslie, who'd apologized just before Kim couldn't remember anything. "I don't think I'll answer her," Simone said.

"Smart," Dalton agreed. He took the phone and put it aside. Then he turned back to Simone. "Forget Jenna. Here's what I think."

He took one hand and slid his fingers through her hair, drawing her toward him. Butterflies suddenly erupted in Simone's stomach and fluttered wildly as he gently pressed his lips to hers. Every nerve in her body trembled, and when the kiss grew stronger and less than gentle, dizziness resulted. His other arm went around her and she melted, glad she was sitting because her legs felt weak. Her arms went around his shoulders and he pressed his lips to hers more intently. When he drew back, he smiled. Then he took the remote and handed it to her without a word.

For a second Simone didn't move. Then she released a breath she didn't even realize she'd been holding and told her heart to stop pounding. After a few blank seconds she started the movie, not that she really watched it. All she could think about was that she'd had her first kiss and it couldn't have been more perfect.

CHAPTER 12

"ALL RIGHT," JIMMY said, cracking his knuckles while standing in Simone's bedroom on Sunday morning. "Rise and shine. There is no avoiding this today."

Simone looked at the clock. It was six a.m. "Are you kidding me?"

"Nope. Time's a wasting. Get up." He pulled away Simone's covers. She pulled them back and rolled over. "Later."

"Later is now." He whipped the covers across the room. Simone sat up. "Let's begin with levitation. That book," he pointed, "flies to that corner. Ready? Go."

Simone made the book fly directly at Jimmy. It soared through him and crashed into a wall. Simone hoped the noise didn't disturb her mother.

Jimmy whistled. "I think you've mastered that. We need to make you mad and have you stay in control."

Simone shook her head. "And burn the apartment down? No thanks."

"That does present a problem."

"I don't think I need to practice levitation. I think I need to sleep." She flopped down, closing her eyes. Jimmy tickled the bottom of her feet. She kicked at him, hitting nothing, of course.

"You need to practice reading minds."

"I try. Sometimes I can do it and sometimes I can't. I can usually pick up emotions, though."

"You need practice, like I said. What am I thinking?"

"That I should get out of bed."

"Excellent."

"It was a tough one."

"What is Jenna thinking?"

Simone opened her eyes. "She isn't here, is she?"

"Of course, not. Just because someone isn't with you doesn't mean you can't pick up their thoughts. Look at cell phones. Look at computers."

"Is there a satellite up there for mind readers?"

"Clever, Simone. Come on. Picture Jenna. I just left her. She's up."

"At this hour?"

"She just came home from a party."

"She went to a party after the movie?"

"She's a night owl. Now. Picture her as pure energy and her thoughts as part of that energy merging with yours."

"You take a class in this or what?"

"I looked into it. You might not be able to read her even with practice, but you won't know until you try."

"Jenna in the morning. More potent than coffee." Simone sat up and wrapped her arms around her knees.

"That's my girl."

Simone closed her eyes.

"Relax," Jimmy said.

Simone sat cross-legged.

"Relax," Jimmy said again. "Let your mind go blank."

And don't fall asleep. Simone smiled and took three deep breaths.

A few seconds passed.

"If a thought comes to your mind, release it," Jimmy instructed. "Just breathe."

Simone did as Jimmy asked and after a couple of minutes, she felt at peace.

"Now picture Jenna. Don't judge. Just accept."

Simone saw Jenna standing before her in her mind's eye. Slowly, emotions drifted toward Simone.

Resentment.

Jealousy.

Simone didn't judge or analyze what she was feeling. She just accepted.

Jealousy was joined by anger. They churned like a roiling sea. Jenna's thoughts, however, remained unknown.

The anger intensified until it was explosive and overpowering, and Simone became uncomfortable. Jenna's emotions scared her. She opened her eyes, unable to take it.

Jimmy smiled at her. "Well?"

"That was awful."

"Did you pick up her thoughts?"

"No, just her emotions."

"Then you need to do it again."

"Not happening."

"Simone—"

"No." Simone hopped out of bed and grabbed the covers. She wrapped them around her and lay back on the mattress. "I'm done." She closed her eyes and when she heard nothing more from Jimmy opened them. He was gone. Simone sighed and went back to sleep.

§ § §

Simone's phone chirped and woke her up around eight-thirty. She took it from her nightstand while rubbing her eyes. There was a text from Anna: *Checking in. Going straight to work from here. XX Mom*

"Okay, Mom," Simone said. "Wherever 'here' is."

She put the phone back on the stand and climbed out of bed. On her way down the hall, she saw that her mother's bedroom door was open. Yep. Anna hadn't come home last night. Simone sighed. Sometimes it felt like she didn't have a mother. Staying out all night was something Anna did quite often.

Simone poured a bowl of cereal and ate while she gathered her thoughts. The only thing she really had to do today was homework . . . and think about Dalton. She smiled, remembering their kiss.

He must have had a lot of practice.

She shooed the thought away.

"*Cyrano* awaits!" she called out, dropping the bowl and spoon in the sink before marching off to her room.

Erickson's assignment was for students to choose something they didn't like about themselves and make fun of it with the same bravado Cyrano had shown with his nose. She had to come up with no fewer than ten jokes.

"What if you're not funny?" one of the students had asked.

"I think," Erickson told them, "once you get started, your creativity will take over."

They also had to write a paragraph analyzing what Cyrano was trying to accomplish by making fun of himself. What were Cyrano's true feelings?

Simone wasn't particularly bothered by her physical traits. It was her so-called gifts she hated, and how could she go public by making fun of them? The students were to act out what they'd written as if they were Cyrano and Valvert in front of the class.

Feet, she decided. Her feet were large for her height. She wore a ten and a half. She could make fun of that.

She sat at her desk, the laptop before her, and stared at the screen. It took a while for her creative juices to flow because her mind kept flip-flopping around to thoughts of Jenna and Dalton and her mom.

Jimmy, too. And then there was Kim who knew she was dead but then sometimes thought she was dreaming.

Simone reached for the keyboard.

Feet. Think feet.

After several futile attempts, she came up with something.

Inquisitive: Excuse me, where do you find shoes for those? At the local clown store?

Discovery: Wait! Wait! I need my camera. We have proof that Bigfoot does exist!

Sympathetic: What did you do to deserve those?

Governmental: Do you need a license to walk down the street with those things?

Insolent: Have you ever put someone in the hospital after doing the rumba?

Simone laughed. This was turning out to be fun.

Familiar: Cinderella's stepsisters got nothing on you.

Simple: Why, Gothilocks. What big feet you have.

Practical: If you ever murder someone, don't leave any footprints behind. The cops will know it could only be you.

Envious: Oh, man. If I had those I wouldn't need to pay for skis.

Curious: When your feet get dirty, how long does it take to clean the bathtub?

"Pretty good," she said as she saved the list. Then she

suddenly wondered if she could come up with jokes for what really bothered her.

I see dead people.

She put her hand to her head and concentrated. It wasn't too long before ideas came to her and she started typing. After an hour she had ten and stared at the last thing she'd typed.

Practical: At least being a ghost-seeing freak means you will have friends for eternity.

It was too harsh and not in the spirit of the assignment. She took out the word "freak" and closed the computer. That was enough. She might play with it later.

Then again, she might not.

Sunday evening around six, her cell rang. She smiled when she saw Dalton's name on the ID.

"Hi," she said a little more coyly than she meant to.

"What a day!" Dalton replied. "John called in sick so we were shorthanded and everybody and their brother must have decided to work on their cars because the place was nuts. And, guess who popped in for a visit? Well, to buy some windshield wipers."

"Jenna," Simone said quietly.

"Correct. Anyway, she had her new guy with her."

"Chris," Simone replied.

"Yeah. Chris. You asked her about him last night. How did you know?"

"I saw them kissing at school."

"Really?"

"Yeah. On Friday."

"I've come to the conclusion that she's crazy. I've made it more than clear that I'm not interested, but I'm pretty sure she brought Chris to the store to make me jealous. I'm starting to think I'm in my own personal version of *Fatal Attraction.*

Well, without the psycho ending. What did you do today?"

"Homework. I have my Cyrano self-mockers."

"Self-mockers. You have your very own word. Very cool. Bring them to school tomorrow? I'll work on mine tonight. I still don't know what I'm going to make fun of." He laughed.

Simone smiled. *I missed you today*, she thought but didn't say.

"I'll pick you up at seven-twenty."

Simone nodded.

"Is that too early?"

She shook her head.

"Simone, are you there?"

"Uh-huh. Seven-twenty. Got it."

CHAPTER 13

FROM THE MOMENT the two of them stepped out of the Camaro and Dalton took her hand for all the world to see, Simone heard the snickers and saw the incredulous stares from the students at school. Dalton with Simone? Really?

"Hey, Dalton. You slumming?"

"Shut up Dickerson, you moron. Get a brain."

Simone felt the blood drain from her face. Dalton was popular, but could that popularity withstand being with her? She tried to slip her hand from his, but he held tight.

"Don't worry about him. He's a jerk and everybody knows it."

"People are staring," she whispered.

"People are jealous. They only wish they could be with someone like you."

That was laying it on thick, and Simone didn't believe it for a second, but she smiled for a moment anyway.

As they walked down the hall toward their English Lit class, she spotted Jenna with Chris. It immediately struck her as a calculated move on Jenna's part. She'd never seen Jenna by first period before. Lynette and Shelly, yes. Their leader, no.

Just as she'd seen them near the gym on Friday, Jenna's back was to the wall of the building, her arms hung over

Chris's shoulders. Only this time her eyes flitted away from Chris's and locked with Simone's. "Hi Simone. Hi Dalton," she cooed.

Simone nodded, but Dalton gave no reply, not even a glance in Jenna's direction. It had to be the coldest shoulder given in the history of cold shoulders. Simone didn't have to ask why; Dalton provided the answer. "Give her an inch, she'll take a mile."

He led Simone inside the classroom and found that none of the other students had arrived. Mr. Erickson was absent as well. They took desk chairs next to each other, scooting them closer together. He took a neatly-typed page from his backpack. "All right. This might be a little obscure. But the thing that bothers me the most is, as I already confessed, I always come in second."

Simone nodded. She understood his feelings but at the same time thought he might not be recognizing all the places where he came in first. He was definitely first with her. And what about all the other people who liked him? He probably took popularity for granted. When you never lacked for something, you often didn't appreciate it.

She looked at his paper. He had written two put-downs.

"I'm stuck," he said. "I'll keep at it. But what do you think?"

Practical: Losers line up over there.

Sympathetic: Did you almost drown back there? Why so far behind?

Simone couldn't imagine that Dalton thought of himself as a loser. She looked at him and wasn't sure how to approach telling him what she thought.

"No good?" he said.

"They're not exactly funny."

"Yeah. They didn't seem all that funny to me either." He seemed discouraged.

"See. They're not an exaggeration of the truth, which is what makes the put-downs in Cyrano funny," Simone explained.

He frowned.

"Cyrano did have a big nose. So he makes fun of what stupid people might think about that and when the person insulting him can't come up with something clever, he shows them how it should be done, which puts the insulterer down for not being good at insulting. Is insulterer a word? No. It's insulter."

"I get that last part, but making it funny . . . "

"Personally, I think you should choose a different sore spot. You aren't a loser or mediocre, so making fun of that can't possibly be funny no matter what you say." She gave him back the paper.

He was quiet. "I really was struggling."

"Pick something else."

He nodded. "What about you? You said you finished."

Simone pulled the folded list of insults she'd printed and handed it to him.

"Now you've done it."

Simone looked behind her. Jimmy sat with his butt on the back of a chair and his feet on the seat. His grin was so wide, the rest of his face almost disappeared.

"What are you—" She stopped herself and turned back to Dalton who was reading the second sheet of paper she'd given him. He lifted his head and stared at her.

Simone's blood pressure surged and she felt her face blanch. She had to be as white as the proverbial being she didn't want to mention. She'd printed the jokes about seeing dead people without realizing it.

"You see ghosts?" Dalton said.

"Ummm." Should she admit it or not? She'd planned on telling him some time, when the timing seemed right. This seemed all wrong. She couldn't read his face. Was he annoyed? Disgusted? Did he think she was nuts? Or just a liar?

"You know, at the swim meet I saw you up in the bleachers talking to thin air. And just now, you almost did the same thing."

She looked down. "I didn't mean for you to read that."

"So it's a joke?"

"No . . . " *Say something, dummy*, she told herself. Her mouth dropped open, but nothing came out.

"I don't believe in ghosts," he said. "I think it's something hotel owners make up to get gullible people to spend the night."

She stared at him. It was hard to breathe. How could she tell him now? She couldn't.

"Oh, yeah?" Jimmy said. He slipped the paper with Simone's ghost jokes from Dalton's hand, tore it into tiny pieces, and rained the confetti all over Dalton.

"I do, on the other hand, believe in telekinesis," Dalton said, none too happy as he brushed the paper from his clothes and hair.

A number of voices hit the room as students arrived in clusters. Mr. Erickson's voice rose above the pack. "Okay, all you meatheads. Let's get settled in. All phones off and stowed in backpacks."

Dalton stared at her. Was he glaring? She saw his brow furrow, and then watched him straighten his desk. Every part of her felt him turning away. Did he think she was lying? Did he think she was strange? She couldn't take it if he . . . She couldn't even finish the thought. She snatched her backpack and rushed out of the room.

She hurried down the corridor where a few stragglers were running to get to class before the bell rang. Simone ran to get away. She would take the bus home, skip all classes as well as detention, and whatever happened, happened. She'd trusted someone for the last time.

Everything looked blurry because of the tears in her eyes. As fast as she wiped them away, more reappeared. She'd been wounded before. By others and especially by Chris. But this hurt worse. She darted into the girls' restroom to calm down before she would make her way to the bus stop. She dropped her backpack and collapsed to the floor with her back against the wall. She drew her knees up and rested her elbows as she continued to wipe away tears. The bell rang just as Jimmy materialized before her.

"Look, Simone. You have to—"

"Quit giving me advice, Jimmy. I hate you. I hate everybody. You're the reason I'm so weird. But you know what? If I could make my mind reading stop, then I bet I can make ghosts disappear. I'm going to ignore you, Jimmy. You and Kim and anybody else who comes along. I'm going to pretend that you aren't there. So don't talk to me. I won't answer. And, you know what? For all I know, I *am* crazy. You aren't real and I'm just seeing things."

"Buggers. I thought you were cooler than that." The goth kid she'd seen smoking a cigarette the day she'd split the Jeapests' pants appeared beside Jimmy.

"You're a ghost, too?" Simone stared.

He shrugged. "Don't categorize me. I define myself."

Simone suddenly laughed. "Right."

"I'll handle this, Ash."

Ash flicked his cigarette away and it vanished into thin air just as Ash disappeared as well.

"Don't mind him," Jimmy said. "He liked school. When he died in a car wreck he didn't want to go to the light anymore than I did."

"I thought you didn't see the light."

Jimmy shrugged. "I lied."

"So we're both liars. Dalton thinks I'm one."

"He's not a bad guy. He doesn't believe. So what? Most people don't. I didn't when I was alive."

"How many ghosts are at this school, anyway?" Simone asked.

"Last count, seventeen. Some choose to stay invisible. Some move on. Some drop in decades after they graduated just to take a look around."

"I guess I came to the right school. Ghost Central."

"All schools have ghosts. Some more than others. It's rare though, to find a live person who can see and talk to us. You're one in a million, Simone."

"Whoopeee."

"Simone—"

"He thinks I'm a freak and I am. Go away, Jimmy. I'm going to work on *not* being weird, and that can only happen if you and Kim—and Ash now—leave me alone."

"Or you could just know that you aren't weird. You need to work on liking yourself. Then it won't matter what anybody else thinks."

Jimmy vanished and Simone sat. "I do like myself," she said. "Sometimes." She sighed. After a minute, she calmed down.

If I go home, I'll just sit and brood. At least at school I'm busy.

After a few more seconds, she picked herself up off the floor and moved to the mirror. Tears had streaked her makeup. She repaired the damage and went back to class. If she received another detention slip, that was okay with her. At least she hadn't completely run away. Her stepfather would have been ashamed of her for even thinking of it.

She walked into class and when Mr. Erickson looked at her, he said nothing. Not even a sarcastic, "Nice of you to join us, Simone." His thoughts, however, did reach her.

Kids are so emotional. I'll let her slide this time.

Thank you, Mr. Erickson, she thought with relief.

He did a double take with a perplexed expression. Simone held her breath. She'd heard him; had he heard her?

Students were in study groups of four and she immediately noticed that Dalton's group was full. In fact, it had five students.

"These two groups only have three. Pick one," Mr. Erickson instructed.

Simone could see by their faces that nobody in those groups wanted her. She screwed up her courage and joined one, but she wouldn't talk. She would not spew forth her pearls of wisdom, she thought sarcastically. These kids were out of luck. And she wouldn't glance over at Dalton either. She would sit there and stew. That was the best she could do right now.

CHAPTER 14

SIMONE SAT ALONE at lunch and thought it must be the longest day of her life. Dalton had the same lunch period as she did, but she never laid eyes on him.

Not that I want to, she told herself. *I never want to see or talk to him again.*

Of course, that was impossible. They were a team, as far as the Cyrano assignment was concerned.

She also didn't mean it.

She wasn't hungry and threw her lunch sack away. It wasn't her fault that she saw ghosts. She'd been born this way.

"It isn't the cards you're dealt," her stepfather used to say. "It's how you play them."

Simone felt like screaming. *Can't I feel sorry for myself for one minute?*

"Thirty seconds and then move on." Her stepfather wasn't there, but everything he'd ever tried to teach her continued to bombard her thoughts.

His number one rule: Never feel sorry for yourself.

"That's easy for you to say," she told him once.

"Now why would you think that?"

"Because your life is perfect and probably always was."

He laughed and then he looked the sorriest Simone had ever seen him. He didn't explain, so Simone asked her mother about it later.

"He had a wife who left him and took their two kids. He doesn't know where they are."

Maybe seeing ghosts isn't so bad, Simone thought. *It's just when other people know about it.*

She looked over at a group of goth kids and saw Ash smoking a cigarette. No one saw him and he didn't care. He was with the people he related to, and that was all that mattered to him. *Maybe for eternity,* Simone thought.

"Hey, girlfriend."

Simone stopped looking at Ash and saw Jenna and Chris standing in front of her. Each had one arm wrapped tightly around the other. "Hey, Spooky," he said with a sour smile.

Simone frowned. "That's not my name. What do you want, Jenna? Mrs. Nagel told you to leave me alone."

"Oh, that was before. She'd like to know we're friends now."

"We aren't friends and we never will be."

Jenna sighed dramatically. "You know what your problem is, Simone? You don't like anyone and that's why you have no friends. I feel sorry for you. I really do." She looked around. "Where's Dalton?"

Simone wondered if Jenna—and the rest of the world— knew they'd had a falling out.

"I don't know."

Jenna raised her eyebrows as if she found that bit of information very interesting before she and Chris walked on.

§ § §

Simone was happy to see Kim in World History. She wanted to talk to someone, even if it was only about the number of little holes in the ceiling.

Kim! Do you hear me? Simone thought.

Kim turned around with a perky smile. "Of course I hear you. Where have you been?"

What do you mean? I've been at school all day. Were you looking for me?

"No. I meant over the weekend. I wanted you to go to a party with me."

Party? What kind of party? How can I go to a party with you?

"Just get in the car and drive."

I can't drive.

"I can. Wait." Kim's eyes drifted as she went deep into thought.

Simone saw Dalton studying her with his brow dipped. Even with her lips not moving, her face was no doubt giving her away.

Great. He doesn't believe in ghosts. Thinks I'm a liar. And thanks to Jimmy, he thinks I tossed confetti all over him.

She opened a book and looked down. *Kim. What are you thinking about?*

"Mrs. Nagel's party."

Simone's head jerked up. *Mrs. Nagel?*

"I guess you couldn't go to that, right?" Kim was no longer perky. Her expression said she was trying to get things straight in her head.

I didn't know the dean threw parties for students.

Kim shook her head. "She isn't the dean. Why'd you say that?"

Oh. This is a party in your day.

"My day. Yeah." Kim suddenly looked scared.

Kim. What's wrong?

Kim didn't answer and faded from sight.

It was difficult to pay attention in class after that. Mrs. Kent lectured more than usual and between her high-pitched voice and Kim's frightened expression, Simone couldn't keep her mind on the past ills of the world. She was grateful when class was over, even though detention awaited her.

§ § §

Simone entered the library, pleased with the setting that would surround her for the next hour. Woodruff Senior High had been built in 1909 and the library might have been upgraded a time or two, but not fully. The dark-wood floor crackled in places when you walked. The lighting consisted of hanging lamps that looked like large upside-down candle holders, the wiring upgraded to allow for energy-efficient bulbs. A bank of windows along the west wall helped illuminate the room. A media center near the back offered ten computers.

Four tables had been strategically placed near the reference desk where Mrs. Nagel stood with her arms crossed. She would preside over the detainees this afternoon.

Simone was not the first to arrive. Three kids she'd seen around campus but didn't know—two boys and one girl—sat at two of the tables checking information on their phones. Simone took a table that was empty. One more boy entered and sat at the other empty table.

Simone glanced up at the large ornate clock on the wall behind the checkout desk. One more minute and it would be a quarter to three, time for detention to begin. That's when Chris Hecker sauntered into the library, ball cap on head and a smug smile on his lips. Simone groaned silently to herself. He took one look at her, grinned, and sat in the chair beside hers.

"Hey there, Spooky."

"Quiet," Mrs. Nagel snapped.

Chris had no books with him. He leaned back in the chair, stretched out his legs and locked hands behind his head. His jaw worked feverishly on the gum in his mouth and he snapped it loudly.

"Gum in the trash, Mr. Hecker."

Chris stood and strolled to the receptacle. He was about to spit out the offending chew when Mrs. Nagel handed him a tissue.

"Wrap it first."

Smiling, Chris took the gum from his mouth and did as he was told. Clearly happy to be the center of attention, he strolled back to the chair next to Simone.

"Phones off," Mrs. Nagel instructed. "Completely off. For one hour they don't exist. All phones will be confiscated until the end of the week if I hear one ding, buzz, chirp or sing-song."

Phones might be a pain in the ass for authority figures these days, but they were also good for leverage. Simone watched everyone turn off their cells to a chorus of shutdown sounds. Hers was already off.

"This doesn't have to be an unpleasant time. In fact, you are welcome to read or do homework. You can even get up and take a book from the stacks. No talking, however."

Mrs. Nagel sat behind the desk and watched the students. Chris leaned his upper body on the table and rested his head on his arms as if he might take a nap. He kept his face turned toward Simone and stared at her, a stupid smile clinging to his lips.

She stopped looking at him and half-heartedly pulled *The Outsiders* from her backpack. She didn't feel like reading, though. She wanted to know why Kim was so confused and upset. She looked at Mrs. Nagel. And what sort of teacher threw a party for kids? Of course, it might have been an open-house-type thing at the school. Kim could have been confused about that. Whatever it was, Simone was curious.

Maybe there were clues in the 1969 yearbook, she thought. She hadn't been able to find it online like she had Jimmy's senior yearbook. Maybe the library had a copy. If so, it would be in the reference section.

Simone scooted her chair back and immediately thought better of leaving her backpack within Chris's reach. Even with Mrs. Nagel in charge, he might try something. Simone hung it on the seat opposite hers as she walked into the stacks.

She found yearbooks for the school all the way back to 1912. Locating the year she wanted was a breeze. She grabbed the book and went back to the table where she found Chris still sprawled with eyes closed.

She sat and opened the book.

"Notice something, Spooky?" Chris whispered.

Simone glanced at Mrs. Nagel who gave no reaction; Chris had whispered softly enough. Simone looked across to her backpack. It appeared to be undisturbed. Then she remembered she hadn't put *The Outsiders* away. It was missing.

Creep, she thought, picking up her stuff. She moved to the table with the lone student who now had his nose buried in a superhero magazine, and sat. Now she faced Chris, but that was preferable to sitting next to him. He raised his head and smiled arrogantly at her with his chin held high. Then he lifted her book so she could see he had it and placed it under his butt. He let loose with a fart.

You can have that book now, Simone thought as the students in detention laughed.

Mrs. Nagel stood, eyes appalled and flashing.

"Sorry," Chris called out. "You know you can't always help it."

"Help it," Mrs. Nagel instructed. "One more sound out of you and you will have detention for the rest of the week."

Chris pursed his lips, apparently weighing whether the punishment was worth further crime.

Simone stared at Chris and told herself it would be wonderful to be such a nice, forgiving, kind person that she never gave a thought to getting even. But the more she thought about how he'd betrayed her at the last school, and how he called her Spooky when she told him not to, and how he'd desecrated her book, the more her senses stirred with resentment and she found herself wanting to strike back.

He liked making trouble. Well. She could make trouble, too. Had he forgotten about her special skill?

Simone focused on Chris's hat, and it slowly began to slide down his forehead. He grabbed it and pulled it back up. Simone refocused and this time jerked the hat down so that the brim covered his face to just below his nose. She held it there. No matter how he tried to pull the hat off his head, he couldn't, which caused him to make all sorts of noises which quickly spurred Mrs. Nagel into action.

"I don't know what you're trying to prove, young man," Mrs. Nagel said harshly. "But you just bought two more days of detention. Take that hat off your head immediately."

"I'm trying!"

"If I have to walk over there and remove it myself, that will buy you another day."

Simone suppressed a grin. She was happy for him to earn additional stints in detention, although like a lot of criminals (not that Chris was a criminal—yet), he probably didn't mind doing time. He probably saw it as a badge of honor.

Simone didn't let up and Mrs. Nagel strode over to Chris. The moment she touched his cap, Simone stopped holding it in place. Chris fumed as the dean took the cap with her. "You can have it back on Friday."

"It's not fair," Chris started to complain.

"Oh, sometimes it is," the woman explained.

Chris turned his eyes on Simone whose back was to Mrs. Nagel. "You did this," he mouthed.

"Don't mess with me," she mouthed back.

Chris had lost and he knew it, judging by the feelings Simone was picking up: self-pity and fury, a dangerous combination if ever there was one. Chris would get his mojo back in time and then who knew what he'd pull? But for now, anyway, Simone was on top, and there was nothing Chris could do.

She opened the yearbook before her. Thumbing through, she came across the pages for homecoming. One full page in black and white showed Kim hearing the announcement that she was queen. Her gloved hand lay over her open mouth and her eyes were wide with excitement. The four princesses—two on each side—looked genuinely happy for her. All five wore sleeveless gowns and long white gloves. Their hair was piled up on their heads in rats and rolls that included the help of wiglets to get that big-hair look.

The next two pages were in color and offered shots of each princess arriving with her escort. The escorts all dressed the same: black pants, white shirt, black bow tie, and a double-button royal-blue coat with a single white carnation on the left lapel.

The next pages showed a dance. Girls were with guys. You couldn't go to the dance if you didn't have a date of the opposite sex. You couldn't go if you didn't have a date, period. Kim was in a couple of photos with a boy named Scotty Ohanian.

Page after page after page was devoted to all the sports activities. Four pages covered drama and the plays that had been performed. And then there were the different clubs: community service, art, future teachers, future nurses, scholarship, Spanish, French, reef divers, science, glee, folk music, Campus Life. It seemed like there was something for everyone and if there wasn't, you could form a club.

She found Kim's picture among the seniors where it listed her activities: ASB Secretary, Homecoming Queen, Future Teachers, Song Leader.

Simone turned the pages devoted to the pep promoters. She found flag twirlers, cheerleaders, and song leaders. That was interesting. The song leaders were another form of cheerleader and all five of them were the homecoming princesses and queen. They sat on the steps of a bell tower in short dresses with flare skirts and puff sleeves clutching white pompoms. Over each dress was a ruffled apron that tied at the waist and extended over the shoulders. A white "W" for Woodruff Senior High was displayed on the bodice of the outfit. All of the pep promoters were color coordinated in orange and white.

It fascinated Simone to look into the world where Kim had lived. It seemed as long gone as the nineteenth century.

She remembered that Mrs. Nagel had been a teacher back then and took a look at the educators. Mrs. Nagel taught twelfth-grade English, was a counselor, and sponsored the future teachers club. She wore her hair as she did now and didn't look any older than the seniors in the yearbook.

Boy, was she young.

Simone went through the book again and found no memorial page for Kim. She thought that was odd, especially for a student who had been so involved in student activities. As she peered into a time that had long since disappeared, she heard Mrs. Nagel announce that they could go. Detention was over.

Simone closed the book and waited until Chris and the others headed for the door.

"See ya around," Chris said with an ominous tone that Simone knew meant trouble.

When everyone was gone, she took the yearbook to Mrs. Nagel.

"Yes, Simone?"

"I was wondering why there isn't a memorial page for Kim Blue."

"Excuse me?" Mrs. Nagel's brow dipped. "What did you say?"

"Kim Blue. In this yearbook." Simone showed it to Mrs. Nagel and then opened to Kim's senior picture. "Her. Why isn't there a memorial page? You were a teacher back then, right?"

Mrs. Nagel nodded. "It was my first year."

"And you were a counselor and a mentor."

"I was ambitious." Mrs. Nagel took off her glasses and leaned back in the chair and looked Simone squarely in the eye. "How do you know about Kim?"

"I just heard about her." Simone shrugged, trying to think of a plausible answer. "You know, people say the school is haunted."

Mrs. Nagel pursed her lips with a sour expression. She put her glasses back on. "Well, that's simply ridiculous. Kim was a sweet, sweet girl. It was a shame when she disappeared."

"I thought she died."

"No. The general consensus was that she ran away. Her parents were divorcing and I believe a boyfriend had broken up with her. You can't have a memorial page for someone who went missing on her own, now can you?"

None of it sounded right to Simone. "When did people realize she was gone?"

"Oh, I don't remember any details like that."

"Did the police search?"

"Certainly people were questioned. I was even questioned. Friends. Family. Her father believed the mother took her to another state. The mother denied it. And they didn't find her with the mother, although I suppose Kim could have been hiding."

"Hiding?" Simone frowned. Kim hadn't mentioned anything about a divorce or a breakup. But then, lately, Kim acted confused. "Why would the mother take her away when Kim was almost done with high school? I mean, she was eighteen and could do what she wanted, right?"

"I certainly can't know what her mother was thinking." Mrs. Nagel gave Simone a grim look.

"And she went with the mother because her boyfriend broke up with her?"

"Are you studying to be a detective?" Mrs. Nagel's face remained hard. "I can only tell you what I heard. Why are you so interested?"

Simone shrugged. "It's kind of fascinating is all."

"I find it's best to keep your mind in the present." Mrs. Nagel took her purse from a drawer. She was ready to leave.

"What about learning from the past?" Simone hoped she didn't sound disrespectful.

"You mean Kim? What could you possibly learn from

that?" Mrs. Nagel looked exasperated. Simone knew she'd asked one too many questions.

"Thank you, Mrs. Nagel. I was curious about her. That's all."

She returned the yearbook to the shelves and left the library feeling she was no closer to knowing what happened. If anything, she'd uncovered a bigger mystery.

CHAPTER 15

DALTON CLIMBED OUT of the pool and yanked his swim cap from his head. His time in the 100 free was abysmal, he knew it. He didn't even have to be told. Egan had beat him by half a body length.

Practice was over and he headed for the lockers with everyone else.

"Worthy! Over here."

Dalton stopped in his tracks, turned around and looked at Coach for a second before walking over to him. What could Coach say to him that he hadn't already said to himself?

"What's going on with you, Worthy?"

"Coach?"

"That last swim, I saw you give up."

"Well—"

"Well, nothing. You don't give up. You never give up! I took you off the relay for a reason."

"Andy's time—"

"Forget Andy. It had nothing to do with him. I wanted you to get your head out of your ass. You need to be determined. Aggressive. Focused! But that's not what I'm seeing. Whatever your mind is on, it isn't swimming and it isn't winning. It's on losing. I've seen it in other kids and I see it in you. Let me ask you a question. Do you think you can improve?"

"Of course."

"You think you can beat Browning?"

Dalton took a deep breath. He'd love to beat Browning, but Browning was the best on the JV team. If he said yes, wouldn't Coach know he was lying?

"That's what I thought. I don't think you can either. Not because it isn't possible, but because you've decided it's impossible."

"I'd love to beat Browning. I swim as hard as I can."

"No. Not even close. You know what I see? Someone who's had things handed to him, and if he has to work for something, say like a better time or beating the best, he says, 'Woe is me' like a little girl. And gives up."

Coach's remark stung. How could he think that? Dalton wasn't afraid of hard work and never had been. He decided to fight back, carefully minding his words. "That's not true, Coach. Nothing's been handed to me."

"No? What about that fancy Z twenty-eight of yours? Glossy purple. Souped-up engine."

"Are you kidding? That car was a junker. I earned money any way I could and I paid for it. I might have gotten a few Christmas and birthday gifts to help me along the way. But that car is mine. I restored it. I cherried it out."

"Well, good for you." There was sarcasm in Coach's tone.

Dalton felt his pulse rise. Why pick on his Camaro?

"When I see the kind of passion you have for your car in your determination to be a great swimmer, then maybe you'll get somewhere. I want you here in the morning."

"Varsity practices in the morning."

"You get five gold stars for knowing that. Five a.m. Five to seven. And you'll still be practicing with JV as well. That's all." Dalton must have looked pained for Coach to suddenly shout, "Stop thinking like a loser!"

Dalton's stomach lurched and his eyes blinked. He turned and walked toward the locker room, unsure if what happened was a good thing or a punishment. He'd probably look like a fool swimming with varsity.

As Dalton toweled off and then dressed, his mind drifted to Simone. He'd told her he'd give her a ride to school, but after what happened in English Lit—whatever it was that actually happened, he wasn't quite sure—he didn't think she was expecting a ride. He needed to tell her just the same and decided a text would do for now. They needed to talk, but that could happen later. He kept the message brief, merely saying Coach had him practicing with varsity and he couldn't give her a ride to school. He was sorry.

He almost added that they needed to talk, but something held him back. Probably that angry look she'd shot him in English Lit.

§ § §

Simone read the text from Dalton then dropped the phone onto her bed. Monday morning had begun so well and had ended in disaster. She could strike Dalton off her Christmas list, she thought, trying to put some levity into the situation. But the joke didn't even merit a smile.

She looked at Dalton's jacket hanging on the back of her desk chair. She'd never even tried to return it. She sank into the chair, pulled one of the sleeves around her and lifted it to her face. The jacket smelled like him, sweet and irresistible. She closed her eyes for a while, remembering their one kiss. Her first kiss. It had been so perfect. She stared at the wall in a bit of a stupor and sighed.

The sound of the front door opening and closing drew her attention with a start. No one else should be in the apartment. Simone shot out the door into the hall and immediately detected her mother's perfume. "Mom?"

"Yes," her mother responded. "It's me." Anna's voice was weak and filled with fake cheer.

"What's wrong?" Simone stepped into the living room and found her mother standing in the middle of the room, her eyes red and puffy. "Why are you crying?"

Anna took a shaky breath. "I stopped crying a few minutes ago, right after the cop took pity on me and let me off with a warning."

"What?"

"I missed a stop sign." Anna threw her purse on the sofa.

"And why *were* you crying?"

"He broke up with me."

No one ever broke up with Anna, at least not since Simone's biological father rejected the responsibility of parenthood. Anna always broke up with the guy.

"I really liked him," Anna said, a tear trickling down her cheek. "But that was the problem. I didn't love him, and he's looking for love. Maybe it's for the best. I don't know. He was a really good guy, though. You know?" Anna looked at her daughter, a begging quality in her eyes.

"I never met him, Mom. You never brought him home."

"You're right, I didn't. I sort of knew this would happen and I didn't want you getting attached. I know how much you loved your stepdad."

"That was different. He died."

Anna shook her head and slumped to the couch. "Gone is gone. Anyway, I was too weepy-eyed to work. I thought we could go out to dinner. You and I. And do a little shopping tomorrow."

"I have school."

"I can write you an excuse. I need you right now, baby."

"Okay," Simone said. "I don't mind missing school." *In fact, I think I need a break,* she thought but didn't share.

Anna held an arm out toward her daughter. Simone joined her on the couch and nestled in as Anna stroked Simone's hair. "You are such a good girl. I want you to know I appreciate you very much."

"I know, Mom."

Anna was cheerful the rest of the evening, bubbly even. Their waiter at Olive Garden was cute and flirted with Anna shamelessly, even though he was probably closer to Simone's age than Anna's.

"Thank you, ladies." He gave them both a cheeky grin, took the menus from the table. "I will be right back." He walked away to place the order with the kitchen.

"He's adorable," Anna said. "I just love dimples. You should talk to him. Let him know you're interested."

"But I'm not interested and I think you're more his type," Simone said.

"Well, if you didn't try to make yourself look like death warmed over, you could be his type." Anna took a tube of lipstick from her purse and applied scarlet color to her mouth.

Simone flipped her hair over her shoulder and kept quiet. She wasn't her mother. Could never be like her mother. And it would be impossible to explain all the complicated thoughts and feelings that dominated her psyche.

Anna tossed the lipstick tube back in her bag and seemed to understand that she'd said something hurtful. She reached across the table and patted Simone's hand. "I'm sorry, honey.

You're such a pretty girl and you hide it behind all that pasty makeup. I don't understand it. I try. I really do. But it makes no sense to me. What did I do to make you want to dress this way?"

"You didn't do anything, Mom. I promise."

Anna perked up. "Well, I didn't mean to pick a fight. I love you. You know that. I only want what's best for you. My coworker Sally has raised five kids. She says it's a stage and you'll grow out of it."

Simone almost laughed. Some teens might hate their mothers talking about them, but Simone thought it was wonderful her mother cared enough to say something behind her back.

The waiter brought Anna her salad and Simone a bowl of soup. Simone was smiling at the idea that her mother cared.

"There you go," said the waiter, gazing at Simone. "I knew a smile wouldn't crack your face."

Simone immediately frowned. Her face was not his business. "Shut up," she said.

"Simone!" Anna was appalled.

"What? He was rude."

"You're right. I was and I apologize," he said, bowing his head slightly. "Can I get you anything else?"

Anna responded sweetly. "No, thank you." Simone said nothing. She didn't even look at him as he walked away.

"You made him feel bad," Anna said.

Simone shrugged. "He made me feel bad. Everybody makes everybody else feel bad. It's the way of the world." Simone dipped her spoon into her minestrone soup.

Anna looked after the waiter with a frown. "Well. He was only joking."

"Can we not worry about Barney? He'll live."

"When did you get so hard-boiled?"

"I think I'm just being real. Anyway, it seems you've gotten your mind off of . . . what *is* his name? You never said."

Anna sat back and half-smiled. "Clarence."

"Really? Is anyone named Clarence anymore?"

"He's a little older."

"How old?"

Anna suddenly laughed. "Fifty-five. But he doesn't look it."

Simone didn't flinch.

"I like him. I just don't love him." Anna finally paid attention to her salad, forking small pieces of lettuce and tomato.

It was as Simone suspected. Anna was hurt because he'd broken up with her, not because she cared deeply about the guy. Simone put her spoon down.

"Can we talk about Dad?" She'd always called her stepdad Dad.

Anna nodded. "Of course. I loved Terry very much."

"You hardly talked about him when he died. And now you never do."

"Well. It was a shock when he passed, and I had to think about practical things, like finances. And you were crying all the time for the longest time."

"He was a great dad."

"He wasn't perfect," Anna replied.

Simone felt a small stab to her abdomen. That seemed like an odd thing to say. "What do you mean?"

"Don't you remember us fighting?"

"No. I never heard you fight."

Anna nodded. "I guess you wouldn't have. He always made sure you weren't around when he picked on a sore subject."

"What sore subject?"

"Oh, honey, it's been four years. I don't know."

"I think you do."

Anna put her fork down and faced her daughter. "He wanted to find his kids. His real kids."

Simone felt her insides grow hot with the kind of upset that burned. "He loved me."

"Yes, of course he did. But he wasn't really your father."

"Yes, he was."

"You know what I mean."

Simone did know. But her mother didn't have to say it. She missed him, especially now that life was so confusing. Terry had talked to her—really talked to her—in a way her mother never could.

Sometimes Simone wondered why his spirit hadn't ever paid her a visit. She saw dead people, after all.

Because he's on the other side and at peace, even if I'm not.

Simone's phone chirped, causing Anna to smile. Simone checked and saw she had a text message from Jenna.

hey gf ☺ chris told me what a jerk he was in detention. Clueless!!! told him we're buds now. cuic

"You're making friends I see." Anna beamed.

Simone looked up. "Yeah. Friends."

CHAPTER 16

"THIS LOOKS ADORABLE on you." Anna held a Marc Jacobs little black dress up against Simone. "It's only twenty-two dollars. Thrift stores are a godsend."

"Yes, a godsend." Simone moved away. Her mother could buy the dress or not buy the dress. She'd rather be at Barnes & Noble checking out books.

"I'm getting it." Anna draped it over her arm on top of the two name-brand sweaters she'd found for herself, and threaded through the displays and racks to the checkout counter. Simone followed, holding three novels she'd found in the bargain bin.

"Oh, these are nice," said the store owner as she checked for the price tags and began writing up the sale. "We just got them in, too."

"My lucky day," Anna responded, smiling at the clothes. "We—" Her phone rang. "Excuse me." She reached into her purse and checked the ID. She looked at Simone. "Clarence," she told her before she answered. "Hello."

Clarence must be having second thoughts, Simone decided.

"We can talk," Anna said. "But right now I'm with my daughter."

Anna listened and sighed. She eyed Simone and gave her a feigned smile. "All right. I'll meet you in an hour. Just this once. No. Simone will understand."

She hung up and Simone said, "I *completely* understand." She did, too, but not in the manner Anna would have liked. She understood that in Anna's world, men would always come first.

At the apartment, Anna quickly wrote Simone a note for being absent from school, before kissing her on the cheek and saying, "I'll be home soon." That was unlikely, since she'd dashed off the note before leaving rather than waiting until she was home from seeing Clarence.

Simone sat on the couch, kicked off her shoes, and propped her heels on the coffee table. She took out her phone and took a picture of her bare feet, which she posted to Instagram for no reason other than to do something silly. Homework didn't interest her. Escaping into a book with fictional characters and their issues didn't interest her. Nothing did right now, except for Dalton, and she'd messed that up. She checked her watch. It was lunch time. She wondered who he was with right now.

She thumbed through Instagram photos absentmindedly until she decided to check out Dalton's page. The last one he'd posted was their selfie. She stared at it, which nearly brought tears to her eyes.

Her phone startled her when her *Phantom* ringtone began to play. Her heart jumped when she saw it was Dalton. She bit her lower lip and took a deep breath before answering.

"Are you sick?" Dalton immediately asked.

She almost said "What do you care?" But that would have been the chip on her shoulder talking, and that's the last thing she wanted.

"My mom needed me," she said coolly, hoping to sound neutral: *Oh, you called? That's nice, but I don't really care. I mean, it's okay that you called, but it doesn't matter to me.*

"What's wrong with your mom?"

"Nothing. Now."

He didn't say anything for a second and Simone closed her eyes. She did care. That was the thing. And he was calling and that had to mean something. No, not something. Everything.

"Can I come over later?" he asked. "I'd like to talk."

Simone held her breath.

"I have swim practice and then I have to go home for a while, but after that I can be at your place. Is seven good?"

"Well, what is there to talk about?" Simone asked. Why was she making this difficult for him?

"The reason you disappeared so fast after English Lit, for one thing."

Simone said nothing.

"Don't do that, Simone. We need to clear the air. I think you know that."

She still didn't respond. Her nerves had paralyzed her throat and fogged her brain.

"I'm sorry if I messed things up," he said quietly.

I'm sorry, too, she thought, finally telling him, "Seven is good."

§ § §

Dalton headed for the aquatics building at a heated pace. "What is so special about this girl?" he muttered. "What?!"

Never in his life had he been so baffled by his feelings. She had him chasing after her and saying he was sorry, which he was, but why should he be? Wasn't he allowed to act surprised by something so out of the ordinary, so strange? Sure there were ghost shows on television and the Internet, but that was hocus pocus pretending to be real. He didn't know anyone who saw ghosts.

Except for Simone . . . apparently.

"Uuugh!" He looked up to the sky, even as he kept moving. When his eyes focused forward again he saw Jenna in his path, smiling at him. He stomped straight up to her and barked, "What do you want?"

That wiped the grin off her face. "What's got you all salty? I only wanted to say hi."

"Hi," he snapped, trying to walk around her, but she grabbed his arm.

"Stop it. I want to be friends. What's wrong with you? Ever since you started hanging out with that freak, you've been a real jerk."

"Can't be anything you've done, can it?"

"I've only tried to be nice to you."

"Here's a news flash, Jenna. Don't try anymore. I can't take it."

He pulled his arm from her grasp and continued walking. When he was only a few yards from the aquatics building, he spotted Chris behind another building. Even though he was smoking a cigarette, something told Dalton he wasn't there to smoke. When Chris poked his head around the corner and stared in the direction where Dalton had been, Dalton glanced behind him. Jenna was watching him as Chris watched Jenna.

There was something squirrely about those two, and he wanted no part of them.

Swim practice was rough. Coach seemed to single him out for a particularly grueling workout. At one point, Dalton thought his heart might burst.

"You want it, Worthy? How bad? Show me," Coach shouted.

"Nice finish!" Coach called to Deagon at the end of the 200 fly.

Dalton checked the times on the board. His time had been faster than Deagon's.

"You just gave me goose flesh, Fragoso," Coach praised the swimmer once he yanked off his cap after the 100 breast.

Dalton swam his heart out, but no matter how well he did, who he beat, or if his time improved, Coach responded with, "Let's keep it up. Show me what you got."

Two hours later, Dalton dragged himself toward the locker room.

"What did you do to Coach? He's sure got it in for you," Fragoso said.

Dalton shook his head. "I don't know."

"Does he want you to quit?" Browning asked.

Dalton shrugged. Maybe that was what Coach wanted. But why? Because he'd missed a practice? That was crazy.

"You did good today." Lockwood tossed an arm over Dalton's shoulder as they walked. "I saw it. Everybody saw it."

"Except Coach," Fragoso added.

Dalton nodded. "Thanks, guys."

Fragoso gave him a friendly punch in the arm.

By seven p.m., all Dalton really wanted to do was go to bed. He had to get up at four-thirty to be at five o'clock practice with the varsity swimmers. He'd be there, come hell or high water. He would. But it was just as important to him to talk to Simone face-to-face, and he wasn't going to cancel.

§ § §

Simone was almost in shock when Anna walked in the door at

six fifty-five—humming.

"What are you doing home?" Simone asked, hearing the anxiety in her own voice.

Anna cocked her head and dipped her brow. "I told you I wouldn't be long."

"I just meant . . . all's well?"

"Actually, yes. Couldn't be better."

"Then you and Clarence are back together?"

"Not exactly. We talked. He said he'd made a hasty decision. I'm just not sure if we get back together it wouldn't be a matter of time before he ended it again. I don't think I could take that. I said I'd think about it." She walked into the bathroom and closed the door.

Simone shook her head. Her mother was home and she didn't want Dalton arriving with Anna there. With any luck he'd be late and she could meet him downstairs.

Simone rushed to grab the house key out of her purse and was about to open the door when the knock came.

"I'll get it," Simone called, her adrenaline making her think fast. She opened the door to find Dalton and pushed him back so that she could walk out.

"What are you doing?" he asked, trying to hold his ground.

"Nothing. Let's go downstairs—"

"Honey?" Anna called. "Who's at the door?"

"Uh, nobody. I'm going out for a few minutes."

"Nobody?" Dalton said.

Simone gave him a look of exasperation. "Please," she begged quietly. He moved back, but before she could close the door behind her, Anna entered the living room. Simone tossed a few words over her shoulder. "We're going for a walk, Mom."

"A walk is the last thing I need," Dalton told Simone.

"Practice almost killed me."

Anna appeared beside her daughter. "Hello. I'm Anna."

"Dalton."

Anna smiled wide. "Oh, Dalton! It's good to meet you. Come in." She pulled Simone out of the way. "Honey, don't be rude."

"Mom—"

"Do you two have a date?"

"Mom!"

"We were just getting together to talk shop," Dalton answered smoothly as he stepped through the door. "It is a school night."

"Oh, yes. A school night." Anna's smile stayed put, as if she found the statement amusing. "Well, let me grab a bottle of water and I'll just be in my room."

Yes, where you can hear everything we're saying, Simone thought. "We're going downstairs by the pool." She took Dalton's arm and led him outside.

"It was nice meeting you," Anna called.

"You, too," Dalton replied.

Simone closed the door and Dalton shook his head with a bemused look. "You are so funny." He ambled down the stairs ahead of her.

"My mom." Simone let out an exasperated sigh. "Who knows what she might say?"

"I've met moms before. It's not a big deal."

Simone felt stupid. She had turned his arrival into a major event. Why couldn't she be cool, or at least pretend to be? "Sorry. I got rattled."

"I guess."

They made their way to the pool, turned two chairs so they could face each other, and sat.

Simone felt her heart race. Did he come in person to make their breakup official? How gentlemanly of him. An email might have been kinder. Then he wouldn't see her cry, because she just might. Right now she felt like a big, devastated baby filled with hot, wet tears.

Simone crossed her arms and did her best to hide her feelings. She would say she understood that her freaky abilities were too much to handle and it was fun while it lasted and best of luck and . . . and . . . it was no big deal. Never mind that wasn't how she really felt. She didn't want to break up and she wanted him to believe her about the ghosts.

She cleared her throat. "You're here to clear the air. Do you want to start, or should I?"

Suddenly Dalton laughed.

"What? What are you laughing about?"

"Us. We're so serious. Yes, I read your jokes about seeing ghosts. But . . . " He shrugged. "What made you run?"

"I didn't run."

"No?"

"Okay, I did. For a little while. But I came back. It was just . . . " She sighed and uncrossed her arms. "The look on your face. It was like I'd shot you or something."

"I may have been a little shocked that you think you see ghosts."

"I *do* see them. There. I said it out loud." The weepy feeling she'd worked so hard to contain morphed into resentment.

"How do you know? I mean, for sure."

"For sure? I see them as real as you or me. They talk to me and I talk to them. And not with symbols, like the mediums on TV. They talk." Did he think she was loony?

Dalton stared at her, his eyes questioning.

"Don't ask me if I've seen a shrink," she added.

"I wasn't going to."

"And I don't have a way to prove it to you, either."

"Okay."

They said nothing for several seconds until Simone couldn't take it anymore. "So where does that leave us?" Her face tingled with apprehension and she began nervously rubbing her palm.

Dalton reached out and took her hand. He looked into her eyes. "It's a little bit crazy, but that's one of the things I like about you."

"That I'm crazy?" she said softly.

"No. That you're you. You're different. And if this is part of who you are, whether I believe in ghosts or not, then okay." He shrugged. "I'm a very eloquent speaker as you can see."

She laughed. "Almost as good as I am. So we're still . . . friends?"

"Friends? Is that what you think?" He leaned in and was about to kiss her when Simone stopped him.

"My mother is probably watching from the window."

"That's okay," he said and when he touched his lips to hers, she closed her eyes. He drew back and glanced up at Simone's apartment. "Your psychic powers are indeed correct."

"I'm not psychic. I just know my mother."

He smiled. "You know you drive me crazy, girl."

"I do?" She half-smiled, trying to squelch it. Should she be happy that she drove him crazy? She wasn't sure. This was all new territory.

"You're all I can think about sometimes."

"Really?"

"You don't make things easy."

"I know." She would work on that, she thought. Be better at accepting how he might feel and not just think about herself.

He stood and pulled her up with him. He put his arms around her waist and she placed her hands on his shoulders.

"I wish I could give you a ride to school. If I quit swim team I'll be able to. To and from."

"Why would you quit?"

"Coach seems to have it in for me. It's like he wants me to quit. But I'm no quitter."

She chuckled, pointing to her head. "Case in point."

"Big case." He kissed her nose. "I have to go. I need to do homework and then get some sleep." He released her. "See you tomorrow."

She nodded and watched him walk across the cement courtyard and out the opening to the street before she headed upstairs.

"He's a cutie," Anna said, her eyes dancing with delight as she gazed at her daughter.

"So?" Simone sounded brusque. She didn't want to talk about her boyfriend.

Suddenly a ripple of nerves tickled her. She put her fingers to her temple and started to pace. *Boyfriend. I have a boyfriend. Me. Spooky Simone Jennings.*

Anna cozied up on the couch. "Why were you keeping him a secret? Last I heard he was ditching you for a party."

Simone stopped pacing, fingers still at her temples. "That was a week ago and he didn't ditch me after all."

"And you didn't tell me?"

Simone looked at her mother. She was grinning as if Simone had just come home with a straight-A report card. Correction, grinning like someone else's mother would if their child came home with a straight-A report card.

Simone dropped her hands. "Can we not talk about it?"

"No. I need to know what's going on with you."

Really, Simone thought. *Because it involves a guy, now you need to know what's going on with me?*

"I think it's wonderful. And he's adorable," Anna said.

"He's not a puppy."

"I know he's not a puppy. But this is your first crush and I'm excited for you."

"Don't gush."

"Then start talking, my little pumpkin face."

Simone grimaced. Now her mother was addressing her the way she'd done when she was five. How dumb was that?

And I need to stop acting like an eight-year-old at Christmas.

"He's . . . he's . . . I don't know Mom. I never felt like this."

Anna continued to smile from the couch, a glow to her face.

"I told him about, you know. Those things I can do," Simone confessed.

Anna lost her smile. "Oh, Simone. Why did you do that?"

"You think that's bad? I mean, it just came out. And shouldn't he know?"

"Well, he didn't run." Anna perked up.

"He almost did. The ghost thing totally freaked him out. In fact, he'd rather think I'm a little crazy than believe there are such things as ghosts."

Anna looked concerned. "Do you still see ghosts?"

They hadn't talked about Simone's "gifts" for years. The subject of ghosts made Anna uncomfortable. Once Simone was old enough to understand that, she'd quit talking about it.

"I see them." She looked at Anna. "*You* believe me, don't

you, Mom?"

CHAPTER 17

DALTON DRUMMED HIS fingers on the desk in his bedroom and stared at the computer screen. He was having trouble buckling down. He kept thinking about his conversation with Simone at the pool. He felt better now that they'd talked. He didn't want their relationship to be over. They'd hardly had a chance to get to know each other.

Still. He had some concerns. Did she honestly believe she saw ghosts and could talk to them? Apparently so. In fact, she was rather passionate about it. His sister would like that. Cindi watched all those ghost shows and he always made fun of her for it. He wouldn't be able to tease Simone, though. That was clear. As long as ghosts weren't the focus of everything, he supposed he could accept it. He'd have to if they were to remain together.

Okay. Get to work. Ten jokes. Ten. That's all you have to come up with. Ten jokes that Simone will think are funny.

He'd been putting off the assignment because—and he laughed at the thought—he was mediocre at it. Mediocrity was an abstract thing to pick on, but it was what bothered him. And, he imagined, it bothered a lot of people.

He frowned at the computer. It was too abstract. He needed something less intangible and more concrete or he'd never think of something.

Swimming. Coming in second, never first.

He started to talk the assignment out. "Valvert says, 'Sir, you just lost as usual.' To which I point out he could have said something clever like . . . " Dalton paused and then he laughed. "You flounder in the pool. But at least you swim like a fish." He laughed again. It wasn't bad.

Okay, one down and nine to go.

An hour later, he had ten funny put-downs and felt proud. He'd never write jokes for a living, but these were okay. Good enough for school.

Simone. He needed to read them to Simone. Maybe they could do the assignment tomorrow and be done with it. He grabbed the phone and called.

§ § §

"All right," Mr. Erickson said. "We have our first Cyranos."

Simone put her hand to her stomach to settle her nerves. She'd memorized everything. They were supposed to act it out. But she was no actress, and being in front of the class was a little scary.

"Dalton and Simone have asked to go first." Mr. Erickson motioned for them to come forward.

Simone and Dalton looked at each other with anxious smiles and approached the front.

"They'd like the desks moved around so that it's similar to the tavern in the movie. And all of you are encouraged to laugh."

A hand went up as the students slid their desks.

"Yes?" Erickson asked.

"Do we get points for laughing?"

"If it seems genuine to me, then possibly. No snickering!

Dalton. Where's your phone?"

Dalton went and grabbed it from his backpack.

"Anyone into playing cinematographer?" Erickson asked. No less than twenty hands went up. He handed the phone to a responsible girl and added, "No one else." He looked at Dalton. "If you like it, post it. If not, do what you want. Ready?"

Simone nodded. Dalton said, "Yes."

"Who's going first?"

"I am," Dalton said.

"And what feature have you chosen to annihilate?"

"Coming in second."

A few of the students snickered.

"Quiet, meatheads. I suppose those of you who laughed always win."

The class was silent. Erickson looked at Dalton. "Interesting and original. Let's hear it." He glanced at Simone. "Valvert. Shall we begin?"

Simone nodded and, drawing on her best acting skills, walked close to Dalton and said, "Sir, you just lost *as usual*."

"Thank you for pointing that out." Dalton began to walk away.

"Loser!" Simone called.

"Loser? Is that all you have to say?"

"Yeah. Loser."

"How original. What if you had said something more original? Like, let me see." Dalton pretended to think and then he began: "Ah ha. We'll begin with the obvious: Excuse me. Was that the Australian crawl or were you just crawling?"

The class groaned.

"Laughter, people. Laughter," Mr. Erickson instructed. "Think about when you're up here."

Dalton took a breath. "Philosophical: Always the champ's groom never the champ."

The students laughed, but only because they'd been told to. Simone began to wonder how the class would react to her. At least they liked Dalton.

"Advice: If you want to win, just swim by yourself."

Now the laughter sounded real.

"Punctual: Well the others were on time, but I guess they have longer arms.

"Complimentary: You're so polite. You always say, 'You first. Please, I insist.'"

Dalton smiled when he could tell the kids liked that one. He became more animated.

"Envious: Oh, I wish I were you. To be able to nap while you swim. Scientific: I know what's wrong. Your bones are made of lead. Kind: You flounder in the pool. But at least you swim like a fish. Inquiry: Have you tried swimming with the little children? They're very, very slow."

Dalton held up a finger. "And now. For the pièce de résistance. Fashionable: Wear some Speedos two sizes too small. No one will notice how slow you go."

Laughter erupted, several hoots included. Dalton made a sweeping bow and the clapping began.

Mr. Erickson wore a broad smile and clapped a few times himself. "Well done, Dalton." He looked at Simone. "Ready?"

"Yes," she said while nodding her head.

"And what characteristic will you make fun of today?"

"Feet."

"Ah." Mr. Erickson's tone lacked enthusiasm. It seemed he'd heard about feet before. "Perhaps you can dazzle us with some originality."

Originality? Simone wasn't so sure. Now if she made fun

of seeing ghosts? That would be original.

"Go Simone!" Jimmy shouted. He and Kim had appeared and were sitting in thin air side by side, smiling. Kim gave her a thumbs up. Their support was nice, but the sight of them made her even more nervous somehow.

She looked at Dalton and took a breath. "Okay," she said.

Dalton walked closer and looked down at her feet. Playing the part of Valvert he said, "My dear, your feet are rather large."

Before Simone could give her reply, the sound of the door opening destroyed her concentration and drew the attention of the students. Mrs. Nagel marched in on clickity two-inch black pumps.

"I'm sorry to interrupt, but I need Simone to come with me to my office." Her tone was authoritarian, and when she finished talking, her painted mouth rested in a severe straight line. She remained near the door, dressed in one of her prim and perfect pantsuits, manicured hands clasped before her, hair combed in that old-fashioned French roll she always wore.

Simone had no idea what she'd done to merit the dean's fired-up attention. Mrs. Nagel had never acted friendly, but she'd never taken on the persona of Attila the Hun before, either. She glanced at her teacher when one of his thoughts slipped into her head.

And you had to show up personally, disturb the class, and embarrass her?

"I don't know what the urgency is," Mr. Erickson began, "but she's in the middle of something. I'm sure you can appreciate how difficult it is for some students to talk in front of the class."

"I prefer this not wait." Mrs. Nagel's chin jutted forward.

"Then I'd like an explanation. What's so imperative you

feel the need to disrupt the proceedings?"

It was a standoff, and Simone didn't know who had more clout. She supposed the dean, but Mr. Erickson's backbone appeared to be made of titanium.

"She has an unexcused absence," Mrs. Nagel stated.

"Oh! I forgot." Simone rushed to her backpack. She hadn't turned in her mother's note. She gave it to Mrs. Nagel and hurried to stand near Mr. Erickson again, where she felt much safer.

The dean looked the paper over, folded it and slid it into a pocket.

"Don't we have five days to hand in an excuse?" a student dared ask.

"I believe that's the rule," Mr. Erickson confirmed.

Mrs. Nagel began, "I'm afraid in Simone's case—"

"Her case?" Erickson repeated. "Was a special statute penned just for her?"

"No. Of course not. If you would just let me take her to my office—"

"You have her note."

"She was also not in class after the first period bell last Monday. *You* of all people should be aware of that."

Simone immediately wondered how Mrs. Nagel knew. Someone must have snitched.

"Simone went to the restroom for a few minutes with my blessing. Sounds like a lot of to-do about nothing."

Mrs. Nagel's reply was to cross her arms. She stared at the English teacher who was giving her such a hard time, and finally said, "I'll wait."

"She looks so old," Simone heard Kim say. "And she's mean. Back in my day she wanted to be everybody's friend."

Simone glanced at Kim, who appeared pensive. Then

Simone looked at Mrs. Nagel.

"What's going on, Simone? Why is Mrs. Nagel after you?" Jimmy floated down out of the air and stood next to Simone.

I don't know. Unless . . . maybe this has something to do with our conversation in detention.

"What conversation?" Jimmy wanted to know.

I asked her about Kim.

"Simone. Are you ready to make fun of your feet?" Mr. Erickson asked.

She felt herself pulled in two directions. She needed to start her performance, but Mrs. Nagel's threatening manner was creating a fight-or-flight response within her and when that happened, Simone knew something out of her control might happen—like split pants or broken noses. She needed to take action to relieve the pressure. She also needed to protect herself from this woman.

"So you asked her about Kim," Jimmy said. "And?"

I think I scared her because she knows what happened back then.

"Simone," Mr. Erickson prodded.

Her insides felt like a geyser ready to explode. *Maybe, if I scare Mrs. Nagel even more she'll back off.*

Then again, maybe not, but she had to do something.

"Simone," Mr. Erickson said more forcefully.

"Simone, are you ready?" Dalton asked.

She looked at Mr. Erickson, then Dalton. This would throw him for a loop but she had to do something now! "Ghosts," Simone blurted. "I want to make fun of the fact that I can see ghosts." She looked at Mrs. Nagel. "And that they tell me things."

The pressure was still there. This was either going to be the bravest thing she'd ever done or the stupidest, but she had to follow through. If Mrs. Nagel was going to come after her, she was going to fight back. Knowledge was power, her stepfather used to say. She was putting Mrs. Nagel on notice that she knew things and she'd better stop harassing her.

The class was snickering, but the seasoned administrator remained still as a stone.

"What are you doing?" Dalton whispered.

She couldn't answer him. Not now. "Yes, Valvert. I see things and you can call me crazy."

"You are crazy." Dalton looked baffled.

"Is that all you can say? Not very clever. Here. Let me help you. I will give you ten ways to cleverly put me down."

Simone pretended to think. "Confused! If you see dead people, how do you know you're not dead? You do look a little pasty around the gills." Simone touched her face, pale with makeup.

The class chuckled.

"Curious! If you've seen one dead person, have you seen them all?"

She received a couple of groans.

"Play on words. What kind of *dead* beat takes advice from a dead person?"

There were more groans, but some laughter, too.

"Scientific! Did your mother take drugs when you were in the womb and you're still hallucinating?"

The class liked this joke. They clapped as they laughed.

"Accusatory. I know. I know. You want to be the first teenager with her own ghost-sighting show. Practical. At least you will have friends for eternity. Inquiry. Excuse me. Is it true ghosts only haunt houses on dead ends?"

The laughter grew louder.

"Know-it-all. I bet all the ghosts call you ghoul-friend."

Groans.

"Uptight. If I spend the night at your house, can I sleep in the *living* room?"

As the kids laughed, Simone turned her eyes on Mrs. Nagel. "And finally, suspicious. I suppose ghosts never lie to you, since you can see right through them."

The class chuckled and then clapped. Jimmy cheered. Kim had disappeared.

Mrs. Nagel walked out the door.

Simone put a hand over her mouth and took a deep breath. What was going to happen now? Would the dean leave her alone? Or had she made things worse? The kids might make fun, but they did that anyway.

Mr. Erickson said, "Thank you, Simone. Dalton. Nice work."

CHAPTER 18

"SIMONE," MR. ERICKSON called out. "May I have a moment of your time?"

Simone looked up from grabbing her backpack. Dalton threw his over his shoulder. "I'll meet you outside," he said.

She watched him leave the classroom. He was still talking to her. But after what she'd sprung on him, was he upset? She couldn't tell.

Sheepishly, she approached her teacher. As was his habit, he stood next to the wall with his arm resting on the shoulder-high sill.

"Simone. Your presentation was entertaining. I enjoyed it. But I have a question." He paused and put a hand to his chin. "You were supposed to joke about something that bothered you about yourself."

"I know," she answered softly.

"So . . . what you're telling me is, you *can* see ghosts."

She nodded.

He thought for a second, started to speak and stopped.

Simone's stomach churned as she began to worry about what he might say.

Mr. Erickson rubbed his chin and took a deep breath. "I'm not quite sure how to ask you this." He paused again. "If you really can see ghosts, does that, um . . . ?" He paused again.

"I'm not psychic, if that's what you're trying to ask." She didn't want to tell him about the telekinesis or mind reading. One supernatural skill was enough.

"It isn't, but, well. I have an issue. I don't know if you can help me with it or not." He checked his watch. "You need to get to class, but would you come talk to me at the break? I'll explain then."

§ § §

Dalton was waiting for her, just as he'd said. A couple of his swim buddies were with him, joking and talking. When Simone joined them, the levity stopped. They said hi and left.

At least they said hi, thought Simone.

"What did Erickson want?" Dalton asked as they started to walk. He didn't take her hand, and Simone couldn't help but think it was because of what she'd done.

"I won't know until break." She didn't try to take his. And she didn't look at him either.

But then he stopped walking and turned to face her. "When did you decide to, you know?"

Now she looked at him. She searched his eyes. "Let on that I see ghosts?"

"Yeah."

He couldn't even say the word. *Ghosts.*

"Last minute," she said.

"Why?"

To answer that question, she'd have to explain about Kim and Mrs. Nagel and the sudden desire to protect herself. If admitting to the world that she could see ghosts bothered him, telling him more could make him say, *It's been nice knowing you.*

She shrugged.

There wasn't time to try to talk. They had different classes and they needed to beat the bell. There was no parting kiss. Nor even a hair tug. It appeared they were back to square one. If she had it to do over again, would she do it? It was too late to think about that now.

§ § §

"Hey, Dalton. You heard this one?" Dalton's science partner asked.

"Huh?" Dalton looked up from the plate, food coloring, bowl, cups of water and plastic wrap on the table before him. Experiment day in science class was supposed to be fun, but he wasn't having fun. He couldn't stop analyzing Simone. Why had she suddenly confessed to everyone that she could see ghosts? And why did Mr. Erickson want to talk to her?

"Yo. Dalton. Listen up. In biology class the kids did a new kind of frog experiment."

"Yeah?"

"They stood around a live frog and told it to jump. The frog jumped. Then they cut off a leg."

Dalton grimaced.

"Yeah. They cut off one leg and yelled at it to jump. It jumped. So they cut off a second leg. And yelled 'Jump. Jump!' and the frog could hop a little."

"Is this a joke?"

"Yes. It's a joke! Finally, they cut off all four legs and screamed at the frog to jump, but it just sat there. It didn't jump. So you know what they concluded the experiment proved?"

"That if you cut off a frog's legs it can't jump?"

"No. That if you cut off a frog's legs, it goes deaf."

Dalton didn't smile. He shook his head. "That's demented."

"I know. That's why I like it."

Dalton finally chuckled.

"Ah ha. He's back."

Dalton looked intently at his lab partner, a guy he liked but didn't really know. They were partners by the luck of the draw. "Hey, Chuck. I have a sort of lame question for you."

"What's that?"

"Do you think people really see ghosts? I mean, not all people. The ones who say they see them."

"I don't believe in ghosts, so the answer would be a definite, absolute, positive no."

"Well. Why would people say they see them if they don't?"

"Who knows? For attention probably. Or they're crazy and they do see something. You know, like in that movie where the math genius sees people who aren't really there. He wasn't crazy like psycho-crazy. But he was schizo."

Dalton wouldn't have thought Simone was seeking attention, at least not before English Lit this morning. She'd seemed to hate attention, but then she made fun of herself in front of the entire class for . . . But if attention wasn't what she was after, and she saw people, or dead people rather, who knew what that meant? Could she be schizophrenic?

"Why you asking?" Chuck said.

I think I'm in love with a crazy girl, Dalton thought. "No reason," he said.

§ § §

At break time Simone entered Erickson's classroom and found the teacher at his desk reading papers. He took off his glasses when he saw her and motioned to a chair in the front row.

"I found your presentation enlightening, Simone. Clever. But enlightening most of all."

"Thank you, I guess."

Mr. Erickson smiled, something he rarely did. "We only have a few minutes so I'll come right to the point. You strike me as a serious type of person, not prone to jokes. That's why I dared to ask you if you really saw ghosts."

She waited for him to explain more.

"At first I wasn't sure if you weren't just piggybacking on the fact that this school is supposed to be haunted."

"Oh."

"But then I reminded myself about the type of person I believe you to be." He paused to think. "I've been a teacher here for three years. At another school for seven. I've run into students who claim all kinds of things. That was my initial worry."

Simone nodded.

"Here's the deal. When I came here I was asked a very peculiar question. Could I handle a classroom that no other teacher wanted any part of?"

"I don't understand." Simone cast a glance around the room.

"Neither did I. But they said they couldn't really explain. They wanted me to discover it for myself. They didn't want to taint the water, so to speak."

"I don't find anything strange about this classroom."

"Because it's only during fifth period and I don't want to say any more to you."

"So *you* don't taint the water."

"Exactly. If you're willing, I will have a chat with your fifth-period teacher so that you can come here. Observe. And tell me what you see. Is that agreeable?"

Simone shrugged. "Sure."

"Today?"

"Okay."

Simone told him who her teacher was.

§ § §

Simone smiled when she saw Dalton coming toward her on the outskirts of the quad. For a while there she thought she would be spending lunch alone. The expression on his face worried her a little. Was it her imagination, or was there something different about him?

She spoke first. "Everything okay?"

"Yeah. Sure. Of course." He took off his backpack and sat next to her on the bench. "Except I think I totally blew my science experiment."

Was that why he seemed different? "What happened?"

"Oh, I don't know. Maybe I have water on the brain from too much swimming." He took out a sandwich and bit into it. Every time he looked at her and she looked back, he glanced away.

Simone studied him. He couldn't be that bothered by what she'd done this morning. But he was holding something back. Then again, so was she. She decided not to push it.

"What did Erickson want?" Dalton asked.

Simone took out a tortilla rolled up with jelly. "He wants me to observe his fifth-period class."

"Why?"

"He didn't tell me. He didn't want to taint the water."

"Taint what water?"

Simone laughed. "That's the figure of speech he used. Did you know that teachers don't like to teach in that room?"

"What's wrong with the room?"

"I think that's what he wants help with."

"But how can you help?"

"I don't know. Maybe I can't." She started to eat. She wanted to change the subject. Mr. Erickson's invitation had something to do with the paranormal and she already knew what Dalton thought of that. "He sure helped me today with Mrs. Nagel," Simone said.

"Wow. Yeah. That was odd. It was like she wanted to string you up and throw darts or something."

"I know. She seemed normal before. When I was in her office and then in detention. Not nice, but like I was any other kid."

"I didn't know you were in detention."

"Oh, yeah. On Monday. Mrs. Calhoun wrote me up for being late to class."

He stared at her and then a small, smirky smile came to his lips.

"What?" Simone asked.

His mood had changed. He was still different, but in a lightened-up way. "My little girlfriend is a bad girl after all." His eyes were warm. Affectionate, even.

Simone giggled. "Yep, that's me. Bad to the bone."

§ § §

When Simone reported to fifth period, she was told she could head on over to Erickson's classroom. Mrs. Lively also handed her a pass.

Upon entering the classroom filled with seniors, Erickson motioned for Simone to come forward. A chair had been placed near his desk in the front of the room and she sat. The students huddled in clusters of four and were engaged in lively discussions. Several curious eyes briefly turned Simone's way, but Erickson gave no explanation as to why she was there. Instead he called out, "Twenty minutes, scholars! The orphan archetype. As many characteristics and examples in literature and pop culture as you can come up with."

He roamed the room, listening and answering any questions the kids had. Simone heard him say, "Absolutely. That's a perfect example." She heard him tell someone else, "That one might be more of the innocent. See what else you can come up with."

She eyed the room, thinking this might be a wild goose chase. Everything looked in order, the same as first period when this was her room. Bland beige walls paired with an off-white floor. A bank of windows with closed white blinds to block glare from the sun. Framed posters of famous authors and classic books on the walls.

Simone watched the students work. These were honor students, captivated by what they were discussing, and Erickson acted different around them. Seniors were more mature than sophomores, and Erickson treated them with more respect and less jocular severity.

Ten minutes in and all was normal. Simone buried a sigh. She picked up a little of what the groups were discussing, but not enough to keep her from getting bored. She put a hand over her mouth to stifle a yawn. That's when everything changed and the hairs on the back of her neck rose.

The two groups in the front just right of center began to murmur, and a panicky hand shot up. "Permission to move,

Mr. Erickson. All of us."

Erickson glanced at Simone. Did he expect her to blurt out what she was feeling? She doubted it. So she nodded instead, to indicate she was aware that something was happening.

"You may."

The sound of desks scraping the floor along with a swell of off-topic chatter rattled the room. An open space was left where no one wanted to be.

"Eight more minutes, scholars," Erickson called. He wasn't going to let them focus on whatever had disturbed the room.

Simone caught her breath as she watched a luminescent Kim Blue grow more and more solid in the center of the empty space. Only it wasn't an empty space any longer. It was as if someone had cut a hole in the atmosphere and she could peer into the past.

Simone glanced around. The kids closest to the cutout huddled away from it. No one stared into what had to be an empty-looking space for them. All of them wanted nothing to do with it.

Simone returned her attention to Kim. She sat in the sort of desk chair the school used back in 1968, notebook before her and a yellow pencil in her hand. There were other students at desks in the space as well, although some were cut off at the edges of the "hole." All of the kids were paying attention to someone in the front of the class who was outside the cutout.

Kim. Kim!

Simone received a slight reaction. Kim cocked her head, but only for the briefest of moments. Apparently this was a one-way picture. Simone could see in. Kim didn't see out. But Simone was fairly sure Kim had heard her, if only as a distant voice. Maybe one in her head.

Somehow Kim's world had converged with the present and apparently did so with enough regularity to bother the teaching staff who didn't want to teach in the room. Ten points for Mr. Erickson, who could handle it and had for three years.

Kim's hand went up. Simone heard the teacher speak: "Yes, Kim."

"What time is your housewarming on Friday?"

"Seven o'clock and all are invited. No need to bring anything. Just yourselves. There will be plenty to eat. I'm happy to be at this school and I want to show my appreciation as well as get to know all of you a little better."

The voice belonged to Mrs. Nagel. But it was younger and cheerful. It was friendly.

"I'll be there," Kim said in that perky tone Simone remembered from the first time they'd met.

Kim, Simone thought.

And just as Kim cocked her head again, she vanished along with everything else that belonged back in 1968.

The energy in the room returned to normal, and Simone sat wondering if what she'd witnessed happened daily.

"All right," Mr. Erickson directed. "If you would return your desks to their proper places, we'll get going with the class discussion."

He crossed to Simone as the class reorganized. "You felt the energy shift in the room?" he asked, his voice low.

Simone nodded.

"Anything else?"

Simone nodded again.

"You know what's happening?"

She squeezed her lips together nervously. What would he think if she told him what she saw?

"I think so," she said.

He nodded and looked toward the sea of students. All eyes were on the two of them. "Can you come by after school today?" he asked quietly.

"Sure."

Erickson turned for the whiteboard at the front of the class and Simone walked out, hoping, hoping, *hoping* that Kim showed up in sixth period. She had a few questions for her.

CHAPTER 19

KIM NEVER SHOWED, and Simone had to settle for actually paying attention to Mrs. Kent, or at least the film she showed that day.

After class she waited at the door for Dalton. He was doing his best to disengage himself from Jenna and her wagging tongue. The girl clung to his side like an annoying gnat as he made his way to Simone, at one point even trying to lock her arm with his. When they reached the door, she gave Simone a bright smile.

"Hey, girlfriend. Dalton's so cute how he always works you into the conversation. Do you think he's trying to convince himself of something?"

There it was. The real Jenna. Simone could only shake her head.

Jenna mouthed a kiss at Dalton and pranced away.

Dalton took Simone's hand. "I don't work you into the conversation. She does all the talking and always brings you up. What's her problem? Why doesn't she take a hint? More than a hint. I've told her outright to leave me—us—alone. It's getting ridiculous."

"You broke up with her. She can't take it."

"No. She broke it off and it was just a friendship."

"She wants you back."

"She has Chris."

"Yeah. I bet he loves how she's always after you."

There was one good thing about Jenna being such a pain. It took Dalton's mind off of Mr. Erickson's request for Simone to observe his class. It was like he'd completely forgotten, and Simone didn't bring it up.

§ § §

Simone watched Mr. Erickson motion to a desk in the front of the classroom. Simone took it, while he leaned against his desk, using his hands for support, and faced her. He took a deep breath. "So. What can you tell me?" he asked.

She wasn't sure how to begin. Did he just want to know what she saw, or should she tell him who Kim was and what happened to her? At least as much as she knew about what happened to her.

"Well," Simone began. "Even though I can see ghosts, I don't know a whole lot about these things." She was stalling. Worried. She felt as if she were skating on thin ice. How open was he about the paranormal, really?

"Understood." Mr. Erickson removed his glasses, held them by one of the temple pieces and put the temple tip in his mouth. Simone suppressed a smile. The move seemed akin to sucking one's thumb. She'd never seen him do this in class and it occurred to her that he might be just as nervous as she was.

It was her turn to take a deep breath. "There is a ghost."

"You saw one?"

She nodded. "And in my opinion it's not a residual haunt."

"What's that?"

"That's like a recording in the atmosphere that plays from time to time. The ghost is just a picture."

"But you say it isn't a recording. What exactly did you see?"

Without mentioning Kim by name, or Mrs. Nagel, Simone did her best to explain what she saw, adding, "I think it's a piece of the past coming into the present for only a minute or so before it disappears."

Mr. Erickson quietly drummed the fingers of the hand still supporting him against the desk, his gaze to the side. *Farfetched*, he thought. *But I see how the class reacts. And I know what I feel.*

"Farfetched or not. It's the truth," Simone stated, pushing to be believed after having picked up on his thought.

At the word "farfetched," Erickson's gaze rose to meet hers. "How do you know it isn't just a residual haunt?"

"Because . . . " Why was she holding back? She'd already told everyone she could see ghosts and he believed enough to ask for her help. "Because the ghost heard me."

"Heard you?" He frowned. "You didn't say anything."

"No. I thought it. I thought her name and she reacted."

He remained silent for a couple of seconds, then he said, "You know the ghost's name."

"It's Kim Blue. She died in nineteen sixty-eight. This was her classroom and the teacher was Mrs. Nagel."

Unbelievable, he thought.

"Why do you think it's unbelievable? I told you I see ghosts."

Mr. Erickson's jaw went slack and his eyes narrowed just as both of them heard the door open and a laser of sunlight shot into the room. Mrs. Nagel's heels clicked on the linoleum as she entered.

"Oh! This is fortunate," she said with a smile that made Simone uneasy. The dean's eyes veered to Mr. Erickson and then back to Simone. "To find the two of you together." Her tone made it sound like they were doing something wrong.

Simone cringed but tried not to show it.

"I came to apologize, Mr. Erickson," Mrs. Nagel said, the bite in her tone now covered with saccharin.

She's like good-cop, bad-cop rolled into one, Simone thought.

"I wasn't thinking when I burst into your classroom. It was a mistake and I want you to know it won't happen again."

"Thank you." Erickson put his glasses back on.

The dean gave him time to say more, but he didn't. So she turned her attention to Simone. "And I wanted to apologize to you as well, Simone. But I need to do it in private. It requires some explanation. Please come to my office when you've finished whatever you're doing here." Once again she looked at Mr. Erickson and then Simone. "And I'll make my amends."

"That's okay," Simone answered without thinking. "I don't need any amends." She sounded rude which wasn't how she wanted to sound. Antagonizing Mrs. Nagel was like poking a snake.

"This isn't a reprimand. I'm concerned about you and need to make sure that all is well."

I know you're concerned. That's the problem. Simone stared at the floor. She wasn't going to get out of this that easily. "Okay."

"Well. I'll let you get back to it," the dean said with one brow raised.

"Mrs. Nagel." Mr. Erickson stopped leaning and took a few steps toward her. "I've just learned that this was your classroom many moons ago. Is that true?"

The dean gave Simone a quick glance. "It was. For one year. My first year, as a matter of fact. Why do you ask?"

"No reason. No reason at all."

But there was a reason, Simone thought. To fact-check my story.

§ § §

Simone's crossed arms betrayed the calm she wanted to convey to Mrs. Nagel. Her foot shook like a cold puppy, and no matter how much she wanted to stop it, she couldn't. She didn't like the way Mrs. Nagel smiled at her from across the desk. It appeared sincere, but Simone was suspicious. She refused to be as gullible as she'd been before.

The dean tented her fingers and leaned back in her imposing black chair. "I am very sorry we got off on the wrong foot, Simone. Frankly, I'm always worried when a student has been suspended from one school and been sent to mine. Breaking another student's nose is serious business, but the fact that you were merely moved within the same school district means it was a first offense and the administrators have some faith in you. I'm sorry I didn't show you that same faith."

With every word, Simone's guard went up. Mrs. Nagel had a tough reputation. Tough people like her didn't say they were sorry. It was a sign of weakness.

"I'm offering my heartfelt apology, Simone. I hope you accept it, and next time I won't be so quick to judge."

Next time? That sounded ominous.

"Does that sound fair?"

Simone pressed her lips together and stared at Mrs. Nagel's desk as she nodded. She wanted to leave, go home to her room and close the door.

"Good. Then we've wiped the slate clean. I won't even

worry about that one detention you have on your record now."

Simone looked up. There it was. The knife she'd been hiding. Why bring up detention if she'd wiped the slate clean?

"I have to admit," the dean went on. "I found your presence in detention to be a red flag after having cleared you of those other charges."

And now you're twisting it, bringing up Jenna's pants.

Simone's foot shook harder and she couldn't stop from defending herself. "I was just late for class. Time got away from me. It could happen to anybody."

Mrs. Nagel sighed. "Now, see. That is the sort of disrespectful retort that can hurt you." She paused for a second. "But I do understand. It *could* happen to anyone."

Simone didn't say anything. She felt like a mouse caught in a corner with a very large alley cat swiping at her with its paw.

"That's pretty much all I had to say," the dean told her.

Simone lifted her eyes to Mrs. Nagel's. Would she let her leave now?

"Except. Well." Mrs. Nagel stood and walked around the desk. She placed her hands behind her and towered over Simone, her stare direct and daunting. "Simone. Now I know there is nothing untoward going on between you and Mr. Erickson."

Simone's heart leapt into her throat. "What?" She felt her face flush.

Mrs. Nagel lifted a hand. "Now don't get upset. I wouldn't be doing my job if I didn't broach the subject. Mr. Erickson has a fine reputation, but in today's world, I don't think it wise for him to meet alone with one of his female students."

"What?" Simone uttered again.

"I'd like to know what you were meeting about," Mrs.

Nagel said gently but forcefully.

"Schoolwork. What else?" Her voice had gotten louder and defiant. Simone stood up. She wasn't one to challenge an authority figure, but she wanted to leave.

"Sit down," Mrs. Nagel commanded.

She's changing tactics, Simone thought. *Now it's hardball.* She sat and looked at the administrator. If the expression in Simone's eyes was challenging, she didn't care. Mrs. Nagel had crossed a line.

"Now," Mrs. Nagel began. "He asked me if I'd taught in that room, which gave me the impression that you were talking about me. I'd like to know why."

Simone thought carefully how to answer. She couldn't tell the truth without making Mr. Erickson look foolish. Closed-minded people always thought people who believed—or even explored whether the paranormal *could* be real—were idiots. Mrs. Nagel was sure to use it against him.

"He said he'd been given that room because none of the other teachers liked it, and I told him you'd taught there. That's all."

One of Mrs. Nagel's eyebrows went up as her mouth pressed into a thin line. "And how did you know I taught in that room?"

Simone thought fast. "You told me. In detention that day."

"I most certainly did not."

Simone shrugged and said innocently, "How else would I know?"

What could Mrs. Nagel say to that?

CHAPTER 20

SIMONE WALKED OUT of the administration building onto the empty campus of Woodruff Senior High. The sun might be bright and the skies brilliantly blue, but the atmosphere lazed with gloom as if the day were tired and wanted to be left alone so it could nap.

Simone's mind tumbled with questions. Should she go to Mr. Erickson's classroom and tell him what Mrs. Nagel had said? It was a veiled threat, and he should know about it. If Mrs. Nagel decided to go after her full throttle, it could hurt him.

She decided she wasn't brave enough. It was too embarrassing. If something happened and she had to tell him, she would. The best thing for now was to just avoid being alone with him.

"Hey, gorgeous," Jimmy said, making a sudden appearance. "What's up with the long face?"

Simone shrugged. "Things."

"Oh, okay. That clears it up." He was quiet, waiting. But she said nothing. "What are you still doing at school?"

"I thought you saw everything."

"Haven't you been listening to me? I can't be everywhere at once."

Simone stopped walking and looked at Jimmy

thoughtfully. "Where do you go when you're not with me?"

"Sometimes I watch other situations on campus and try to help. You know, scare a bully away. That sort of thing. I'd be better at it if I could make people see me."

"So when you're not with me, you're with other people."

"Not always. Sometimes I'm nowhere. I think I must sleep or something. Except I'm dead, so why do I need to sleep?" It was the most serious Simone had ever seen him.

She started walking again and Jimmy floated along. "I think you should go into the light," she quietly told him.

He looked hurt and playfully put his hands over his heart. "Just when I thought we were friends, you want to get rid of me."

"It's not that. You want Kim to be at peace. You should be at peace, too."

"I am at peace. I help. It's called a calling."

Simone didn't really understand. He did help just by being there sometimes. But he couldn't help with Mrs. Nagel. He didn't see the future to know what was going to happen so she could avoid the bad. He needed to help himself.

"Simone, you know I drowned in the pool. What you don't know is, it wasn't completely an accident."

She stopped and stared at him.

"I went to the pool to dye the water green with my best friend. Only we got drunk first. And I, in all my teenage wisdom, decided it was the perfect time to tell him I was dating his ex, Kaci. He had a lot of exes, but she was the one that got away. We'd only gone out a couple of times, but we really liked each other."

"And he didn't take it well."

"He went crazy, yelling and punching me. I'd never seen him act like that. I tried to calm him down, but nothing I said did any good. And so I started yelling back, calling him stupid names. Just 'cause he'd dated someone, that didn't mean she was his for life. Finally, he landed a blow to my jaw that spun me around. I fell to the ground and I remember seeing his shoes revolving like a gyroscope. I tried to get up, but I couldn't, and he took off. And then, nothing. I must have rolled into the pool."

"And drowned."

"Didn't feel a thing."

"What happened to your friend?"

"He's kind of a mess. I think because he's never admitted that what happened to me was partly his fault. Things fester, you know. I feel sorry for him."

Simone studied Jimmy with fresh eyes. "That's very forgiving of you."

Jimmy shook his head. "Nah. He was my friend. We screwed up."

She started walking again with no thought to where she was going.

"So that's why," Jimmy said, "if I see a kid starting to drive drunk, I steal the keys. Or if two kids get in a bad fight, I do what I can to break it up."

"And if you see someone like me getting picked on . . . I get it." It had to be exhausting, Simone thought, trying to be responsible for what everyone else did wrong.

"And now that I've bared my soul, don't you think it's time you shared what's on your mind?"

She decided not to tell him. What could he do about Mrs. Nagel? And she didn't want to add to his burden of taking care of everyone. She could take care of herself.

"Kim haunts Mr. Erickson's classroom."

"That's what the long face is about?" He waved his hand

like it was nothing. "She haunts your history classroom, too."

"It's different."

"How can it be different?"

If anyone could understand, it would be Jimmy.

"Well, here's the thing. I've seen Kim in her time, nineteen sixty-eight, twice. Once, the first week of school when she was walking down the hall with two girls who dressed like she did. It was super quick and I didn't know what I was looking at because I didn't know Kim was a ghost.

"The second time . . . " She stopped and looked around. She was near the aquatics facility where Dalton was. She hadn't even been thinking about him.

"The second time?" Jimmy asked.

"In Erickson's fifth-period class. I guess it happens a lot, only the kids don't see it. They feel it."

"You see nineteen sixty-eight?" Jimmy gave her an incredulous stare.

"What? *You* don't believe me?"

"Are you kidding me? Of course I believe you. Do you know what this means?"

"That I see nineteen sixty-eight."

"You can help Kim cross over. This is great." He was so excited he began to buzz back and forth, a ghost version of pacing. It spent his energy, and before he could explain, he vanished.

"Jimmy." Simone shouted. "Jimmy!"

CHAPTER 21

"JIMMY. JIMMY!" CALLED a mocking male voice. "Oh, Jimmy, where art thou? Who's Jimmy?"

Simone narrowed her eyes at Chris, who was lurking near a building and had gone unnoticed. He began walking toward her with that sappy smile he liked to bestow on everybody. Simone decided to ignore him and made a beeline for the pool building. Chris had to jog to catch her.

"Hey, where you going, Spooky? Still up to your old tricks? I heard you told everyone you can see ghosts. Guess you talk to them, too."

Simone kept walking, nostrils flaring. "Don't make me mad, Chris."

"Sweet ole me? You're breaking my heart." He fluttered his eyes at her.

"You don't have a heart."

He put fingers to his chest and groaned. "Now, see. That hurts."

She needed to calm down and not allow Chris get to her. She slowed her pace, eventually stopping. "What is it you want?"

"A driver's license. A shiny new Mustang. And a million dollars."

"Then I don't know why you're hanging around me. I'm

fresh out."

"Yeah. I was afraid of that."

Simone shook her head. "Well, 'bye." She started walking, but Chris stayed by her side.

"I'm actually waiting for Jenna," he said.

Simone slid a look his way.

"She was supposed to meet me when . . . " He cut himself off, his eyes searching the school grounds.

Simone finished his sentence for him. "When you got out of detention."

He shrugged. "Calhoun had the honors. She's mean. No sense of humor what . . . so . . . ever!"

"What'd they ding you for this time?"

"Nothing. It's all one giant conspiracy." He smiled good-naturedly.

Simone could see that Chris didn't give a hoot about punishment. It was all a game to him: Breaking the rules. Getting caught. Not getting caught. Harassing her.

His phone chirped. He pulled it from a pocket, eagerly checked it, and frowned. He texted something with nimble thumbs and waited for a response. None came, that Simone could see.

"Trouble in paradise?" Simone asked.

"Nah." Chris sounded irritated, but didn't explain. Neither did he leave Simone's side.

"You're like a lost dog," Simone said. "Go home. Shoo. Shoo."

Chris responded with an obnoxious puppy whine.

They arrived at the aquatics facility, where the scent of chlorine greeted them along with the sound of short whistle blasts, the splash of water being entered by a several bodies at once, and the shouts of the coach urging the swimmers on. The pool, which was outdoors, couldn't be seen. A gray brick wall surrounded it. To get to it, they had to pass through the aquatics lobby, which they did.

The pool was state-of-the-art, fifty meters long, with water the appealing crystal blue of all well-kept pools. Thick black lines on the pool bottom helped swimmers swim straight. There were no floating rope dividers for working out.

With Chris still stuck like glue, Simone stood near the first set of bleachers and caught sight of Dalton along with seven other swimmers standing at the far end of the pool. Eight teammates lined the close end while eight were in the pool sprinting toward Dalton's end. As soon as all the swimmers touched the wall, the coach blew his whistle and Dalton's group dove in and swam as hard as they could.

"Go Dalton!" a female voice screamed.

Simone looked over and could hardly believe it. Jenna sat with Shelly and Lynette half the way up on the second set of bleachers.

"Go Dalton," Shelly and Lynette echoed their leader.

Simone glanced at Chris. He didn't look happy. He wasn't grinning, that was for sure.

The line of swimmers reached the wall, the whistle blew, and the waiting third dove in. Dalton's group immediately climbed out.

"Great job, Dalton," Jenna yelled. "Woo hoo!" Shelly and Lynette gave a thumbs up.

Dalton ignored them. Instead, he and all the others stood ready to go again.

Chris raced up the bleachers to his girlfriend while Simone grabbed a seat on the first bench rung and turned to watch what she thought might be fireworks. She was close enough to hear what they'd say.

Jenna was quickly on her feet embracing Chris, but he was having none of it. He put his hands on her arms and pushed her away from him. "What are you doing here? You were supposed to meet me."

Jenna gave him a pouty face and kissed him, paused, then kissed him again. He stood there, stiff and silent, allowing her to kiss him over and over, until finally he caved. His arms went around her and he hugged her tight. With her eyes looking over Chris's shoulder, Jenna saw Simone. She stared, but didn't acknowledge her. Finally, she took Chris's arm and led him down the benches to the deck. Ignoring Simone and acting like Chris was the love of her life, she leaned her head against his shoulder as they left the pool area.

Shelly and Lynette trailed behind with Lynette looking rather bored, but Shelly checking out the swimmers. Pausing, Shelly yelled, "Go Andy!"

Lynette grabbed her by the arm and pulled her out the exit.

§ § §

Having forgotten that Simone was perfectly capable of opening a car door for herself, Dalton unlocked her side first, opened the door, allowed her to step in, and closed it before walking around to his door and climbing in.

He looked at her. "In case I didn't mention it before, this was a nice surprise."

"You mentioned it." She grinned.

He started the car. The engine growled to life with a surge of power, the mellow exhaust throbbing gently. Dalton put the Camaro in gear.

"How was the meeting with Erickson?" He drove toward the exit.

"Mrs. Nagel crashed it."

"What?"

"Yeah. She showed up to apologize and then she asked me to come see her."

"Did you?"

"Yep. She apologized to me, but it didn't seem genuine." Simone fell silent. She needed to spill her guts and tell him everything. But was he ready for it?

"Well? What did she want?"

"She's afraid I know something she doesn't want me to know. And even though I know a little bit about it, I don't know everything. And I don't know enough to know why she's threatening me."

"She threatened you?"

"In a veiled sort of way."

Simone studied Dalton's face. Was he ready to hear it all? She wasn't sure, and all her insecurities seemed to be rising up inside her.

"Simone, what?"

"I want to tell you. I do. But . . . "

"But you don't trust me." He sounded hurt and Simone closed her eyes for a second.

"I trust you. I trust you more than anyone I've trusted in a long time." She opened her eyes and caught that he was pulling over to the curb. He shut off the ignition and turned toward her.

"What can I say that will help?" he asked.

"I don't know. I'm weird. I'm just weird. And it's catching up with me."

"Okay, you're panicking." He took both of her hands and squeezed them gently. "This is me. This is me telling you as plain as I can that I won't hurt you. If I don't believe your story because I think there must be some other rational explanation, that's all it is. I know you aren't lying to me. I know that. And I won't repeat what you tell me to anyone else, either. But if Mrs. Nagel is threatening you, we need to do something."

"I think she's going to find a way to expel me," Simone explained.

"Why?"

"Because I know about Kim."

"And Kim is?"

"A ghost. She died in nineteen sixty-eight."

Dalton was silent and Simone didn't know how to read his face. At least he continued to hold her hands.

"How do . . . " He paused.

"How do I know?"

He nodded.

"Kim told me, in a roundabout way."

Dalton didn't talk.

"See. You think I'm crazy," Simone said.

"No. I don't. There must be something to what you're saying if Mrs. Nagel wants to get rid of you. And if Erickson wanted you observe his class."

His words felt like a smack in the face. "So because they believe me, you're going to cut me some slack?"

He looked at her hard. "Don't do that, Simone. Don't turn what I'm saying into something bad. It isn't. You should know that."

"Okay," she said softly, a streak of guilt running through her, causing her to look away.

"This may be a stupid idea." He placed his hands back on the wheel.

Simone glanced at him.

"But would you like to meet my sister? She believes in ghosts."

CHAPTER 22

"AND THEN MRS. Nagel said not to get upset; she wouldn't be doing her job if she didn't bring up the subject." Riding in the passenger seat of Dalton's Camaro, Simone hugged herself and repeated the dean's exact words. "'Now I know nothing untoward is going on . . . '" Simone growled. "It was the way she said it, insinuating something *was* going on."

Simone glanced at Dalton. With eyes on the road and hands on the wheel, he was nodding, like he completely understood.

Simone dropped the topic of Mrs. Nagel. She felt secure enough to explain about the strange time warp in Erickson's fifth-period class and what she thought it meant. Dalton listened attentively without interruption, all the way to his house.

He parked in the driveway behind a white Avalon that looked new.

"Mom's home," Dalton said easily. "She usually isn't. She teaches first grade and likes to spend a lot of time in her classroom." He checked his watch. "But then again, it is a bit later than I usually get home."

Simone thought the car looked rather expensive for a teacher's salary.

"My dad's a lawyer," Dalton continued. "He has his own

practice."

That explained it.

The house was a one-story, ranch-style structure with lots of curb appeal thanks to perfectly groomed landscaping and a lush green lawn. It looked like it had been built several decades ago but had upgraded windows, doors, roof and trim.

Dalton put his arm around Simone and led her to the front porch. He opened the door and they went inside. The inside was as pleasing as the outside. It had modern furniture and hardwood floors. The many windows allowed lots of light.

"Hey, Mom," Dalton called. "There's someone I'd like you to meet."

Simone almost bit her tongue. She hadn't expected to meet anyone but a twelve-year-old girl.

Mrs. Worthy stepped into the living room, an apron covering beige slacks and a simple sage-green top. Her brown hair was pulled back in a low ponytail, leaving an open view of her face. Simone instantly realized where Dalton got his good looks.

"Oh, hello," she said. "I was just starting to make dinner. We like to eat around five so the kids can run off and do whatever. Are you Simone?" She extended her hand and Simone took it, nodded and smiled.

"I'd like to say Dalton has told me so much about you, but the truth is, he can be a very secretive son."

Dalton shook his head with a serious expression. "I'm not so sure that's true."

"For the most part. Like all teenagers." Mrs. Worthy addressed Simone again. "I'm glad he brought you home so I could meet you." She smiled warmly and didn't even seem to notice the goth attire Simone wore. Perhaps Dalton had warned her. Or perhaps, being a teacher, even a grammar school teacher and raising kids, she was used to running into today's counterculture.

"Can you stay for dinner, Simone?"

"Oh. I . . . I don't know," Simone stammered. "Um."

"What are you making, Mom? Simone likes what she likes."

Simone's eyes widened in humiliation. Yes, she was a picky eater but she knew how to be polite. "Dalton," she whispered in angst.

"Well, don't we all?" was Mrs. Worthy's understanding response. "Anyway, everyone likes spaghetti and garlic bread."

"I like spaghetti," Simone concurred.

"Oh. Cool. You're batting a thousand, Mom." Dalton smiled. "We're going to go say hi to Cindi."

Mrs. Worthy retreated to the kitchen. Dalton led Simone to Cindi's door and knocked. "Hey, brat. I have someone for you to meet."

"I'm busy!" came the response.

"Too busy to meet Simone?"

There came a rumble, as if Cindi were scrambling to put things away, and the door flew open. "Hi!" Cindi said, wide round eyes on Simone. "Wanna come in?"

"Uh," Simone said, a bit shocked at Cindi's eagerness.

"Maybe," Dalton replied. "How messy is that pigsty?"

Cindi stuck out her tongue and also made a face that caused Simone to smile. Dalton chuckled and they stepped into little sister's inner sanctum. Cindi plopped onto a bright pink beanbag chair and sank in deep, while Dalton and Simone sat beside each other on the bed. "My brother really likes you," Cindi started in.

"Hey!" Dalton replied playfully.

"Well, who knows if you told her?" She shifted from Dalton to Simone. "He's weird sometimes. But we keep him around anyway. Like a pet."

"Oh," Simone said, eyebrows raised. "Like a pet." She was getting the gist of their banter and was willing to play along.

"My friend saw you guys together at Wendy's and—" Cindi suddenly stopped as if she'd caught herself starting to say something she shouldn't.

"And what?" said Dalton.

"Nothing. I forget."

"I didn't," Dalton said.

Cindi shot daggers at him with her eyes, but then sloughed it off and turned to Simone. "Okay. I called you a geek. But that's just me. I call people names. Anyway, Dalton said you weren't. I could tell he didn't want me to say anything bad about you. Which I didn't after that because he likes you. He really does. Look. He's not even turning red and he usually turns red if I mention any of his personal business."

Simone looked at Dalton, who smiled at her. He motioned with his hand under his chin as if to say: *Nope. Not red. I like you. I don't care who says it or knows it.*

Cindi wrinkled her nose at him and he wrinkled back.

"As charming as your chatter has been," Dalton declared, "I brought Simone here because you, my dear sister, believe in ghosts, and I think it would be good for her to have someone to talk to about that."

Cindi suddenly looked disenchanted. "You mean she can't talk to you because you don't believe? That's bogus, Dalton. I wouldn't blame her if she dumped you right now."

Simone broke in. "I think what he means is, you might have a better understanding of what I say, and that would make it easier for me to share my experiences."

Sharp-eared Cindi perked up. "Experiences? You have experiences?" The excitement in her voice almost bounced off the walls. "Then, yes. I'm the one to talk to. All my friends talk to me about their stuff. I mean, seriously."

"Okay, then," Simone said, amused at this little ball of personality.

"Okay, then," Cindi echoed. "Why don't you sit on the floor with me? And tell me. What ghosts have you seen? Do you go ghost hunting? Does it scare you?"

Simone laughed. "No, I don't go ghost hunting."

"Why not?"

Simone turned to Dalton wondering how funny he found this conversation. She knew he hadn't brought her here as a joke. He was trying to help. But there was no way she was going to tell Cindi her troubles.

"Don't worry about him," Cindi said. "He's hopeless when it comes to this stuff."

Simone hoped that wasn't true. She didn't see how their relationship could survive if his mind was so made up he couldn't even consider that the ghosts she saw were real.

Simone turned back to Cindi. "Have you ever seen a ghost?"

"Um, no."

"Then why do you believe?"

"Because it just makes sense! When we die, we go to heaven or hell or somewhere else. Ghosts went somewhere else. Here!"

Simone smiled and Dalton laughed. Even Cindi laughed.

§ § §

Everyone sat at the dining room table for dinner. Except

for Mr. Worthy. He was working late and Simone would have to meet him another time, she was told. Dalton's home life was certainly different than hers. A mother who made dinner and kids who actually sat together to eat it? Honestly, it felt a little weird to her; she was so used to being alone.

"Mom. Mom. Simone sees ghosts," Cindi said brightly.

"Oh?" Mrs. Worthy responded with one raised eyebrow, passing a bowl of spaghetti to her son.

Shocked, Simone looked at Cindi, as did Dalton. "You were sworn to secrecy," Dalton said, scooping out spaghetti.

"Oh, yeah. I forgot." Cindi sat back in the chair with a sheepish expression.

"Wait until your friends hear that you can't keep a secret." Dalton handed the bowl to Simone.

"I keep their secrets," Cindi defended herself. "They're about boys and stuff."

"Which is more important, I guess," Simone said quietly, placing food on her plate. She gave the bowl to Cindi who looked very distressed.

"I didn't mean to tell," she told Simone. "It was an accident."

"Your grandmother saw ghosts," Mrs. Worthy said matter-of-factly, tearing a piece of garlic bread in two. "Well. One ghost, anyway."

"What?" Cindi said, her perkiness filling the room. She put the bowl on the table. "Why didn't you tell me?"

Dalton said nothing, although he stared at his mother as if she were an alien.

Mrs. Worthy shrugged. "It's not something I ever think about. You can ask Grandma about it next time you talk to her. She'll tell you."

"You tell us," Dalton said.

She put the bread down instead of taking a bite. "This was when you were little," she said, looking at Dalton. "She and your grandfather moved into a hotel room for a couple of weeks. Their house was being tented and some repairs were needed, too."

"And the hotel had a ghost?" Cindi asked.

"Evidently. They'd leave and when they came back all the drawers in the dressers would be pulled out, or the chairs would be on top of the tables."

"So someone could have been doing it. They didn't actually see a ghost," Dalton pointed out.

His levelheadedness bothered Simone. He was being logical, sure. But after all she'd told him, he still wouldn't consider the possibility there was a spirit world.

"Grandma thought that. And Grandpa, too, of course. But then, this one day, Grandpa was at work and Grandma was in the bathroom when she heard the furniture being moved. She ran out to the living area just in time to see one of the chairs slide into the middle of the room."

"And nobody was there?" Dalton asked.

"Nobody was there."

"Cool," Cindi said. "Too bad she didn't see the

ghost."

"She did. The last day of their stay, she was closing the door. She poked her head in to have a last look and she saw a woman. The woman raised a hand as if to say goodbye, and when your grandmother started to reenter, the woman faded away right before her eyes."

The dining room was silent. Even Cindi was at a loss for words until she said, "Creepy."

Simone laughed. How were you supposed to keep up with the changing mind of a twelve-year-old?

§ § §

Dalton and Simone avoided the subject of ghosts, and put Mrs. Nagel's threat on the back burner. They sat on the floor at a coffee table in the den, reading and discussing study questions for *The Outsiders*. After an hour, having only read a portion of the book, and being ahead of schedule in terms of needing to have it read, they decided they should work on other assignments.

"Need a break? Want some water or something?" Dalton asked.

"I'm good," Simone responded.

"Me, too." He smiled and then turned to his science book while Simone reached for her algebra papers. She found it tough to get going. She couldn't stop looking at Dalton as he concentrated on his work. With his sight lowered she couldn't see the blue of his eyes but could see the dark lashes that outlined them. His nose was straight and perfect. Even now, as he studied, there was thoughtfulness in his expression.

His neck was thick, but not too much so, and she knew

from having seen him in Speedos that his arms and chest were muscular under the t-shirt he wore. He had a lot of upper body strength and could probably do chin ups without breaking a sweat.

Dalton pressed the book flat against the table and Simone stared at his hands. She couldn't see evidence that he worked on cars, except for maybe the one-inch scar below the thumb near the wrist. His nails were clipped and clean.

Those hands had touched her face, she thought. They'd pressed her against him when they'd kissed. She was ready for him to kiss her again. A kiss like their first one . . .

"Hello," she heard him say, and she looked up to see he was watching her. He smiled and she gulped. She hoped she didn't blush.

"Algebra tough?"

"Nope. Nu-uh." She shook her head and looked down at the problems she needed to solve. But they just looked like gobbledygook. She gripped the pencil more tightly and stared at the paper.

"Find the solution," she whispered and allowed a silent sigh.

"Simone," he said. She looked at him. They gazed at each other for a couple of seconds before he leaned in close and said very softly. "I stare at you sometimes, too."

She smiled. And then he pressed his lips to hers and held them there tenderly. She closed her eyes, loving the feelings that seemed to touch every part of her.

"Mom's making popcorn if you want some." Cindi giggled from the doorway.

Simone and Dalton separated. Simone didn't look at the twelve-year old, but Dalton did.

"We don't need any popcorn," Dalton said. "Just privacy."

"Good luck with that," Cindi said.

After a second, Dalton told Simone, "She's gone."

"I think I should go home," Simone replied.

"Because of Cindi?"

"Because all I want to do right now is kiss you and that's not homework."

§ § §

Dalton walked Simone up the stairs to her apartment even though she told him he didn't need to. She saw no reason for him to get out of the car when she came home by herself all the time. But then again, this let them be together longer.

"You sure have good manners," Simone said.

"My father taught me well. He said it's how he won over Mom. She wouldn't go out with him at first."

"Really?"

"Yeah. She thought he was full of himself."

They reached the landing and Simone unlocked the door. "Do you want to come in for a second?"

"Of course I do. But I better not." His eyes shimmered by the light of the porch lamp and his mouth bore a slight smile.

"We didn't talk about Mrs. Nagel. And you haven't said anything about your grandmother's ghost story."

"If we didn't talk about it at my house, I don't think we'll talk about it here. At least not tonight."

She knew what he meant. Her emotions were running amok and his were too, it seemed.

"There's probably a logical explanation for the ghost story," he said.

"Yeah, probably," Simone responded, silently adding "not."

He reached out and tugged her hair. No kiss this time, just a warm smile as he turned and began to lope down the stairs.

Simone waved at him when he reached the bottom and he waved back.

She closed the door behind her and was met with "It's about time you came home."

Jimmy had his arms crossed and was in a mood.

"What's your problem?" Simone asked. She headed for her room.

"Kim. We can help her now and you're off gallivanting." He appeared in front of her, slowing her down, but not stopping her. She continued to walk as he floated backward.

"As it turns out, I like gallivanting." She smiled at Jimmy with satisfaction. She'd had fun spending time at Dalton's and sure wasn't going to apologize for it.

"Okay, okay. You deserve some gallivanting time, I'll give you that. But now let's talk about Kim."

"What about her?"

"You need to talk to her. She needs to tell you where that party was—"

"Housewarming."

"Whatever. She needs to tell you where it was so you can meet her there and do your thing."

"What thing?"

"See the past."

"I have no control over that." Simone took off her boots and sat at her desk.

"You don't know until you try."

"And how will that help Kim?"

"You'll see what happened to her. And, if I'm right, you'll find out what happened to her body. She doesn't know where it is. But if you find out, she can rest and cross over."

"And it might stop what happens in Erickson's fifth period," Simone added softly. She remained quietly thoughtful.

Her body.

Simone had never thought of Kim's death like that. Her body'd been disposed of. Maybe tossed out with the trash. *Poor Kim.*

"What if I can't find out?"

"Then Kim may roam the school forever in that confused state of hers." Jimmy's tone was caring.

"I bet Mrs. Nagel knows where it is." Simone's eyes swept back and forth. "That's what she's afraid of. She's afraid I'll figure it out."

CHAPTER 23

SIMONE CLIMBED INTO bed with a lot on her mind. If Jimmy hadn't shown up worried about Kim, she might have gone to sleep dreaming of Dalton. As it was, she needed to find a way to talk to Kim. Lately her appearances in World History had been hit-and-miss. If Jimmy was right about things, Simone couldn't just go about her business *hoping* for Kim to show.

She turned onto her back and looked up at the ceiling buried in the dark. She closed her eyes.

Kim. I need to talk to you.

She paused, waiting. She felt nothing, heard nothing.

Kim. If we're as connected as you said we are, then please, come and see me. It's important.

She paused again, but still the ghost did not show.

Simone curled onto her side and sighed softly.

Kim, I'm just going to talk to you and hope that you're listening from wherever you are. Remember you wanted to invite me to Mrs. Nagel's housewarming? You wanted me to go with you? Well, I'm ready now. I want to go with you. I want to see what happened to you.

Simone wondered how blunt she should be. Kim knew she was dead but then she'd get confused, and she never, ever mentioned that she didn't know where her body was. It was

Jimmy who thought that was Kim's problem, and maybe it was. But even if it wasn't, finding out what really happened to her was something that needed to be done.

Kim . . . Kim, do you wonder what really happened to you? Do you wonder where you're buried?

Of course, she might not be buried. Heck, her body could be anywhere. But if it was really hidden well, or somehow destroyed, what was Mrs. Nagel so worried about? Could be that Kim's body was close to home.

Kim . . . Kim. I think I can help you if you take me to that housewarming.

Kim never answered, and Simone grew sleepier and sleepier, all the while with Kim on her mind, Kim's name on her lips. Finally, she fell asleep.

§ § §

Simone sat in the backseat of an unfamiliar car. It was an old-style car although it looked new. The interior was red: carpet, roof liner and vinyl bench seat. Simone stroked the material. The windows had hand cranks. She reached out and touched the one closest to her. It all felt solid and real.

She looked at the driver and saw Kim. Another girl sat in the passenger seat. A radio played through speakers in the front, the sound not of great quality. A female voice sang, "Stars shining bright . . . "

Was this a dream or had she, somehow, wound up in 1968? If this was a dream, it was more real than any she'd ever had.

It was dark outside. The car rolled past streetlights that lasered on the window glass. A few other vehicles were on the road, but not many; they were in a residential neighborhood.

The car came to a four-way stop, stopped, then went straight. Simone checked the street signs. They were traveling on Fidler.

"I love your Malibu, Kim," said the passenger.

"Birthday present!" Kim squealed.

"Your dad spoils you."

"I know. It's a perk of divorce. Your parents fight over you. They want you to like them best. Of course, I wish they had stayed together. Except they couldn't get along. My sister went to live with Mom in Denver. I miss them."

The divorce Mrs. Nagel had mentioned was true, Simone thought.

"K . . . R . . . L . . . A" sang a canned male voice on the radio. "Serving Southern California from Pasadena." A song started with piano notes, then violins, and a woman began to sing, "Once upon a time . . . "

"You sure you want to go to this dumb party?" Kim's friend asked.

Mrs. Nagel's housewarming, Simone thought. It's where she'd asked to go as she was falling asleep. But she'd never imagined it would happen like this. She'd been transplanted into the scene and it was a little scary.

"We could go to the drive-in and meet boys," the girl continued. "They'd die for your car. They'd come buzzing around like bees."

"I have a boyfriend, remember?"

Simone thought, *Boyfriend breakup story not true.*

"Besides," Kim continued. "I told Mrs. Nagel I was coming. What if everybody who said they were coming didn't come?"

"She's a teacher. Why is she inviting kids to her house anyway? It's kinda dumb."

"It's her first house. That's what people do. I think she wants all the kids to like her. Be her friend."

"That's dumb, too."

"Well, it's a party, even if she calls it a housewarming, and you like parties."

"Only if cute boys make the scene."

"You mean if Randy is there." Kim laughed. Her friend laughed, too.

"Kim," Simone said uneasily, wondering if she'd be heard. "I'm in the backseat. Can you see me?"

"There's the house." Kim pointed.

I guess not, Simone thought.

"It just looks like a house," Kim's friend said, completely unimpressed. "Not even as good as mine."

Kim laughed. "Were you expecting the Taj Mahal?"

"Maybe."

A few cars were parked near the house, enough to know guests were over, but not so many you'd think there was a party. Kim was even able to park in front of the house. Some people must have left. She unbuckled her seatbelt.

"Hey, there's Kenny's truck," the friend said, unbuckling hers.

"Debbie, don't go running off with him the minute we go in."

Debbie laughed. "I won't, Miss Homecoming Queen. Like you won't have a million friends inside to hang out with."

"I don't think a million friends are here. And I'm thinking of Mrs. Nagel."

Debbie sighed. "That's why you're Homecoming Queen. You're so sweet! She'll be fine if I leave."

They stepped out of the car.

Simone reached for the door handle, but wondered—since

Kim didn't hear her, and it seemed she couldn't see her, could anybody? What if someone saw the door open and close by itself?

Well, what if they did? What else could she do? She couldn't move through glass and metal. She opened it and jogged to catch up.

"You brought a gift," Debbie said, noticing a wrapped, small rectangular box in Kim's hand.

"It's customary. It's just a little picture frame."

"See? Homecoming Queen. Sweet."

Kim and Debbie stepped onto the porch and just as they were about to open the door—a handwritten sign said to come on in—out popped a couple of guys, one tall and one short.

"Kenny. I didn't know you were here," Debbie said coyly, smiling at the tall guy.

He smiled back. "Hey, babe. How are you? RJ and I were just going to get something to eat. All she's got . . . " He motioned toward the house with his thumb. "Well, I don't know what that stuff is. But pardon me if I don't eat it. Hey, you want to come with us?"

"Well, yeah." Debbie glanced at Kim with a look that begged forgiveness.

"Sorry. The truck only holds three," Kenny said. "But RJ probably wouldn't mind riding in the bed."

"Doesn't bother me," he replied.

"It's okay," Kim said. "I'm good being here."

"It's your funeral," RJ said. "It's dead in there."

Simone cringed at the foreboding words no one knew were foreboding but her.

Kim went inside, Simone right behind her. Music played from a radio in the stereo. "America's festival of hits," a ditty informed anyone who was listening, and then a pop tune began. The music was different from what Simone was used to. She liked it okay. The song was catchy.

As Debbie predicted, Kim found friends right away and joined them in a corner of the living room after dropping off her gift on a table designated for that purpose. Simone recognized them from the yearbook. They were the homecoming princesses and the pep squad song leaders. Three of them, anyway. Simone stuck close to Kim and out of the path of anyone who might walk by. She wasn't sure what would happen if she was in the way. Could a person walk right through her? Or would that person bump into her and freak out because she was invisible? Simone had no intention of finding out.

"Where's Mrs. Nagel?" Kim asked.

"She's around. Guess what? Leslie's here." This came from Princess Jackie, if Simone's memory was correct. Her hair was long and red.

"What? You're kidding." Kim's mouth dropped. "Where?"

"In the back room, where most of the people are. She's with some boy. I think his name is Vance. And I'm pretty sure he goes to South." This was Princess Lori. Her blond hair was ratted and hair-sprayed to death, but it wasn't piled high.

Death. Simone cringed. It was getting harder to be here, knowing what was coming. Knowing she couldn't do anything about it.

"Good. Maybe she'll cut me and Scotty a break," Kim said. "She's spread enough rumors."

"Don't worry. No one believes them." Jackie took a sip from the cup she was holding. "She's a scuz and everybody knows it."

"I'm not worried about it. I just don't like it."

"She's acting really nice. Even to us," the friend with long brown hair said, a cup in her hand as well.

Princess . . . Simone concentrated. *Linda.* That was it.

"Must be the new boyfriend," Linda added.

"Maybe she's changed," Kim said hopefully.

"You are such a Pollyanna." Jackie crossed her eyes and Kim gave her a playful slap so her eyes went back to normal. "But that's what we love about you."

Mrs. Nagel walked into the room from the kitchen and clapped her hands together once. "Oh, girls. Come on in the back. I have plenty of food there and people are dancing."

She looks so young, Simone thought. Except for the way she dressed, she could have been one of the students.

"Kim. It's good to see you," Mrs. Nagel said. "Your friends were missing you."

Kim smiled brightly.

The hostess turned and walked back into the kitchen.

"We've been here forty-five minutes," Jackie said. "Where were you?"

"I got a late start. Debbie wasn't ready," Kim answered.

"Where is Debbie?" Lori asked.

"She ran into Kenny."

All the girls nodded like they understood.

"Well, I'm just telling you we aren't hanging around much longer," Jackie said. "She made these fancy hors d'oeuvres with calves liver. She actually told us that. There's all this fancy stuff. She doesn't even have any chips."

It really was a sad little party, Simone thought. Mrs. Nagel was trying so hard, but it appeared all the kids were ready to bail.

"You missed the good stuff," Lori said.

"I wouldn't call it good," Linda replied.

"You know what I mean."

"What?" Kim asked.

"Mr. Nagel was here," Lori told her. "They had a fight. Sounded like he didn't want her throwing this shindig. That's what he called it, a shindig. She said, 'It's a housewarming.' And he said, 'In my eye.' He had their kid in his arms and he stormed out of the house."

"There were only a few of us here, so I don't think Mrs. Nagel was too embarrassed," Linda added. "She smiled at us and said he didn't like parties. Like that made it okay."

Simone remembered the framed photo in Mrs. Nagel's office. That had to be her daughter.

The four girls, along with Simone, made their way to the rumpus room. It had been added onto the house, otherwise the place would have been as small as it looked from the front. And just as Mrs. Nagel had said, there was dancing. About eight teens were wiggling their butts and swinging their arms to a song on a record player that urged everyone to dance to the twist, the stomp, and the mashed potato.

Mrs. Nagel had her arms crossed and nodded her head to the music.

Simone looked around, hoping to figure out who Leslie might be. When she spotted a girl, the rat pile on her head possibly the highest Simone had ever seen, holding hands with a boy, but staring at Kim, Simone was sure she'd found her.

The song ended and Mrs. Nagel took another record from its sleeve. "Anybody know the Watusi?" she said.

"Let's dance," Kim told her friends. "It'll make her happy." She took hold of the wrists of two princesses and pulled them onto the "dance floor." Dropping their hands, she motioned at Linda to join them and she did.

A song began and now twelve people were dancing, a

record for this party, Simone thought. She kept her eyes on Leslie who stared at Kim the way a lioness might stare at her prey. Either Kim didn't notice or she pretended not to. She smiled and laughed as she danced with her friends.

Not long into the song a sweet, pungent odor infiltrated the room. It was a smell everyone could instantly recognize: pot. Potheads might have just entered the house. The door was open to anyone. Or they could be in a bedroom somewhere.

"Keep having fun," Mrs. Nagel instructed, "and I'll take care of this." She left the room to investigate.

"Have fun?" Jackie stopped dancing as did all the others.

"We should go," Lori said. "We've been friends to the lame long enough."

"That's not nice," Kim said. "And I just got here. I need to stay a little longer. Look. Everybody's leaving. This is so sad."

"Leslie and her new boyfriend aren't," Linda pointed out.

Kim shrugged. "I'll just stay until Mrs. Nagel comes back. Then I'll make an excuse."

If only she'd listened to her friends, things might have turned out different. Simone could feel her eyes tearing up and tried to push her feelings aside.

"We'll meet at my house," Jackie said. "We'll go to the movies or something."

"Okay," Kim agreed. "See you in a little while."

The princesses left along with most of the others who'd been dancing. Kim went to the punch bowl and ladled a drink into a cup. She sipped it and turned to look around the room that was emptying out.

Leslie pounced. Simone almost threw her hands over her face, the way she might in a horror movie just when the knife was about to plunge.

"Hi, Kim." Leslie smiled broadly, stepping in front of

Kim.

"Hello," Kim answered, politely.

"Can we talk? I mean really talk?"

Kim shrugged. "What's there to talk about?"

"I want to apologize."

"That's nice," Kim replied.

"No, really. I'm very, very sorry. I went too far and I know it now." Leslie's eyes held Kim's as she crossed a hand over Kim's cup and took her wrist.

Simone's breath caught in her chest. *That's when she did it. That's when she drugged Kim's drink.* There was no telling with what.

"I'd like us to be friends, even though I know it's too late for that." Leslie let go of Kim's wrist, grabbed a cup for herself and poured some punch into it. "Can we at least toast to the fact that I've said I'm sorry?"

"Sure," Kim replied and they both took a drink. Leslie smiled, lifted her glass and drank more, causing Kim to do the same.

Kim's reaction to whatever had been put in her drink happened quickly. She began to sweat and she put her hand to her stomach, leaning over.

Leslie stepped out of the way, but Kim didn't throw up. Her eyes drifted to the side, and her breathing grew labored. She tried to walk on unsteady feet.

Leslie's expression changed. "What's wrong?" she asked. "Here, let me help you." She led Kim to the only couch in the room and sat beside her. Kim lay on her shoulder with her eyes closed. She gulped for air like a fish and thrashed back and forth.

Leslie looked up at Vance, panic all over her face. "I think I gave her too much. I just wanted her to throw up in front of everyone and be embarrassed."

Really? Simone thought. *Because everybody's gone.*

"Well, it didn't go as planned, that's for sure," Vance said. "You should have done it sooner and not given her so much."

"I know that!" Leslie snapped. "Oh, my God. What should we do?"

"We? This wasn't my idea." Vance shook his head.

"You're not helping!"

"Why'd you need to drug her anyway?"

Leslie growled, like that was a stupid question. "She just bugged the crap out of me. Miss Goody-Two-Shoes. I hate her. But I wasn't trying to kill her. I swear. She's turning blue! Kim. Kim!"

Simone felt anger rise within her. *She bugged you because she was nice? She bugged you because Scotty liked her better, and maybe that's because she was nice.*

"She can't even get sick right," Leslie said, apparently covering her fright with anger.

Kim stopped thrashing. Her breath grew shallower and shallower.

Vance stepped closer. "She looks bad," he said. "Like she really might die."

Leslie looked at him, panic once again the foremost expression on her face.

"I think we need to get out of here before Mrs. Nagel comes back," Vance said.

"You're right." Leslie pushed Kim's head aside and stood.

"Well, I took care of that little problem," Mrs. Nagel said, entering the room. She looked squarely at Leslie since there was no one else to look squarely at except Vance. "Found the little punks in my bedroom closet. I'm going have to buy new clothes. Maybe furniture. The whole house reeks . . ." She noticed Kim lying on the couch. "What happened? Is Kim sick?"

"We don't know—" Vance started to say.

"Um." Leslie stared at Mrs. Nagel. "She . . . she took something."

Simone could see the wheels in Leslie's head turning. The spiteful teen had moved from panic to survival mode.

"What?" Mrs. Nagel looked worried.

"Some pills," Leslie asserted. "I don't know what. I saw her do it. Everybody thinks she's so great, but she's really a druggie."

Horrified, Mrs. Nagel hurried to Kim and knelt beside her. "She's not breathing." She took Kim's arm and placed two fingers on her wrist. "She has no pulse. Call an ambulance. Hurry!"

Mrs. Nagel pinched Kim's nostrils together and breathed into Kim's mouth. She pressed on Kim's chest, then breathed for her again.

"Call an ambulance!" Simone shouted aloud, although she knew she wouldn't be heard.

Leslie looked at Vance. She moved close to him and whispered. "We can't call an ambulance. The cops'll get involved and they'll figure it out."

"What, then?" Vance whispered back.

It became clear to Mrs. Nagel that Kim was gone. She looked over at Leslie. "Did you call?"

"Um. No, I'm sorry. I . . . "

"We didn't see a phone," Vance added.

Simone felt like crying, and apparently so did Mrs. Nagel. She saw her eyes glisten as she got to her feet.

"I'll call," Mrs. Nagel said. "Although . . . " She didn't finish, but swallowed instead.

"Is she gone?" Leslie asked.

Mrs. Nagel nodded.

Leslie took a deep breath. "Maybe you shouldn't call."

Mrs. Nagel stopped and stared at the girl, numbly.

"If they can't do anything to help her and the cops come . . . "

"I want the police to come," Mrs. Nagel said. "This is a tragedy."

"I know, but . . . " Leslie rubbed her hand over the side of her head. She glanced at Vance and back again. "Your house smells like marijuana. Kim died of a drug overdose at your party. What's going to happen?" Leslie asked.

"To you?" Vance added.

Mrs. Nagel blinked. Clearly, she hadn't thought of that.

Simone knew she wasn't going to call now. She wondered what might have happened if she had. Maybe Kim wasn't beyond help.

Leslie took a step closer to the teacher and pressed her lips together for a second. She was on a roll and knew what she wanted. "You might go to jail. And it won't bring Kim back."

"But . . . " Mrs. Nagel looked frightened. "Oh, my God." She rushed to the back door and opened it to air out the room.

"I don't think that'll help," Leslie said.

"What do I do?" Mrs. Nagel stared at the floor, frozen. A tear trickled down her cheek. She finally looked at Leslie, her breath exiting in short bursts.

"Maybe Vance and I can do something. I mean, I'd hate for you to go to jail for something that's Kim's own fault."

Mrs. Nagel looked at Kim. "It *was* her fault," she said softly before taking in a deep breath.

"We'll take care of Kim. You don't need to worry."

Mrs. Nagel sank to the floor. She didn't say okay, but she

didn't say no. Leslie looked at Vance.

"What?" Vance asked Leslie. "What are we—"

"Do you have a shovel?" Leslie asked.

Mrs. Nagel jerked her head up. "What?"

"It's the best way," Leslie said. "Unless you think the neighbors might see."

"No." Mrs. Nagel swallowed. "No. The house is twenty years old. The trees are tall and there's a block wall fence." She shook her head and stared at Kim. "The shovel's behind the garage where I keep the trash cans."

There wasn't much talking after that. Vance retrieved the shovel and dug a grave in Mrs. Nagel's flower bed. When it was deep enough, Vance carried Kim to the hole in the ground and dropped her in. Then he covered her body with dirt and Leslie replaced the primroses.

Leslie stood up and brushed the soil from her pants. She pulled something out of her pocket and held it up—a dangling set of keys. "I remembered Kim had a car. We'll have to get rid of that, too."

CHAPTER 24

SIMONE TOSSED FROM side to side. "Kim," she mumbled more than once until she finally opened her eyes and stared at the ceiling in her bedroom. Feelings of grief overwhelmed her. She'd witnessed Kim's death and it hit her hard—the loss and the unfairness of it all.

"Maybe it was just a dream," she said softly, going over every detail in her mind, none of it scattered or skewed. It had unfolded logically without gaps or strange sidetracks. What she'd witnessed in the dream had to be true, she decided; something easy enough to prove if she dug up Mrs. Nagel's backyard. But how could she make that happen?

Simone jumped out of bed, dressed, and hurried to the bus stop, arriving at school earlier than ever. She knew what happened to Kim and who'd made it happen: a girl named Leslie. What she didn't know was Leslie's last name. Yearbooks were good for that, and the library opened at seven.

She found the book where she'd left it and quickly took it from the shelf.

Leslie . . . Leslie . . . Leslie . . . Standing in the stacks, Simone checked the face of every senior until she found the one she wanted: Leslie Maker. She didn't look for Vance. Lori had said he went to South.

As Simone stared at Leslie's face she wondered if Mrs.

Nagel had stayed in touch. Probably not. There was no reason to that Simone could think of. It didn't matter anyway. Whether she had or had not, she didn't know how to find Leslie and even if she did, what good would that do? Neither Leslie nor Mrs. Nagel was going to confess.

Simone walked out to the quad and sat on a table, her feet on the bench. She rested her head in her hands. All she really cared about at this point was helping Kim find peace. She lifted her head.

Kim? Kim I need to talk to you.

She waited. The school was coming to life with students arriving for classes, teachers walking together and discussing whatever teachers discussed, and a few blackbirds cawing as they whipped from one tree to another. There was also a slight breeze that skittered bits of stray trash across the lawn.

But there was no Kim.

Simone spotted Mr. Erickson ambling down a walkway, briefcase in hand. He strolled with another teacher, but when he saw Simone he excused himself and made his way to her.

"How are you today, Simone?" he asked politely.

"I'm good. How are you?"

His answer was a nod. "I've been thinking about what you told me."

"About the ghost."

"Yes. About that." He paused to think. "I never believed in ghosts. I still don't, honestly."

Simone didn't say anything. It wasn't up to her to make people believe, but it sure felt like it these days.

"I guess, what I'm trying to say is twofold. One, I'd appreciate it if you didn't tell anyone I asked you to come to my classroom to spot a ghost."

"You didn't. You asked me to come to your room to see if

I sensed why none of the teachers want that room."

"Yes, but only after you told everyone you could see ghosts. I don't want . . . "

He allowed the sentence to trail and Simone picked it up for him.

"You don't want people to think you believe in something most people think is nonsense."

He nodded. "That about sums it up. It could tarnish my reputation."

She understood completely. She shrugged and nodded.

"The second thing . . . I wanted to know if you knew how to stop what you saw in my classroom from happening." He nervously squeezed the handle of his briefcase and Simone heard him think: *Oh, boy. Now I sound like a complete hypocrite.*

She glanced away and caught sight of Mrs. Nagel staring at the two of them from a corridor that led to the administration building. Simone felt her stomach do a back-flip.

She's like a stealth bomber and possible as deadly. Kablam!

"Kablam?" Mr. Erickson looked perplexed.

Simone blinked hard and looked at her English Lit teacher. He obviously had some of the same abilities she had, sans the one that allowed her to see ghosts. And he probably couldn't move objects with his mind, either. But he'd heard her. That was for sure. She glanced at Mrs. Nagel again. The woman wasn't going away.

"Did you say something?" Erickson asked.

"No." Simone studied her teacher's face, unsure if she should say anything more. But the dean had made a vague threat that involved him and he needed to be aware of it. He needed to protect himself. He was already freaking out about the ghost-sighting thing, what would he think if she told him he could hear her thoughts? Simone screwed up her courage. "Not out loud anyway," she said.

"Excuse me?" he asked.

"I heard you think, 'Oh, boy. Now I sound like a complete hypocrite.' And then I saw Mrs. Nagel watching us and I thought 'She's like a stealth bomber. Kablam!' And you heard me."

He stared, dumbfounded, not moving a muscle, until his mouth started to move, but no sound came out.

"It happens," Simone said. "You've never heard anyone else's thoughts before?"

Mr. Erickson found his voice. "Uh, no."

"Well. Welcome to my world," Simone said. She wanted to laugh at the expression on his face, but reeled in the urge. She glanced at Mrs. Nagel again. Her arms were crossed, her eyes zeroed in on Simone like the barrel of a shotgun.

Mr. Erickson, let's practice. Simone thought.

He answered very slowly. "Practice?"

She nodded and thought: *We're tuned to the same wavelength or something. Can't read minds with just anybody, you know.*

I didn't think you could read minds with anybody.

I heard that. Simone laughed, then sighed. *I need to warn you about Mrs. Nagel. You probably already figured out that she has it in for me. But the thing is, because of that she might be making trouble for you.*

Mr. Erickson snapped to attention. "What do you mean?"

"I mean she's watching us right now." She looked at Mrs. Nagel and Mr. Erickson turned to look as well. Whether his glance was confrontational or not, Mrs. Nagel raised her chin, uncrossed her arms and walked in the direction of the administration building where her office was located.

"She thinks I told you something she doesn't want anyone to know. Something that happened a long time ago."

"How—" He cut himself off. "Never mind. I'm not sure I want to know. It seems I've opened Pandora's box."

Simone laced her fingers together and stared at them. "We shouldn't talk except in class."

When he didn't ask why, Simone felt sure he understood what she meant. She looked up. "And I'm trying to help the ghost in your room. If I figure out how, then I don't think you'll have that problem in fifth period anymore."

She'd stunned him into silence and she couldn't read his thoughts right now. He looked like someone who knew he had a problem—Mrs. Nagel—and was trying to figure out how to deal with it. He turned from her without a word and ambled in the direction of his classroom.

She looked over and saw Dalton. The bounce in his stride told her he was happy about something. She hopped off the table and hurried over to him. She planned to tell him about her dream. She'd tell Jimmy, too, if he ever showed up again.

Dalton grabbed Simone's hands and swung her halfway around. "Guess what?"

"What?"

"I've shaved enough off my time in the one hundred free that Coach is thinking about putting me back on the JV relay team as the *anchor*!"

"That's great."

"All I have to do is beat Browning in a head-to-head. After school at practice. Tomorrow."

Simone nodded and bit her tongue. Her news would have to wait.

He put his hands over his face and leaned his head back. "Augh! I have to win. I *have* to!"

"I believe in you," Simone said. "You've worked hard."

He lowered his hands and looked at her, his eyes filled with excitement. He seemed to have forgotten all about her meeting with Erickson, and Mrs. Nagel's threat. With swimming the only thing on his mind, Simone wouldn't dampen his mood with any talk of ghosts, dreams, or murder.

CHAPTER 25

SIMONE OPENED THE mailbox when she came home from school and found it empty. Not even a piece of junk mail lay inside. Shrugging it off, she climbed the stairs and opened the door to the apartment.

"Hello, honey." Anna rested against the arm of the couch with her feet on the cushions. She had a fashion magazine in her hands and was looking at the pictures. She smiled softly at her daughter and put the magazine down.

"What are you doing home?" Simone asked.

"I live here."

"I know, but . . . "

Anna nodded, then shook her head. "I know what you mean. I'm not home a lot." She patted the cushion. "Come sit."

Simone took her backpack off and placed it on the coffee table. A sick feeling clawed her stomach. Anna shouldn't be home at this time of day. Plus, her smile looked forced. She was being careful about something.

Simone sat beside her mother and waited. Anna looked at her daughter's face and put a hand to Simone's hair, stroking a lock of it.

"Is something wrong?" Simone asked.

"You know, I'm not sure. I think I know you. I mean, I do know you. But you're on your own so much and you've changed the way you dress."

Simone's concern heightened. "What is it?"

"I got a call from the school today."

Nothing out of the ordinary had happened at school, except for Mrs. Nagel's frosty stare. Simone couldn't think of a single reason for anyone else from Woodruff to call Anna.

"Let me guess," Simone said. "It was from Mrs. Nagel."

"Yes. She acted very concerned about you."

Acted. Yes, it would have had to be an act. Simone bit her lower lip.

"She seems to think you're getting too close to a teacher. And, well . . . " Anna took a breath.

Simone felt her eyes grow hot and moist. She pulled away. "Mom, I'm not."

"She said she was worried—"

"You can't believe a word that comes out of her mouth."

"Well, if you have an explanation, please, tell me what it is. She wants me to transfer you to another school before something happens and she has to expel you."

Simone let out a short, false laugh. How nice of Mrs. Nagel to try to save her from the embarrassment of expulsion. *How nice of her . . .*

The tears came now and she couldn't hold them back. Her mother quickly put her arms around her daughter and Simone hugged back with all her might. "I'm sorry, Mom. I'm sorry."

"What are you sorry about?"

"I'm sorry I'm such a terrible daughter. A terrible person. I'm sorry I'm so weird. I tried to keep to myself. I promised myself I would this school year. But everything's fallen apart and I'm trying to straighten things out. But everything keeps getting worse."

Anna let her daughter cry for a while before she spoke.

"I don't ever want you to be sorry. I love you. You're not a terrible person. And you're definitely not a terrible daughter. I couldn't ask for a better one."

Simone hiccupped now. Anna held her away from her body and wiped Simone's tears with her thumb. "And the only thing weird about you is your makeup since I bought you nice black clothes."

Simone giggled through tears that finally started to subside.

"Now. Tell me about this Mrs. Nagel. Because if you say not to believe her, then I believe you."

Simone looked at her mother. "It involves seeing ghosts. Can you handle it?"

Anna smiled. "I've handled it since the day you were born."

Simone hesitated. She wasn't one hundred percent sure Anna would accept everything as true. But once the words started to come, it all spilled out: why she'd been talking to Mr. Erickson, the ghosts, the dream and Kim's awful death.

Anna listened intently and never interrupted. The expression on her face was hard to read.

"What do you think, Mom?" Simone asked.

"I think you've been dealing with a lot of stuff."

Her words felt noncommittal. Did she believe her or not? Simone waited for Anna to say more.

"What does Dalton think of all this?"

Of course you worry about him. Simone gritted her teeth and hid her irritation. "He's kind of busy with swim team right now, so he doesn't know everything. And I'm not sure he'd believe me about the dream. He's made it clear he doesn't believe in ghosts."

Anna nodded. "Well. It would be nice to tell the police

about Kim. But how would you explain knowing? They'd never believe you saw it in a dream. As for Mrs. Nagel, I don't want you to worry about that. I'm going to call her back and tell her in no uncertain terms that you told me why you met with your teacher and that I believe you. I'll also tell her that if she tries to make something out of nothing, then we'll fight it and everyone will learn what kind of person she is."

Simone smiled. She didn't know if that would bring an end to Mrs. Nagel's harassment, but at least she knew her mother was on her side and that felt wonderful.

"Hey. Are you in the mood for a Fred Astaire movie?"

"Mom. When am I ever in the mood for that?"

"Okay," Anna replied. "I'll watch alone."

"And I have homework to do." Simone walked into the kitchen and heated a cheese pizza while her mother searched Netflix.

Simone retreated to her room with her dinner. She heard *Swing Time* begin just before she closed the door.

"Where's mine?" Jimmy was back, grinning as usual, in a playful mood. He lay on his side, head on one hand, his body floating through the air.

"Ha. Ha," Simone said. "Where have you been?"

"Around. I do have other missions."

"Oh, yeah. The James-Bond-of-spirits thing." She bit into her pizza.

"Well. What's the buzz? Have you been able to help Kim?"

"I haven't seen her." Simone didn't realize until this minute that she was a little mad at Jimmy. He'd pushed her to find out what happened to Kim and then he'd just disappeared. She turned away from him and opened an algebra book.

"Is that it?" Jimmy asked.

"For now."

"Why are you being so weird?"

Simone turned back to Jimmy. "I know where she's buried, but I can't tell her because she's disappeared on me."

"You know?" His grin returned. "That's fantastic!" He started to dart through the air like a goldfish in a bowl that was too small.

"And you disappeared on me, too. I wanted you to help find Kim."

"Woo hoo," Jimmy rent the air with excitement, continuing to flit like a fish. "She'll turn up. She always does."

"Will you stop that?" Simone said rather forcefully. "You're making me queasy."

Jimmy settled down and sat midair. "I'm proud of you, gorgeous. Really proud."

She glanced away. "Thanks. I guess."

When she looked up, Jimmy was gone.

Unenthusiastically, she returned to her homework and found it hard to concentrate. Thank goodness her mother supported her. But Kim was still missing. Mrs. Nagel was still on the warpath. And Dalton? Well, it remained to be seen if he'd survive her latest saga.

Dalton. I had this dream . . .

Her phone rang and she checked it. It was Dalton.

"I can pick you up for school tomorrow."

"I thought you had practice."

"Nope. Coach just texted me. I don't. So I'll pick you up same time as before."

"Okay." She would be glad when this race was over and she could tell him her secret.

"Sweet dreams," he said. "See you tomorrow."

CHAPTER 26

SIMONE PUT ON her game face and smiled at everything Dalton said as he drove them to school. She'd done enough thinking about Mrs. Nagel. As she'd dressed that morning, she'd wondered what would happen once Anna called to say she was backing her daughter.

He pulled into the parking lot, all smiles, until he discovered that someone had parked in his usual spot. Everyone knew Dalton parked there and because he was well liked, no one stole it. This was the first time someone else had claimed it.

"Not a big deal," he said. But his smile was still gone.

"It's odd, though, isn't it? That it happened today," Simone said. "Maybe Browning had a buddy park there to mess with you."

"Browning can joke around with the best of them, but he wouldn't do this." He put his smile back on. "If it was to mess with me, it's not going to work. It's just a parking space." He pulled into a nearby spot.

Simone sighed. It *was* just a parking space. But when you needed all the concentration you could get, small things mattered. She half-smiled, glad to see that it truly didn't seem to throw him off his game. He put his arm around her and they started toward their first period class. Everything felt normal.

Until they both saw the swim coach standing up ahead, hands on hips, his glare frosty as winter glass.

"You forget something this morning, Worthy?" Coach glanced at Simone but otherwise didn't acknowledge her.

"What do you mean?"

"I mean practice."

Simone saw fear cross Dalton's face. "You sent me a text. You said I didn't need to come."

Coach maintained his severe expression. "Let me see that text."

Dalton found it for him.

Coach read it quickly. "That's not my account." He handed back the phone.

Dalton studied the message. "But it says it's from . . . You have to know I would have been there—"

Coach threw up a hand. "Someone's screwing with you, Worthy." He shook his head once and raised his chin. "All I can say is I hope you've got what it takes."

He walked off.

"Coach believes you," Simone said.

"Yeah. But I wonder who did this. It could have been a disaster if Coach hadn't given me a chance to explain—"

"Don't think about it. Stay focused."

Dalton smiled at her. "Yeah. Stay focused. Focused— that's my middle name."

§ § §

During first period Mr. Erickson had a hard time even looking in Simone's direction. She didn't know if it was the lie Mrs. Nagel had cooked up about them or if he worried she might be reading his thoughts. She watched him talking in front of the students and for the first time realized how nerdy he was, in a Fred Astaire sort of way. He was nothing like Terry, but still. She wondered if Anna could ever like a guy like him.

Once, a couple of years ago, Simone had watched an old Fred Astaire-Ginger Rogers movie on TV with her mother and Anna had commented, "I love their old movies. They're so sweet and sassy together. Someone once said Astaire gives her class and she gives him sex appeal."

Maybe she could like someone like Mr. Erickson.

With that, Mr. Erickson tossed a look at Simone that said, "What are you talking about?"

Oops. She'd spaced out and forgotten that he might be able to hear her thoughts. She'd have to look into how to keep that from happening. There had to be techniques.

§ § §

Seated under a tree beside Dalton, eating lunch, Simone received a text from Anna: *Called Nagel. All's well.*

Somehow Simone doubted that. But at least Mrs. Nagel knew whose side Anna was on. And with Erickson aware that they should only talk to each other in class, that avenue of attack seemed closed to the dean.

She put her cell phone away.

"Who was that?" Dalton asked.

"Mom. Telling me she loves me."

Dalton smiled. He looked like he might say something, but then he didn't. He leaned in and gave her a small kiss on the lips instead.

They were staring at each other when a male voice drew their attention.

"Hey, Worthy, I just heard what happened." Browning had

walked up with a buddy by his side.

"What?" Dalton got to his feet.

"Someone's been messing with you and I don't want you thinking it was me."

"I don't."

"Good. Because when I beat your ass, I'm gonna do it fair and square."

They shook hands, although neither smiled. Simone could see that this race was serious business to the two of them.

Browning walked off with his friend.

Dalton sat down again. "Told you it wasn't him." He looked at Simone. "If I win, we'll go to the football game Friday night."

"And if you lose?"

"I'll stay in my room crying and we'll miss half the game."

Simone giggled. At least he was joking.

§ § §

You would think they were racing for Olympic gold, Simone thought, looking at the stands of the aquatics venue as she entered. They weren't packed full, but tons of people had turned out. She saw a camp for Browning and another for Dalton. People carried signs and horns and everything. If she were a proper girlfriend, she might have made a "Go Dalton" sign as well. But it had never crossed her mind. She had no idea so many people would be here.

She looked for Jenna. She didn't see her in the bleachers filled with Dalton supporters, but did find her seated beside Chris amid those rooting for Browning. The ever-present Shelly and Lynette sat directly behind them. Jenna held a sign in her lap—a small one, but a sign nonetheless.

Strange, Simone thought. The other day the Jeapests had been at the pool to cheer for Dalton at practice. Maybe, just maybe, Jenna wanted to prove to Chris she didn't care about her "ex."

This would be an excellent time to read minds, Simone decided as she concentrated on Jenna. *One more time. Just one more time let me see if I can hear what she's thinking.*

She opened herself up to Jenna's energy. But just as before, she only picked up Jenna's emotions, and they were no more pleasant now than the last time she'd experienced them. Simone immediately put a stop to the experiment. It was like getting a transfusion of nauseating poison.

Suddenly another thought came through—from Shelly: *I'm getting sick of this. I'll be glad when tomorrow night is over and we'll be done with all this crap.*

What happens tomorrow night? Simone wondered.

Suddenly the crowd came to life with clapping and shout-outs as Browning and Dalton walked toward the pool. They both wore latex caps and goggles. Browning looked a lot more relaxed than Dalton. He even waved at the crowd.

Browning has less to lose, Simone thought. She quickly nabbed the closest open space to sit. *If Dalton wins, Browning will still be on the relay team. If Dalton loses, Dalton remains off.*

Browning stepped on the racing block for lane four, and Dalton took lane three. Both of them swung their arms and shook their muscles to stay loose.

Ten seconds later a voice came over the speaker: "Take your marks."

Dalton and Browning bent over. Hands touched the blocks. Each of them pressed his right foot against a slanted component of the block that would help him spring forward into the water.

A horn beeped and they dove in, Browning's start quicker than Dalton's. They had to swim two lengths of the pool. Up and back. That was all. But it meant pacing yourself and knowing when to swim all out.

Simone felt nervous knots in her stomach. "Go Dalton, you can do it," she shouted as loud as she could because she wanted him to win, but also because she needed to expel some of that tense energy.

Other people shouted.

"Go Dalton!"

"Go Jay!"

"Go! Go! Go!"

They were halfway down the first length and Dalton lagged behind by a quarter body length.

"Go Dalton!" she screamed. She could hear whistles from the crowd.

Browning reached the wall first, but Dalton gained a little ground on the turn. They both dolphin-kicked under the water three times before rising to the surface to give it their all. Simone almost couldn't watch. No matter how much she screamed, the knots in her stomach made their presence known.

Dalton caught Browning three-quarters of the way to the wall, but didn't pass him. Both of them turned it on, their strokes fast, smooth, and strong. Their kicks left white churning trails behind them.

The screams of the crowd pierced louder. The race couldn't be any closer. Touch pads were in the water. The one to make contact first won. There would be no human error like in the old days when judges used stopwatches.

Both swimmers reached the wall amid deafening screams. With the human eye it looked like Browning might have come in first. But then the scoreboard flashed, reporting that Dalton had out-touched him by a fraction of a second. Dalton had done it. He'd pulled out the win!

Simone jumped up and down, cheering and yelling, her heart pounding.

She watched Browning and Dalton shake hands. Dalton looked for her in the crowd. Somehow he found her and waved. Simone waved back.

She sat and tried to relax. Some of the crowd stayed in the stands like she did, while others filtered out. As Chris passed with his arm around Jenna, he called to Simone. "He got lucky, Spooky."

Spoken like a true loser, Simone thought. It didn't deserve a response. Dalton had worked his butt off to win this race. But Chris wouldn't know about that. He was one of those people perpetually jealous because he didn't work for achievement. He'd rather complain.

True to form, Lynette and Shelly lagged just a few feet behind. Lynette smirked at Simone while Shelly didn't even look in her direction. Simone stared at Shelly, hoping for a thought to seep through. None did.

CHAPTER 27

SIMONE SWAYED WITH the movement of the rolling city bus, her eyes cast on the Friday morning commuters that crowded the street outside the window. Her mind chased back and forth between images of Dalton and his happiness at having won a place on the relay team and the ominous thought she'd heard from Shelly early on at the pool yesterday: *I'm getting sick of this. I'll be glad when tomorrow night is over and we'll be done with all this crap.*

Tomorrow night was now tonight. Simone had no clue what Shelly might have meant and, like an unsolved puzzle, it nagged her.

She tried to shake off Shelly's words and focus on Dalton's victory. She still hadn't told him about her dream or even that Mrs. Nagel had called Anna. The race might be over, but he was riding high and she'd decided to wait for the right moment.

As she stepped onto the school grounds, a chill iced her skin. The atmosphere struck Simone as unnervingly quiet. Although students crossed the campus every which way, she heard little noise to go with the activity. It just felt strange— muted somehow.

What's going on? she wondered. *Is this the calm before the storm?*

It's your imagination, she told herself. *Stop being weird.*

As the day wore on, her "imagination" subsided. Eating lunch with Dalton, holding his hand, and listening to him crow over his victory, made all the difference in her mood.

But then a strange thing happened. While walking toward fifth period, Simone bumped into Mrs. Nagel—literally. She hadn't been looking where she was going.

"Sorry," Simone immediately said, her voice cracking.

"No harm done," Mrs. Nagel responded with a smile.

If Simone didn't know better, she'd have believed the smile was genuine. She stared after the dean as she walked away, thinking, *Yeah. Friendly like Leslie had been.*

§ § §

"I never asked. Do you even like football?" Dalton said after they were both buckled up in the Camaro in front of her apartment.

"Yeah, sure. I used to watch it with my stepdad."

Dalton started the car and the engine roared to life. He drove faster than usual, and Simone decided his adrenaline hadn't one hundred percent subsided. He was still on cloud nine.

Dalton's usual spot in the corner of the lot, where the Camaro could park in full view of a security camera, remained open for him and he took it. He stepped out of the car and Simone let him open the door for her. They headed for the football stadium, which wasn't far from the lot, just past the basketball and tennis courts. The sound of the high school band—cymbals, drums, tubas and horns—reverberated in the parking lot and grew louder the nearer they came. The rousing song ended, drawing a roar of cheers before a new song began:

The Hey Song.

Simone hadn't been to a football game in a very long time and she'd forgotten how exciting it could be. Inwardly she smiled, her arm around Dalton's waist. She wore his black jacket—the one she'd never returned—and he held her close just as he had that first night on the beach. The days of September might be hot, but after sunset they quickly cooled.

With the bleachers mostly full and all the best seats taken, Dalton and Simone climbed the benches near the far end and found places to sit. They'd arrived late, only ten minutes to kickoff, which occurred at exactly seven-fifteen.

The first half of the game couldn't have been more thrilling. With the teams evenly matched, the score at halftime was fourteen to fourteen. To the music of the band, the drill team began to perform, its members' bright orange costumes sharp and sexy with sparkly silver fringe and white boots. White pompoms shook as the members of the team performed an intricate routine filled with marches, turns, bounce steps and high kicks.

"You hungry?" Dalton asked.

"A hot dog sounds good. Ketchup only, please."

Simone watched Dalton weave through the seated spectators as he made his way down the bleachers. She sat alone for a few seconds before she decided she needed to visit the restroom. She wished now that she hadn't drunk that Coke earlier. Going to the restroom at a high school football game was not fun.

From the bottom row, she hopped to the ground and walked only a few yards before she saw a line over twenty people deep at the girls' restroom. She'd never make it in time. Nearby were the trusted Porta Pottys, ten of them, each with anywhere from five to seven people in line. She'd have to brave the temporary toilets. Thank goodness she carried hand sanitizer in her purse.

Simone tried to be patient as the line she'd chosen inched forward. The school needed more toilets near the stadium, there was no doubt about that. She checked out the other lines to see if she'd picked the best one and saw that they were all bad. Her eyes strayed to the right and she caught sight of Lynette and Shelly standing with Andy about ten yards away. Lynette's gaze was full on Simone and she had a smirk on her face, which only grew wider once Simone stared back. Jenna, Simone assumed, was off somewhere with Chris.

Simone had no doubt Shelly had a crush on Andy. She smiled shyly as Andy did the talking. Occasionally she'd reach out and touch him or she would adjust a lock of her hair. One of her thoughts jumped into Simone's head: *You're so cute. Jenna's crazy.*

Lynette tapped Shelly on the arm and said something that made Shelly look annoyed and say something back. Another thought came through from Shelly: *Why should I? I think it's stupid.*

Lynette tried to pull Shelly away from Andy, but Shelly had a mind of her own. Her voice rose and Simone could hear her. "You do it. I don't want to."

Trouble in Jeapest land, Simone thought.

Lynette stormed off and Shelly continued to smile at Andy.

It took fifteen more minutes for Simone to get back to her seat, and when she reached it she found Dalton waiting for her. He handed her the hotdog, still warm because of the foil wrapped around it. "Bet I know where you went."

"I won't take that bet." She raised the hotdog. "Thank you."

"I ate mine already. Sorry, I didn't wait."

She smiled at him, pulling the foil away.

"I ran into Chris," Dalton added.

Simone's smile faded. "That must have been fun."

"It was bizarre. He was like congratulating me for winning the race and saying how he and Jenna rooted for me."

"They didn't. Jenna even had a Jay Browning sign. I saw it."

"That's what I mean. It was strange. I don't even know the guy but he was saying he had no hard feelings. He knows now that Jenna doesn't have a thing for me and that she never really did."

Simone swallowed the bite in her mouth and stayed quiet. Jenna and Chris were up to something. She wished she knew what it was. She almost told Dalton she wanted to leave right then, but he seemed to be into the game and she didn't want to spoil anything.

The Woodruff Warriors won twenty to seventeen. Most of the game the two teams were tied, but the Warriors pulled it out with a field goal just as the clock ran down.

Amid a sea of others, Dalton and Simone walked toward the parking lot. She felt good inside Dalton's jacket, snuggled against him. Even with the odd conversation he'd had with Chris, nothing bad had happened. Their school even won the game. She turned her head to look up at him and smiled. He was looking down at her.

"The way I see it," Dalton informed her, "we can go to Wendy's and pig out on chicken nuggets or we can go to your place, eat bad cheese pizza and watch a movie."

"Is that all?" she bravely asked, giggling when his jaw dropped in mock shock. They'd kissed, but never again like that first time because they hadn't really been alone. Simone wanted to go with Dalton to her apartment. She felt Dalton tighten his arm around her.

They neared the parking lot and heard a roar of chatter amid the revving of engines. Through a plethora of curses and bad words, Simone heard:

"Look at my car, man!"

"Dude. This is bad."

"Call the cops."

"Already done."

"Hey, Dalton! Check your Camaro."

Still holding on to Simone, he hurried over to his car. Someone had keyed it even under the scrutiny of the security cameras. A long, white, irregular slash was clearly visible from the front driver's panel, across the door, through the rear panel. Childlike scribble etched the hood as well.

Dalton said nothing. He stood in shock—staring—his arm fixed around Simone. She felt his fingers squeeze her waist as if holding on for dear life.

"Looks like yours got the worst of it," a guy said. "I've counted eighteen cars so far. The cops are on the way."

It didn't take long for a black-and-white with flashing blue and red lights to pull into the lot. Two officers stepped out of the car and were quickly met by a mass of students eager to report what they'd found.

"Is this your vehicle?" a young officer asked Dalton. He had a pen and a pad of paper.

"Yes," Dalton answered.

"Nice car." He took Dalton's name and checked his driver's license. "You got insurance?"

Dalton gave him proof of that. "I have comprehensive. The deductible won't be any fun."

"You have any idea who might have done this?"

Dalton and Simone looked at each other. Jenna? Chris? There was no proof, only the fact that they didn't like her or Dalton.

"You got it the worst," the officer added.

Dalton shrugged. "There're people who don't like us being together, but that's the only thing."

The cop nodded as if he understood completely. He glanced up at a security camera. "This will help. We might get lucky." He looked at Simone, studied her a little longer than she might have liked. "I suppose the two of you were together all evening."

Simone didn't answer, but Dalton did. "Why?"

"We received a nine one one earlier. The caller claimed to have witnessed a girl dressed in black, with a purple streak in her long dark hair, keying cars. She said the girl wore heavy makeup with black around the eyes. She was very specific and everything she said, pretty much describes you."

So that was it, Simone thought. A setup. "I didn't do this," she told the officer.

"May I see your ID, please?"

She took it from her purse and handed it to him.

"Simone, I think you should come to the station and answer some questions. Call your parents and have them be present." He motioned toward the police car.

"I'll take her," Dalton said quickly.

"Am I under arrest?" Simone asked.

"No. There's just more questions we'll need answered. Hopefully we can clear everything up." The cop eyed Dalton. "He can take you. Ask for Detective Cruz when you get there. I'll call him and tell him you're coming."

The officer walked away.

"Call your mom," Dalton said.

"She's at work. I'd rather go without her."

"Then I'll call my dad." He took out his phone.

§   §   §

Simone, Dalton, and Dalton's father—dressed, thought Simone, in an expensive-looking suit, exactly as a successful lawyer would dress—sat at a table in a small room across from Detective Cruz. They'd had to wait twenty minutes before Cruz would see them.

"You're sure your mom can't be here?" Cruz asked Simone.

She nodded her head. Simone either fell silent or became too mouthy in threatening situations, and facing a detective in an interrogation room, being suspected of a crime, certainly felt threatening to her.

Cruz slid a pad of paper and a pen toward Simone. "Just in case. Why don't you write down her number?"

Simone picked up the pen and did as she was asked. When she looked up she thought she saw a bit of smugness on the detective's face.

"Thank you," Cruz said.

"Why don't you tell us what you have?" Mr. Worthy urged.

"Sure. Why not?" Cruz pressed a button on a laptop.

"Nine one one. What's your emergency?"

A young female voice responded. "There's a girl going nuts keying cars in the parking lot. I've seen her around school. I think her name's Simone. She has dark hair with a purple streak. She wears black and too much makeup. Lots of dark liner around the eyes. Nobody likes her. That must be why she's doing it."

"Where's the parking lot?"

"Woodruff High. The lot by the football stadium."

"What's your name?"

The caller hung up.

"You recognize that voice?" asked Cruz.

"It was disguised," Simone said. She glanced at Dalton. "It sounded like Lynette."

"Lynette have a last name?"

"Cryer."

Cruz wrote down the name. "Does she have a reason to make this up?"

"We've had run-ins at school."

"So she wouldn't just *think* your name was Simone. She'd know it."

Simone saw Mr. Worthy sit back in his chair and relax. "Anything else?" Mr. Worthy asked. Dalton was easygoing, while his father seemed the opposite. Simone wondered if he'd hold it against her, having to come down here to help out his son's girlfriend at eleven-thirty at night.

"Yes. We have the security footage of the incident." Cruz picked up a remote control device and hit play. A screen in a corner near the ceiling came to life with a black-and-white recording of the parking lot filled with shimmering cars. After a couple of guys walked out of the shot, in walked a person in black jeans and a black sweatshirt with the hood pulled up far enough to hide the face. Just from the way the person walked and moved, Simone could tell it was Jenna.

The vandal held the hood tightly under her chin with her left hand, keeping it in place, as she quickly scratched the first car with her right. Staying low, and weaving between cars, defacing some and not others, she made her way to the Camaro. After checking to see that no one else was in the lot, she went to work on Dalton's purple muscle car. It took only a few seconds before she finished and ran for the gate.

Cruz pressed pause and the image froze. "Do you know who that is?"

"She moves like Jenna," Simone said.

"Jenna?"

"Martin."

"When was the nine-one-one call made?" Mr. Worthy asked.

Cruz smiled. "Eight forty-two."

"That video's time stamped—"

Cruz interrupted Dalton's father. "Eight forty-eight."

"So the caller wasn't calling as the deed was happening, like she said," the lawyer pointed out.

"Nope." Cruz looked at Simone and Dalton. "I have to ask. Were you two together at the time?"

"I went to get hot dogs," Dalton explained.

"I was in line for the bathroom."

"Yeah. Well." The detective reached for the pad of paper with Anna's phone number. "Here's the other thing. The hooligan is right-handed. You're a lefty."

CHAPTER 28

MONDAY MORNING, SIMONE stepped off the bus and made her way to the school grounds, eager to see Dalton. He'd been busy all weekend and they'd only been able to call and text.

"Hey, gorgeous."

Simone slowed her step. She hadn't seen Jimmy all weekend either. He sounded down-and-out, not his normal glib self. "Where you been?"

"Looking for Kim. I can't find her and I'm worried. She's never been missing this long."

"No?"

"Maybe you found Kim's grave too late." He faded from sight in that moment.

Too late? Simone hoped not.

She passed through the gate, onto campus, and as she was about to leave the administration building behind her she heard her name called. "Simone!"

She turned around. Mrs. Nagel stood a mere ten feet away. Simone's heart dropped.

"I need to see you. Now!"

The dean walked into the building. Simone followed her inside, down a short hallway to that bleak office of hers.

"Have a seat." Mrs. Nagel motioned as she stepped around

the big desk and sat in her chair. "It seems I always have a reason to find you in my office."

"I don't understand. What reason is there now?" Simone had lost all respect for Mrs. Nagel, and while she was a little nervous sitting before her, it wasn't like before.

"You know very well. The vandalism during Friday night's game. You were caught on tape."

Stunned, Simone lost her voice until the nervousness she'd felt at first turned to anger. Mrs. Nagel had to know the police had cleared her.

"That wasn't me."

"Of course you'd say that."

"The police know it wasn't me."

"I didn't ask you here for debate."

Simone's stomach burned. Mrs. Nagel didn't care about the truth. She wanted to use this to finally get rid of her.

"I'm very sorry, Simone. But with your history and this latest event, I'm suspending you. I also intend to have you expelled. If your mother wants to find you a school in another district before that happens, then perhaps we won't need to go through the motions of a hearing and all that. We can—"

The rage inside Simone pushed her to speak through gritted teeth. "No. I want a hearing."

"Do you really think that's a good idea? Everyone—"

"Everyone will find out I didn't do this. You know I didn't do this. I'm not going to another school." Simone shook. Her skin was as hot as the desert in August. She needed to get out of there before something happened she couldn't control.

"Young lady—"

Simone rose to her feet and moved as calmly as she could to the door.

"I'm not finished." Mrs. Nagel came toward her.

Simone's anger rose another notch and she looked for somewhere to release it. Just in time, she noticed the vase of pencils on the desk and made it fly through the air so close to the dean the woman had to jump back. It shattered against the wall and the pencils tumbled to the floor like pick-up sticks.

Mrs. Nagel froze. "How did that happen?"

Simone didn't answer. Her heart was beating so hard and fast, she knew had to leave before she broke something else. She stormed out.

"Simone, do not go back to class! You *are* suspended."

Simone's eyes stung. Suspended? She hadn't done anything to deserve the way she was being treated. She turned and glared at Mrs. Nagel. "I know what happened to Kim."

The dean looked shocked at first and then her cheeks flared red. "You couldn't—"

"I know you didn't kill her. But you covered it up."

They stared at each other and Simone saw terror emerge in Mrs. Nagel's eyes.

"I know where she's buried, too."

Simone practically ran, but when she heard Mrs. Nagel coming after her, she spun around and paused to make the door slam in the dean's face. Then Simone sprinted as fast as she could to the bus stop.

It was now or never, she decided. She shouldn't have told Mrs. Nagel she knew where Kim was buried. Knowledge was power, her stepfather used to say. Who knew what Mrs. Nagel would do now?

Simone couldn't wait any longer. How would people find out what happened to Kim if she didn't show them? She needed to get to Mrs. Nagel's house. But how? The house was two cities away and Simone didn't know which buses to take. Besides, riding buses, waiting for buses, changing buses would take time. She could go home and get some money to pay for Uber, but she'd lose time that way, too.

She needed Dalton. She needed him to help her. He'd be in Erickson's class right now, wondering where she was. He wouldn't have his phone though. It would be turned off and safely tucked away in his backpack.

But Mr. Erickson could get a message to him if she could reach him with her mind.

Sitting on the back of the bus stop bench, she closed her eyes and focused on her English Lit teacher.

Mr. Erickson. Mrs. Nagel kicked me out of school. I need Dalton's help. Please tell him to meet me at the bus stop with his car. Mr. Erickson, can you hear me?

She started to repeat her message when she heard Mr. Erickson think: *I'll tell him.*

Amazing, thought Simone. He didn't even ask questions.

Dalton arrived in less than five minutes. He must not have asked questions either. Although he was now.

"What happened?"

Simone jumped into the running car. "I'll tell you on the way."

"Where are we going?"

"To Mrs. Nagel's house. I put her address in the GPS." Simone's phone began to spew directions and Dalton pulled into traffic.

She told him everything. She told him about Kim and Jimmy and her dream. She told him Mrs. Nagel was using the vandalism Friday night to kick her out of school. She told it all and didn't hold back. He could believe her or not. She wanted him to believe, but life would go on if he didn't.

"But if you learned this through a dream, how do you know it's true?"

"Part of it through a dream. Part of it from ghosts. Real live ghosts."

She saw him shake his head. "Dead ghosts."

"Just drive. We'll find out how crazy I am, won't we? I didn't look up Mrs. Nagel's address. We're going to the address I saw in the dream."

"And do what?"

"We're going to dig up Kim's grave."

CHAPTER 29

DALTON PARKED ACROSS the street from the address Simone had provided, and she stepped out of the car. The house looked different from the way it had appeared in 1968. It had a new roof and new windows and was a pastel peach color now, with white trim and olive-green shutters.

"It's the house in my dream." Simone darted toward the driveway that led to the backyard with an unattached garage. Dalton dashed to stay up with her.

A gate barred the way, secured with a slider bolt and a regular lock that needed a key.

"I'll give you a boost to help you over. I can scale it without help, I'm pretty sure," Dalton said.

Simone shook her head. "The lock isn't anything complicated. I'll just use my mind to turn the tumblers . . ." She glanced at Dalton to see if she was making him uncomfortable.

His face gave no hint that she was. In fact, he looked determined and supportive even though they were about to break and enter.

"You don't have to stay with me," she told Dalton. "You could get in a lot of trouble."

"I don't care," he said.

The lock fell away and Simone opened the gate.

Well, maybe they hadn't broken anything so far. She'd merely opened the lock.

Dalton closed the gate behind them so no one would be able to see. "What now?"

"Find a shovel. In nineteen sixty-eight it was behind the garage."

Dalton left to retrieve it and Simone walked over to the flower bed. The yard had been fancied up with brickwork and a nice patio. But the flowerbed still held flowers. Thankfully Mrs. Nagel hadn't poured concrete there. In fact, Simone spotted an angel statue in the dirt. *Sort of a headstone for Kim*, Simone decided.

Dalton returned with a shovel and a spade. He handed Simone the spade. It had a point and was designed for digging. "Two is faster than one," he said.

Simone moved the angel aside and plunged the spade into the dirt.

"What happens if she isn't here?" Dalton asked.

Simone frowned. "We'll find her."

"It was a dream, Simone."

"I know."

"Even if everything you saw was true, Nagel could have moved her."

"It doesn't matter. We still have to dig to find out."

She tossed a scoop of dirt aside.

Dalton stabbed the flowerbed and stepped on the edge of the shovel so it would penetrate deeper. He pulled the handle back toward him and removed a large chunk of soil.

The earth was soft on top, but dense and dry farther down. "Maybe we need to use the hose," Simone said.

"Here. Give me the spade. I can do it."

As he reached for it, the gate opened and in walked two

policemen. The older one looked to be in his forties, while the younger one looked like he'd just graduated from the academy. "You need to stop what you're doing—"

Mrs. Nagel rushed into the yard and went straight to the officers. "Thank God, you're here. I told the operator she threatened me and I knew she'd come here." She pointed at Simone. "Arrest her. She's trespassing. Arrest him, too. But she's the one . . . she's the one. She put him up to this. She's dangerous."

The shrill agitation in Mrs. Nagel's voice made it apparent she was on the verge of hysteria. The stare she gave Simone was menacing. The police turned their attention to her.

"Ma'am. Please quiet down," the older officer said, clearly in charge. He stepped in front of Mrs. Nagel, effectively blocking her view of Simone and Dalton.

"Can't you see what she's doing?" Mrs. Nagel complained.

"It's just a yard. We'll handle it. Calm down."

Simone's adrenaline surged. She quickly dug in and tossed aside two more scoops of dirt.

"Stop her!" Mrs. Nagel screamed, going for an end run around the cop. "She's destroying my property!"

The older officer reacted swiftly, staying in front of her. "Ma'am. Ma'am! Let us handle this. Go stand with Officer Sutton."

Flustered, Mrs. Nagel did not immediately comply. "She threatened me. She's been in trouble before."

"Please, ma'am. Over there with Officer Sutton. Give him your statement."

Mrs. Nagel backed up, eyes on Simone.

The seasoned officer turned around. "Put the equipment down," he said. Dalton dropped the shovel and moved aside.

Simone did not comply. This was her chance. Maybe her only chance to expose Mrs. Nagel and free Kim. How deep had they buried her?

She felt the cop grab her. She didn't kick or fight as he pulled her away. She dropped the spade and kept her eyes on it.

Dig . . . Dig . . . Dig . . .

The officer spoke, but none of his words reached her. All she had to do now was concentrate on the spade.

Dig . . . Dig . . . Dig . . .

The spade rose in the air and slammed into the dirt. A blast of earth was tossed aside.

Dig . . . Dig . . . Dig . . .

The spade rose and plunged again. Then again. And again.

The cop let go of her but continued to talk. He didn't notice what was happening; the other officer did. "Hey, Pete. Do you see that?" He pointed.

"See what?" Pete looked. "What the . . . ?"

The spade continued to dig up the flowerbed with no visible help from a human. The two cops backed away, but Simone moved forward. She allowed the spade to drop to the ground and looked into the wide hole it had dug. There lay a perfect skeleton, much of it covered by the striped dress Kim had been wearing when she died. Next to her lay her purse. Simone knew her license would be inside.

Dalton came forward and looked, too. "You were right," he murmured.

Simone's breathing returned to near-normal as she stared.

"Thank you," came a soft voice. Simone looked up. Kim knelt beside her grave. "You found me. I'm so grateful."

Simone's eyes stung with tears. "You're welcome," she whispered.

With the spade silenced, the older officer came forward and saw the bones, too. He frowned at Simone. "Is this what you were after?"

Simone nodded.

"What is it?" Officer Sutton asked.

"Take a look," Pete said. He pulled out his radio. "This is Officer Rainey. We have a possible one-eight-seven non-emergency. Dispatch ten thirty-one." He gave the address.

Officer Sutton stared at the bones. "They look old."

Dalton put his arm around Simone's waist and held her against him. She didn't need his support physically. She was fine. And she was happy that he'd helped her without ever once trying to stand in her way.

Officer Rainey walked over to Mrs. Nagel, who stared at the grave in silence. "What do you know about this?" he asked.

She shook her head and closed her eyes. "I think I need a lawyer."

CHAPTER 30

SIMONE DRESSED AS Dalton's father had told her to dress: neat, clean, responsible and innocent. Her dark hair was tied back in a ponytail. That morning she'd applied mascara, blush and lip gloss only—no eyeliner, no purple lipstick. Anna had helped her choose her clothes: a knee-length blue dress, a simple lightweight sweater and plain black flats. She wore no jewelry.

Even with Anna sitting on one side of her and her lawyer—the imposing Mr. Worthy—sitting on the other, and even though Mr. Worthy had told her not to worry, Simone couldn't help herself. She nervously rubbed her palms together in her lap and sometimes could scarcely breathe. It seemed that things went wrong through no fault of her own. Otherwise, she wouldn't be at this school-board hearing to determine if disciplinary action should be taken against her. And Mrs. Nagel would have admitted what she'd done back in 1968.

Mrs. Nagel had hired a lawyer who was using every legal maneuver he could to save his client and was claiming, *She didn't know the body was there. She believed Kim Blue had run away.*

The dean still had her job and she still maintained Simone should be kicked out of school. She insisted the delinquent in the security video was Simone despite the fact the local D.A.

refused to press charges.

The only happy thing in the whole mess? Kim had crossed over. Mr. Erickson's fifth period had not been disturbed by her since her grave was found. Simone had no idea how that worked and didn't care. As long as Kim was at peace, that's all that mattered.

The hearing was open to anyone who wanted to attend. Mr. Worthy had thought that best. The small boardroom had filled to capacity. Simone refused to look behind her. She didn't like being the center of attention. To see the faces of curious lookie-loos, some on her side, but most against her, took her breath away. She'd heard their whispers in the hallways at school, a few outright threatening her. Those with cars that had been defaced were eager for justice and wanted her to be guilty.

Dalton sat directly behind her. He occasionally reached out and put his hand on her shoulder. "Don't worry," he whispered. "You're innocent and my dad's the best."

"Yeah, don't worry," Jimmy said, pacing in front of the five school-board members who sat at a long, glossy table facing those in attendance. "This is nuts. I'd like to . . . " He began to act like a boxer, prancing back and forth while striking out at each member one at a time, to no effect.

Simone suppressed a smile. *I don't think I need Rocky right now.*

The fact was she could send a hurricane through the room if she chose to, her powers had strengthened that much since digging up Kim's grave. But that wouldn't solve her problem. And it wouldn't land Mrs. Nagel in prison where she belonged.

The board president, a woman in her forties, sat at the middle of the glossy table rifling through papers.

"This is going to be like shooting fish in a barrel," Mr.

Worthy told Simone.

"What does that mean? Fish can be fast," she answered back.

Mr. Worthy chuckled. "I'm a crack shot. And . . . well, you'll see."

He knew everything about her sixth-sense abilities. Like his son, he refused to believe she saw ghosts, and didn't believe she'd actually gone back in time to witness what had happened to Kim. But, like Dalton, he did accept that people sometimes knew things psychically, and he did accept her kinetic gift. After all, she could prove that at will. She'd done so for him by making one of his big heavy law books float from a bookshelf to his desk and plop open.

"Make the pages move," he'd commanded.

She made it happen.

"Put it back on the shelf."

She did that, too.

"Well, I'll be a monkey's uncle," he'd said. Then he stared at her. "Look. My son likes you and he loves his car. If he says you didn't scratch it up, then you didn't. And I don't like these hoity-toity hearings anyway. It's not like a court where you have to stick to facts. There's always a lot of baloney hearsay."

The board president called the meeting to order at exactly seven p.m. She took roll call, and after business formalities got out of the way, she asked Mrs. Nagel to present the district's case. The dean listed the official rules that Simone had supposedly broken, and for the most part didn't say anything Simone hadn't heard before. Except, she explained, she'd interviewed many witnesses who saw Simone break the girl's nose on purpose at her last school and witnesses who saw Simone vandalize those cars. There was even one student from Simone's first period who apparently did not like Mr. Erickson and claimed Mr. Erickson hadn't excused Simone when she'd run out of the classroom. Of course, Simone had seen this guy from time to time hanging out with Chris.

"This child is trouble. While in detention she was disrespectful to me and confrontational. We have determined that she would be better off at another school. In fact, we would recommend continuation school in another district," the dean concluded.

Board members asked Mrs. Nagel for clarification on several points, including the names of the witnesses who saw Simone vandalize cars. Mrs. Nagel said that for the time being she would not be able to reveal their names.

"Were the names given to the police?"

"They are worried about retaliation on Miss Jennings' part. And until such time as they feel safe, no, their names will not be provided."

Mr. Worthy wasn't allowed to ask questions. That would happen later, if he had any. At this time, he was to give Simone's position in the matter while remaining in his chair.

"Simply put, this is a frame-up on the part of Mrs. Nagel, who has convinced gullible members of the district of her sincerity."

"Excuse me," Mrs. Nagel tried to interject.

"No. Excuse me," he countered. "This is a hearing, not a court. I was quiet during your parade of fact-finding. Now, please extend me the same courtesy."

"Yes, Mrs. Nagel," the board president said. "We need to hear his position. You'll be allowed to speak again."

"Thank you," Mr. Worthy said.

"Those are serious allegations, Mr. Worthy, and must be provable for you to make them."

"I can prove them. We will not present witnesses because

according to your rules, we are not allowed to do that. But please know they are in the boardroom and can back up everything I'm about to say.

"First, we have witnesses that will state for the record, and in fact already have, that the girl whose nose was broken started the fight and did, indeed, throw the first punch. Simone was, in fact, defending herself. This was deemed mutual combat by the administration, and because of a no-tolerance-for-violence policy, *both* students were disciplined.

"We acknowledge that Simone was late for class and deserved detention. That is hardly a reason for her to be expelled.

"Next. Mr. Erickson is in the room and will confirm that Simone had his permission to leave his classroom. If she . . . "

A voice began to play in Simone's head: *I'll be glad when this is over. I'm sick of Jenna. Sick of her. She doesn't own me.*

Simone turned and glanced behind her. In the last row of spectators, she spotted Shelly seated next to Andy. She didn't see Jenna or Lynette. At least not with Shelly. Jenna and Lynette sat with Chris four rows away, not far behind Mrs. Nagel. The three of them looked happy and full of themselves. Jenna threw an amused smirk Simone's way.

It appeared Shelly had broken ranks. Once again, Simone looked at the ex-Jeapest who gazed back at Simone with the tiniest of smiles before turning away.

Simone was beginning to believe Mr. Worthy; she might not have anything to worry about.

"As for the keyed cars—which I'd like to go on record to say, my son's car was keyed and even he doesn't believe Simone did it—we have a witness in the room who has first-hand knowledge of who keyed those cars and, as of this morning, has given that name to the police."

Simone heard someone audibly draw a breath and glanced at Jenna. She didn't look so smug now. Her face had visibly paled. Chris whispered something to her and she shoved him away.

"And finally, as to our assertion that Mrs. Nagel targeted Simone, this witness can also testify, if given the chance, that she told Mrs. Nagel who that person was, why she did it, and that this person had disguised herself so Simone would get the blame."

Jenna, Chris, and Lynette immediately left the hearing. Simone looked from them to Mrs. Nagel. Her expression was blank, but Simone saw her chest rise and fall with anxiety.

Mr. Worthy continued. "In addition to that, we found the people responsible for Kim Blue's death."

Mrs. Nagel's eyes widened at that news. She had to be scared now. She'd been desperate to get rid of Simone. Desperate to ruin her so no one would believe anything she said. And all the time the people who'd conspired with Mrs. Nagel were still out there. The dean should have been worried about them.

Mrs. Nagel suddenly stood. "This hearing is *not* about me and I would appreciate it if the board would keep Mr. Worthy on track."

"On the contrary, I am on track. The girl whose grave was found in Mrs. Nagel's backyard was Kim Blue. And although they aren't here today, testimony is forthcoming as to Mrs. Nagel's part in the cover-up of Kim's unfortunate death. Simone knew that grave was there. And, in fact, led the police to find it. That is the reason for Mrs. Nagel's vendetta against Simone."

"I do not have a vendetta."

"Everything I've said can be backed up with eyewitnesses,

an assertion Mrs. Nagel cannot make herself. If this board sides with the administration and Mrs. Nagel's hearsay remarks, and does not see fit to listen to the witnesses I have with me so that this matter can be cleared up tonight and resolved in Simone's favor, this matter will end up in a courtroom with the board among those being sued. Thank you. That's all."

It was as if he'd dropped a bomb in the room. No one spoke, although the look on several faces spoke volumes.

"Well, I might ask one thing," the board president finally said. "Will Mr. Worthy's witnesses who are in the room please stand?"

Simone turned to look. The first on her feet was Shelly, clinging to Andy's hand. She was followed by Mr. Erickson and three students from Simone's old high school.

"Thank you. Mrs. Nagel, do you have any questions at this time?"

"Not now," she said with a quiet, shaky voice.

"Well, this *is* the time if you have anything to add," one board member said.

Mrs. Nagel merely repeated herself.

"Mr. Worthy. Any questions for Mrs. Nagel or the board."

"No," he said.

It was an open meeting, so the members of the board did not retire to another room to deliberate. The board president looked to each of the other four one at a time and each said they had no questions and were ready to vote.

"This case is dismissed," the board president ultimately announced.

"Fish in a barrel," Mr. Worthy repeated, picking up his papers.

Mrs. Nagel hurried from the room, neither speaking nor

looking at anyone. Simone hugged her mother, who had tears in her eyes. Then Simone hugged Dalton before shaking the hand of Mr. Erickson, who had approached the group.

"Thank you for backing me up," Simone said quietly.

Never shy, Anna stuck out her hand. "Yes, thank you, Mr. Erickson." Anna paused as she took in his appearance. Her expression said she approved. "Do you mind if I ask you, has anyone ever told you how much you look like a young Fred Astaire?"

Simone chuckled and turned to Mr. Worthy. "You found Leslie and Vance?"

"I did. Or rather an investigator I use quite often did. Since you knew their names and they really had no reason to go into hiding, it was a piece of cake. Leslie is dead, as you might expect of someone who was into drugs. However, Lance is very much alive. And, it's interesting to note, he is still in possession of Kim Blue's car, although it's stored away and never driven. If there is anything that ties him to Kim's death, that car does. So it didn't take much to get him to talk. He didn't actually give anyone drugs, according to him, and, I might add, according to your dream—which still amazes me. Since the charge wouldn't be murder in his case, the statute of limitations would keep him from being tried as a conspirator or of obstructing justice. And the whole episode has been an albatross around his neck anyway. He's ready to give it up."

"What's going to happen to Mrs. Nagel?" Simone asked.

"That's up to the authorities. But make no mistake about it, Lance is going to talk. She's in trouble."

"Thank you," Simone said.

"You're quite welcome." Mr. Worthy looked at Dalton. "I will see you at home, son." He took his briefcase and strode out the door.

Dalton hugged Simone. She closed her eyes and relief washed through her. Mrs. Nagel had to leave her alone now. And maybe Jenna would be forced to go to another school. Shelly had turned against her leader. All it took was a boy.

Simone heard her mother laugh and opened her eyes. She was chatting with Mr. Erickson. They had walked a few feet away, maybe subconsciously seeking some privacy. He was smiling and doing all the talking. Simone saw Anna place a hand on his arm.

This will be interesting, Simone thought. *Very interesting.*

CHAPTER 31

SIMONE TOSSED A chicken nugget at Dalton and he caught it in his mouth. She watched him chew with a big grin on his face. He swallowed and then motioned for Simone to lean across the small table where they sat in Wendy's.

"This is the proper way to feed someone a chicken nugget," Dalton said, and he carefully placed one in her mouth. "With decorum."

"Oh, decorum," she said as best she could before she chewed.

"You know what this reminds me of," Jimmy said, having just appeared beside Simone.

Not now, Simone told him, maintaining eye contact with Dalton.

"Oh, what does it remind you of, Jimmy?" Jimmy said in a higher-pitched voice than his own before continuing as himself. "It reminds me of two people at a wedding reception feeding each other cake. I have to hand it to Dalton. He did it with much more class."

Wedding reception? Really Jimmy? Don't go there.

"Hey, I'm just calling it like I see it."

Okay. Simone saw Dalton watching her.

"You know," Dalton began. "When you talk to ghosts, I wish you'd do it out loud so I could hear at least one half of the conversation."

"Uh, oh. You're in trouble now." Jimmy laughed as he vanished.

"What are you talking about?" Simone put her mouth over the straw in her chocolate Frosty.

"What's this ghost's name, anyway?"

Simone took the lid off the Frosty and plunged her plastic spoon into the ice cream treat several times. "You don't believe in ghosts."

"But you do. What's his name? Or her name?" he corrected.

Simone put her hands in her lap and looked him in the eye. "Jimmy. His name is Jimmy. He went to Woodruff. He died in nineteen eighty-eight. He drowned in the school pool. His best friend killed him by accident."

Okay, she'd told him. Now what? Everything between them had been going so well. Her heart beat rapidly waiting for what he might say next.

"Jimmy." Dalton nodded. "Hi, Jimmy."

"He left."

"Oh." Dalton was quiet for a minute. Then he took out a nine-by-eleven-sized envelope and unclasped the clasp.

"What's that?" Simone's eyes narrowed.

"Something your mother gave me a couple of days ago."

"What is it?"

"Well, evidently she's concerned that I don't believe in ghosts."

"Really? Because I'm not sure she believes me. I think she just goes along with it to support me."

"Oh, she believes you. And she wants me to believe it, too. In fact, she says it's important that I do or we might break up."

Simone rolled her eyes. "I'm sorry about that. She means

well."

"I know. She says you've seen ghosts since you were a baby and she gave me some pictures to prove it."

"What pictures? I don't know about any pictures."

He took the first one out. "Here is one of you as a baby in your crib." He handed it to her.

Simone stared. Beside her sleeping figure was a foggy light anomaly, along with what people called orbs. To Simone, it just looked like something went wrong with the camera when it took the photo. "She thought this would convince you?"

He handed her another picture, this one of Simone in a baby carrier. Again there appeared an anomaly, only this time tiny Simone seemed to see something and be reaching for it.

Dalton handed Simone another and then another. Simone as a toddler. Simone as a preschooler. Simone at the ages of five, six, seven and so on. Each picture included strange lights, and some clearly looked like a person was with her. "She says there are plenty more at home, but she didn't think I needed to see them all."

"None of these look familiar." Simone stared at the shots.

"I have one more, but it comes with a story and an apology from your mother."

Simone looked up. "For what?"

Dalton handed her a photo of Simone standing in the living room of their house. She looked to be eleven. Behind her and a little to her right stood her stepfather, Terry. "I've never seen this." She smiled at the picture then looked at Dalton. "That's my stepdad. I guess I told you he died when I was eleven. Probably not long after this picture was taken."

"Before this picture was taken."

"Huh?"

"Your mom says she took this picture after he died. Don't you see the sadness in your eyes?"

Simone looked more closely. She was smiling, but she did look sad. "You'd just come back from Knott's Berry Farm. She'd taken you there to help cheer you up."

"But . . . " She stared at the picture. Terry had never come to her, and yet here he was.

"Your mother says this picture freaked her out and she never showed it to you. And then one night when she was in bed sleeping, he woke her up. She couldn't see him. She doesn't have that ability. But she smelled his aftershave, and she could feel him sit on the bed. When he touched her face it scared her to death, and she asked him not to come back."

Simone felt a surge of sadness, and her eyes immediately grew hot and wet. "That's why I've never seen him? She told him not to come?"

"That's why your mother said she owes you an apology."

Simone pushed the picture away and wiped her face. "It doesn't matter. If he's at peace that's all I care about. He was a great dad. The greatest. I miss him. But that's no reason for him to hang around."

Dalton put the pictures back in the envelope.

"What do you think of those?" she asked tentatively. "Did they change your mind?"

He shrugged. "I don't know about ghosts, but I don't think they should come between us. I'll respect what you say about them and I promise never to make fun of *you*. I'll reserve that for Cindi and the people on TV."

Simone laughed. "Okay, deal."

He gathered up the remnants of their meal and picked up the tray. "Ready to go?"

She nodded and scooted out of the booth. Dalton slid the

trash into the receptacle and left the tray on the counter. He opened the door and they walked out. After they were in the Camaro he turned to her without starting the motor.

"I have one more thing to say tonight."

He sounded so serious it almost frightened her.

"My father was brilliant at your hearing. But he got one thing wrong the day we asked him to represent you."

Simone frowned. She had no idea what he was talking about.

"Remember when he said I liked you and I loved my car?"

Simone nodded. "Yeah. What's wrong with that?"

He waited a moment before answering. "He got it backwards."

It took a second for his meaning to sink in. Simone started to smile, but before she really could, Dalton took her face in his hands and gave her the second most wonderful kiss she'd ever experienced.

At that moment, she knew with all her heart that more were to come.

ABOUT THE AUTHOR

ROBERTA SMITH is the author of the *Mickey McCoy Paranormal Mystery Series, Bouquet of Lies, The Dreamer of Downing Street, Distorted: Five Imaginative Tales on the Dark Side,* and *A Year in the Life of a Civil War Soldier: the 1864 Diary of Frank Steinbaugh.* This is her first young adult novel.

Made in the USA
San Bernardino, CA
23 June 2017